RISK ASSESSMENT

A Mystery

D1602414

ISBN: 979-8-9859339-0-1 (print)
ISBN: 979-8-9859339-1-8 (ebook)

This is a work of fiction. Names, characters, places,
and incidents either are the product of the authors'
imaginations or are used fictitiously. Any resemblance
to actual persons, living or dead, events, or locales is
entirely coincidental. Geographical place names and
descriptions are generally accurate but, in some cases,
small details have been changed.

Printed in the United States of America

*For Jack, Sam, and everyone in the youngest
generation as they explore and protect the world*

Two retirees met at a condo in Florida.

"How did you manage to retire so early?" asked the first man.

"My business was destroyed in a fire and I retired on the insurance money," the second man replied. "How about you?"

"My business was destroyed in a flood," the first man said.

The second man asked, "How do you start a flood?"

Sacramento, California
2015

Chapter 1

Just another day on the road.

Too much time alone in the car; too much time alone in my head. White-line fever was a real occupational hazard. But on an early spring day like this one—with the fruit trees and wildflowers in bloom—getting paid to drive from Sacramento to the California coast was more than bearable. As I headed west on Interstate 80, the first light of the morning spread across the valley, from the coastal hills on the horizon to the orchards of soft white almond trees along the highway.

Working as a lawyer for Farmstead Insurance wasn't my first choice as a job, but it did give me a chance to explore every nook and cranny of Northern California on the company dime. Farmstead, headquartered in Sacramento, specialized in rural homes, farms, and businesses with the proud motto: "Standing up for the Little Guy." I handled cases from around 100 miles south of Sacramento all the way north to the Oregon border. I knew the exact driving time to every courthouse and the best Mexican restaurant in every county seat. The road was my office at least two days a week, and my "beat" could take me to some of the most scenic places in the world.

Today, depositions were taking me to Boonville, a small town almost hidden in the coastal mountains north of San Francisco. My client, Annie Adams, was being sued, and this was the chance for the lawyers to tie down each side's testimony before trial. My hope was that we would finish quickly so I could continue west and spend a few hours fishing on the Navarro River before heading back to the office. Fishing is my way of meditating, and I'd been needing its calming effect more than usual of late.

In the big picture, the case was a routine trip and fall. Like many legal disputes, if the personalities had been different, it could have been avoided altogether with some basic manners and an apology. Annie, a retired schoolteacher, lived on a piece of land that her family had owned for generations. Rural doesn't begin to describe how far from civilization her property was. She lived off a back road between Boonville and the coast, and in those thirty miles of road, hers was one of only two driveways. Her property was insured by Farmstead, which meant that my office provided the lawyer.

The plaintiff, Leslie Watts, was a woman in her sixties with no fixed address. She shuttled around the state staying with friends. Annie could not for the life of her remember when she had first met Leslie, or how it had come to be that she was on Leslie's circuit, but for the past fifteen years or so Leslie had shown up in late August like clockwork.

Annie's pride and joy was her Gravenstein apple orchard—an old-fashioned early-ripening variety that bruises easily, so it doesn't have much of a commercial market nowadays. Most of Annie's trees were older than she was and the orchard was in disrepair, but the trees kept producing. Leslie always left Annie's place with a box of the apples for her next "host." On this visit, she had gone out to pick them, stepped in a gopher hole, and seriously broken her ankle. Now she was suing.

The depositions were scheduled to begin at ten o'clock. I met my client at nine at the Horn of Zeese on the main drag. "Horn of Zeese" means "Cup of Coffee" in Boontling, a local dialect concocted in Boonville around the turn of the last century to amuse the locals and bemuse the visitors, which it continues to do to this day. From there, we went across the street to the back office of a local real estate company that my court reporter had arranged for us to borrow.

Annie was seventy-five, tall, and thin—almost as tall as my slouchy five foot ten. I had been to her house to look at the lay of the land and talk about the case when it first came into our office. At our initial meeting, Annie had been dressed in jeans and a sweatshirt. Today she wore a jean skirt and a crisply ironed button-down shirt, her grey hair pulled back in a ponytail.

Leslie Watts and her lawyer had already arrived. I hadn't met him before, though I had had cases with other attorneys in his office. The attorney, who, based on his age, was newly minted, rose to greet us as we came in. Leslie did not stand, but sat at the table nervously pushing her coffee cup back and forth. She was wearing slacks, with a bulky medical boot on her injured leg. After greeting her lawyer, I extended my hand to her. "Hi

there, Jake Maxwell," I said. "I represent Ms. Adams."
Leslie turned her injured leg toward me and rubbed it
with her left hand as she reluctantly shook my hand with
her right.

Annie had very sharp brown eyes and, when she
wanted to make a point, she had a way of looking over
her glasses that must have been honed during her many
years of teaching. She greeted the plaintiff with "the
look," and I thought she also did a good job employing
this technique during both depositions.

I understand how filing a lawsuit can sour a friendship,
but it was all I could do to control my client. Here's an
excerpt from the transcript of the plaintiff's deposition:

Me: Ms. Watts, can you please tell us how you
injured your ankle?

Watts: I was walking into the orchard to pick some
apples and all of a sudden my foot went into a hole
in the ground.

Me: Was this the first time you had ever been in the
orchard?

Watts: No.

Me: Had you ever noticed holes in the ground on
prior visits?

Watts: I don't remember.

Me: On the most recent visit, the one where you
hurt your ankle, did my client warn you to watch
out for gopher holes in the orchard before you went
out there?

Watts: No.

Me: Ms. Watts, isn't it true that every time you went into the orchard, on every visit, Ms. Adams always told you to watch where you were stepping?

Watts: She never said anything about that to me.

Ms. Adams: I did so! You're a lunatic! You [unintelligible]!

Me: Annie, no! Put that down! [unintelligible].

Me: Let's go off the record.

[Off the record discussion.]

(What the transcript doesn't show: Ms. Adams lurching across the table with a paperweight in her hand and Ms. Watts' gasp of alarm.)

A lot of my cases were like this one—someone slips and falls in a grocery store, a cow wanders through a broken fence and onto the road, one car hits another—the so-called shit that happens. It's business to me, but I know it's personal to the people involved.

The depositions, which should have taken two hours altogether, lasted until almost two o'clock without a lunch break. By the time they ended, I decided I was too wound up for time with the Navarro River to do me much good, so I got in the car, cued up some Eric Clapton, and headed back to Sacramento.

Chapter 2

It's a three-hour drive from Boonville to Sacramento. Between music, my cell phone, and dictating a deposition summary, I managed to occupy myself for a good deal of the trip. But Boonville is a little close to the towns of Mendocino and Fort Bragg on the coast, and lately being anywhere near them dredged up thoughts that I really didn't want to be alone with.

I've been divorced for about a year. My ex, Beth, and I had spent our honeymoon night in Mendocino, and we returned to that part of the coast whenever I had to be there for work. We usually stayed in Fort Bragg, Mendocino's larger and more blue-collar (and therefore cheaper) neighbor. Beth preferred Mendocino, but I felt it was just a little too precious, so I blamed our staying in Fort Bragg on Farmstead's expense account limits. It had been on the day before we were scheduled to leave for Fort Bragg on a holiday last year that she told me she was trading me in on a new model. Since we split up, my life has been limited to work, my dog, and watching sports, and it's pretty easy to get myself into a downward spiral thinking about what I miss.

The road came to an end, as it always does, and I pulled into the Farmstead lot shortly before five. The parking lot, usually stacked up as densely as the cubicles inside the building, had started to break up, and I found one of the premium parking places in the shade of a big valley oak. When I opened the car door, it was quite hot for an early spring day. The sun was still bright, and heat radiated from the asphalt. I loaded up my rolling briefcase with files and headed inside.

The building is located in one of the many business parks in the Natomas area just north of the American River. I sometimes walked along the water at lunchtime to relax. Ever since I was young, I've always loved to fish and, even without my gear, I find watching the motion of the river therapeutic. Farmstead was the first tenant in the park. When we moved in, our building was surrounded by open fields dotted with large oaks. I would often see jack rabbits leaping and burrowing owls peering at me as I walked by. The wildlife is now long gone, and has been replaced by buildings filled with title companies, weight-loss clinics, and insurance brokers.

Farmstead has about 300 employees, which is about twice the number of people the two-story building was designed to hold. The executive offices, along with the claims and legal departments, are on the second floor. Reception, sales, personnel, underwriting, and the cafeteria are on the first. The whole place is full of cubicles and laid out like a huge maze. I sometimes hearken back to a team-building event, initiated by an earnest HR director, where we watched a movie on corporate management called *Who Moved My Cheese.* It used the rat-maze metaphor, though I forget the point. I think it had something to do with accepting change.

As I got off the elevator, it was no surprise to see that most of the lights were already off, but I was confident that Jocelyn would be there, since it was still short of quitting time, and she never left early. I had known her for most of the time I had been at Farmstead. She had started as a receptionist with no legal background and was now working as a legal assistant. She worked for both me and another lawyer, Peter.

When I reached the second floor, I saw that she was at her desk with several files open and was totally absorbed in two computer screens. She was in her forties, about my age. Her cubicle wall was covered with pictures of her three kids, mostly in sports uniforms. Over the years, I think I paid for many of those uniforms with my purchases of their fundraising candy, wrapping paper, and cookies, but I didn't really mind. It was a minute before she noticed me. She looked up while continuing to type.

"Anything I need to take official notice of?" I asked. She finished what she was typing.

"Oh, hi, Jake," she said. She shuffled through a few loose pieces of paper on her desk and handed me a couple of "while you were out" message slips.

"Marge from Judge McTaggart's office called to warn us that they're going to have to bump the trial date in Waters again."

Damn. A good third of the counties I handled cases in had only one or two trial courts, and criminal cases got priority over the civil cases.

"You've called off the witnesses?"

8

"Yes. Luckily, everyone seems to like the idea of going to trial in September better, which is what Marge said would be the likely date. She'll know more on Monday. Hey, what are you doing here, anyway? I thought you were going fishing and I wasn't going to see you until Monday."

"The stupid depos took way longer than they should have. It was all 'she said/she said, yes I did/no you didn't.' I think I heard our seventy-five-year-old client muttering 'bitch' under her breath while threatening the plaintiff with a paperweight."

"What?" Jocelyn said, surprised.

"We're lucky they aren't charging her with assault." I shook my head. "Plus, plaintiff's office sent some freshly hatched kid, and this newbie was so afraid of missing anything that he had to ask all his questions at least three different ways."

Jocelyn sighed. She usually put up with only a few minutes of my complaining before moving her attention back to her work, so I switched to a topic I knew would interest her more. Jocelyn was often my link to the office grapevine, and these days there was plenty to talk about. I hadn't been around too much lately, so I thought this might be a good opportunity to catch up.

The corporate office, which historically had rarely interacted with our division of the company, had been on people's minds throughout the building for the past two months. The whole time I had been at Farmstead, its stock had been widely held (a lot by current and former employees through the 401(k)) and thinly traded. Its share price had moved in a very narrow range, and it paid a not-bad dividend. It was a classic, very safe, very dull, "widows and orphans" holding.

However, several months ago, something called Black Belt Capital, Ltd. had bought a 20 percent share of the company, driving up the price of the stock. Even though that wasn't enough to give Black Belt outright control of the company, it was a far larger chunk than that held by any other investor in the company. In the insurance biz, it's not unusual for a national company to make a play for a regional, niche-market carrier like Farmstead, but Black Belt was a private equity fund with no other toe in the insurance water. No one could figure out what its interest was in our little operation.

In any event, at the next board of directors meeting, management agreed to let Black Belt put three people on the board. With impressive resumes, and lots of letters after their names, the new directors persuaded the board to begin a big shakeup of the staff at the higher levels. Though it hadn't affected us at the lower levels yet, everyone was nervous about the future.

"Any hot news from corporate?" I asked.

"Actually, yeah. Big news. You should have an email about it. Looks like Anton is staying on as company president, which makes a lot of people happy." Anton had been the president for a number of years, and was well liked in the company. "On the other hand, they've hired a new head of claims—a guy named Jim Scanlon. Some of the claims people have heard of him, and the most common word I get back is 'scary.'" Jocelyn leaned back in her chair. She seemed interested in talking, so I sat down next to her desk.

"I like Anton," I said. "Unfortunately, I think they're just leaving him in place to keep the deck chairs organized while Black Belt does whatever the hell it is that they have planned for the ship. Any word about Dan?" Dan Casey was our boss, the head of legal.

"I don't know anything for sure," she said, "but Dan says it looks like he may be leaving. We'll see." She took a deep breath, checked her watch, and began closing the files on her desk. "Anyway, it's time for me to skip. Have a good weekend."

"Well, it's mostly out of my control, but I'll do what I can. Have a good one yourself. Say hi to Doug and the kids for me. I'll proof my depo report. Looks like I'll be the last one standing, so I'll lock up."

All of the attorneys' offices in legal were dark. I knew that Dan was away for a meeting all day. I didn't know offhand the schedules of the other five lawyers, but they often cut out a little early on Fridays. I would miss Dan if he left. He had hired me at Farmstead five years ago when I was desperate to change jobs. It helped that I had gone to law school with one of the other lawyers who was in the office at that time, and it probably helped even more that she was married to Dan back then, but I think mostly he recognized an upside to a dazed burnout case. In fact, all the lawyers who worked for Dan had come to work at Farmstead by roundabout ways. We weren't the classic Hollywood band of misfits, but we all had plenty of battle scars and less ego than a lot of attorneys, a strong streak of intellectual curiosity, and an ability to work together without a lot of competition.

11

Dan had been a lieutenant in the U.S. Marine Corps after his ROTC days at Harvard, and had absorbed the corps' teaching that it was the primary duty of an officer to see to the well-being of the troops before looking out for himself. In a business where "I win when you lose" was the order of the day, his approach was pretty unique. He let us run the office collectively, which suited all of us just fine. He had been outspoken about his unhappiness with the changes ushered in by Black Belt, so it wouldn't be surprising if he were pushed out. But whatever had been going on between Dan and corporate, he had kept it to himself, probably not wanting to involve the rest of the office in his issues.

I switched on the light in my office and turned on my computer. As Jocelyn had said, the email from corporate was there. I skimmed it and read a couple more. By the time I was done proofing my report, the rest of the support staff had left and the office was quiet. I opened my bag, took out the Adams file, stacked it on top of the pile on the credenza, traded it for a couple of others, and headed home.

Chapter 3

I woke up the next day to a beautiful, cool morning. My home is in Curtis Park, a Sacramento neighborhood filled with interesting architecture, much of which dates back to the early twentieth century arts and crafts movement. There are many charming old homes, mini versions of the grand homes in Sacramento's famous Fabulous Forties. Mine wasn't one of them. Built in the 1950s, it had seen some uninspired updates and was now a standard two bedroom/one bath stucco. The distinguishing feature of the lot was an enormous sycamore tree. The deep shade was greatly welcomed in the hot summer, but was a problem when the tree's root system met the aging foundation of the house. Beth had left most of our IKEA furniture when she moved out and I hadn't changed anything since then. I had grown so used to how the house looked that I hardly noticed it.

After a leisurely cup of coffee and a trip to the grocery store, I grabbed Elwood, my dog, and knocked on my neighbor's door. "Hey Claire, would Abby like to join us for a walk?" Claire had a beautiful old craftsman-era bungalow, with a large porch and a well-kept garden, next door to my place. Abby raced down the porch steps, wagging her tail and barking.

"Hi Jake—I think that's a yes," said Claire, handing me the dog's leash. She smiled at the dog's enthusiasm. "Wish I had that kind of energy."

"Me, too," I said.

From the kitchen I could hear her grandson calling, "Grandma, I need you to help me."

"Oops, better go," said Claire. "We're making brownies. Thanks for walking the dog."

Four years ago, when another neighbor, who worked in animal rescue, was finding homes for some puppies, Claire and I each adopted one from the same litter. The dogs are mostly border collie, and Abby had the classic black-and-white markings. Elwood, on the other hand, showed evidence of a golden retriever somewhere in his family tree. Possibly as a result of the golden heritage, both Elwood and Abby were somewhat low-key for border collies, but they were very protective dogs, so I never worried about someone breaking into my house while I was away. Claire was pushing eighty when we adopted the pair, a little old to handle an active dog, but she and I had a symbiotic relationship that worked well. She kept an eye on Elwood when I was at work or out of town. In exchange, I took Abby on the long walks the dog craved but Claire could no longer manage. We even put a gate in the fence between our two yards so the dogs could go back and forth.

The dogs jumped into the car and we headed to the American River Parkway. The capital of California is a major hub in many ways. Interstate 5, the main north-south freeway in the state, crosses I-80, the east-west interstate that travels over the Sierra, in Sacramento. Two railway lines make a similar crossing, and two major rivers—the American and the Sacramento—also converge in the capital. A thirty-mile trail along the American River is well-used by joggers, walkers, and bikers. It is so popular that the park authority has had to put up signs along it showing how people should pass each other, and defining who is supposed to give the right of way to whom on the path. The river is also populated by many homeless people, though their camps are generally hidden behind the thick brush. I kept the dogs leashed and out of traffic as we walked a particularly pretty stretch of the river. A few fishermen cast lines along the banks, and a lone egret stood watching the water before leaping into the air in a graceful arc.

Ever since the divorce a year ago, it's been hard finding ways to keep busy, although it helps to have a dog that needs exercise. Beth and I were married for eleven years. We met in San Francisco on the first night of classes in law school. She had an eight-year-old son, Drew, and a part-time job as a legal secretary. She wanted to become a lawyer to change the world. I wanted to become a lawyer to change my own world, particularly by adding some cash to my pocket.

The law school we attended was a night school—unaccredited, downtown, and upstairs—designed to prepare attorneys for bread-and-butter jobs in the legal world. Days and weekends I worked in the Macy's men's department, and the thought of a life in retail sales was enough to motivate me to stay in school. Beth, on the other hand, dropped out after one semester. The rigors of school, single parenthood, and work proved to be too much, even with the help of her family.

We were married eight months after we met. It was a small city hall ceremony, followed by a party at her parents' home in Daly City. Her mom watched Drew as Beth and I took an extended honeymoon, mostly camping along the Pacific Coast from San Francisco to Washington's Olympic Peninsula. I don't think I have ever been happier.

When I finished law school, I took a job with a plaintiff's firm in San Francisco. The office was headed by a lawyer named Tim ("Tim Will Win") Ransom, a charismatic guy who advertised on billboards and television. He was blond, tan, and fit. He had the ego of a rock star and a lifestyle to match. However, while he was good at signing up clients, he was pretty much a disaster when it came to trying their cases. Instead, he would settle them at the low end of what they were worth just to keep the cash coming in. And his management skills were no better. He had a custom carpet in his office with a huge copy of his signature worked into the fabric. Rumor had it that whenever the office staff brought something into his office when he wasn't there, they would grind their heels into that part of the carpet.

At first, my job was mainly to do the legal scut work—depositions, interrogatories, document production requests—you name it. But as time went on, the big insurance companies caught on to Tim's game, and really started low-balling their offers, forcing us to try many of our cases. That task fell in my lap, and since more than a few of the cases were screaming dogs, I considered it a good day when I could meet the client's expectations. More commonly, Tim had talked such a good game when signing up a client that I couldn't get anywhere near what he had told them the case was worth.

Eventually, the increased lead time between signing up a case and getting paid on it caught up with Tim. When our paychecks began bouncing more often than the ball at a Warrior's game, I was desperate for a change. I had reconnected with Sharon, Dan Casey's wife and a Farmstead attorney at the time, on the one case I had against a Farmstead insured, and she let me know they were hiring. Even though it meant leaving San Francisco, the stability it promised was appealing, so Beth, Drew, and I picked up and moved to Sacramento.

I thought things were going pretty well in our marriage for the first few years after the move, so I was completely taken by surprise when Beth began the "it's-not-you-it's-me" talk which, in retrospect, did include a lot of unhappiness with me. She had been working as a paralegal for a divorce lawyer downtown and told me she had met her soul mate, a tall, balding man named Hank who was a client going through a divorce. It hadn't really occurred to me until this happened, but a family law practice must be a pretty good place to meet people on the rebound. The legal part of our divorce was fairly simple. Beth drafted the documents to save money. I kept the house, the mortgage, and the dog. She ended up with pretty much everything else.

Like Beth, her new love was very spiritual (not religious) and into meditation and yoga, which was an area where she and I had differed. They married as soon as our divorce was final, and rode about fifteen miles west into the sunset to the college town of Davis. Drew, now twenty, had already moved to Humboldt County in the far northwest of the state to attend the state college there. He and I kept in touch, mostly by text, and had recently gotten together when he came down for a visit. He was always a sensible kid, and he seemed pretty well-adjusted despite all the upheavals in his life. I missed him terribly and missed being a stepdad almost as much as I missed the sweet warm shape of his mother in bed next to me.

I walked and ran the dogs for a couple of hours until we were all exhausted. When I got back, Claire thanked me profusely and pressed a paper plate with a few brownies on it into my hands as I left.

I spent the afternoon catching up on a few chores, then microwaved something for dinner and lay on the couch with a Diet Coke. I turned on the television, and opened the first of the files I had brought home. Since most the cases I handle involve bodily injury claims, much of my work involves reading reams and reams (or, more commonly these days, screens and screens) of medical files. As technology has developed over the years, handwritten medical records have become a thing of the past, so they are easier to decipher, but no less boring. I like to watch sports while dictating my summaries to help pass the time. Baseball is the best. I can read medical records during the long, boring sections of the game and turn my attention to the screen when I hear the announcer's voice rise in excitement. Tonight's game was the first broadcast from spring training. Management had promised that the established players would play at least the first three innings, so it was nice to get reacquainted with the Giants.

The records show that claimant was first seen on the night of the accident in the emergency department with primary complaints of neck pain...

...and he's out at home! The score is 5-4 with Buster Posey coming to bat...

...X-rays were negative for any bony pathology...

...he hits it high, he hits it deep, and it's out of here to dead centerfield!

I've read that the brain doesn't really multitask but that our attention moves back and forth between the separate tasks. But despite the sharp differences in my two areas of attention, somehow I've made an excellent and complete adaptation. I watched the game until the Giants won 8-6, closed the file, and decided to call it a day.

Chapter 4

Monday was the regular office staff meeting. Farmstead keeps its lawyers on the road, so it was a rare day where all six of the trial lawyers were together and today was no exception. Sam, Peter, and I were the only attorneys present. Missing were Rosa (our civil procedure and appeals specialist), Larry (another generalist like me), and Charlene (our newest attorney, who also doubled as our technology guru).

Sam, a former Air Force pilot, was the most serious of the bunch. He had come to Farmstead from years of practice as an assistant district attorney at the north end of the valley, making the move after an unsuccessful election bid to replace his boss as the county DA. He knew just about everything there was to know about picking and relating to a jury during trial.

At fifty-seven, Rosa was the oldest in the group. She had begun her career as a corporate attorney and then realized that the ladder she was climbing was not headed where she wanted to go. While her job with Farmstead was a huge cut in pay, it allowed her the time to pursue other interests, including a passion for golf. Larry was our resident socialist. He had worked for years in the world of nonprofit legal services. After being laid off periodically as funds fluctuated, he appreciated the steady paycheck our practice provided.

Of the lawyers at Farmstead other than Dan, I probably felt closest to Peter. He had been at Farmstead for a long time, and had helped me learn the ropes when I first arrived. We shared an interest in sports as well as in seafaring novels, particularly those written by Patrick O'Brian. Peter was usually willing to be distracted from his files, and talking about the 49ers or Jack Aubrey and the Napoleonic Wars was a welcome respite from the battles of litigation. Another facet of Peter was his side gig doing stand-up comedy at open-mic nights around Sacramento. I had never gone to see him perform, but he often publicized his plans among the office staff.

Lately, I had found myself talking more and more with Charlene. Though she was a lot younger, and seemed to be from a different generation in many ways, she was funny, friendly, and smart. Charlene grew up in San Francisco and was a proud product of some of the best of the California public education system. She went to Lowell, the city's premier high school, and then to UC Berkeley and King Hall law school at UC Davis. She had recently gotten married, and her husband worked in Silicon Valley. From what she told me, he didn't go into the office very often, but, when he did, he could often ride with a friend who owned a small plane and commuted by air from the UC Davis airport to Palo Alto. She had clued me in on a number of very cool apps, and provided a window into a tech world where I knew I would always be an outsider.

Although Dan was technically in charge of the office, he didn't usually take part in the staff meetings. As always, the first order of business was assigning new cases and, unlike most offices, we decided who got which cases as a group. Running the sessions usually fell to Sam and he sat at the head of the table in his usual khaki pants and plaid button-down shirt like a blackjack dealer. The absent lawyers were represented at the meeting by their legal assistants.

"Okay," Sam began. "I've got eight cases to assign: A fender-bender in Stockton, a dog bite in Calaveras, a slip-and-fall in Yuba City, what looks like a premises liability case in Eureka, a broken tooth at a Mexican restaurant in Red Bluff, a mobile ag collision in Colusa, part of a chain-reaction pile-up in Modesto, a multi-party construction defect case in Sacramento, and, last but not least, a cow-out in Jackson." Cow-out cases, where someone's livestock gets hit by a car while it's out on the road, were one of our strong suits, if not our downright specialties. They went by various names among us—Bovine on the Blacktop, Angus on the Asphalt, Ruminant on the Road, Heifer on the Highway, Steer on the Street—and responsibility often turned on arcane fencing and open range laws. I wound up with the Mexican restaurant and the case in Eureka.

We then turned to the issue of Black Belt's takeover. Sam had gotten a little news since Friday. "I called a claims guy I know over at Grange Insurance, because I heard that he'd worked under Scanlon for awhile. From what I gather, we can expect claims to be a lot less settlement-minded, so we'll probably be going to trial more often."

This was disturbing. Farmstead was already known throughout the state as a company that tried more cases than most. Our resources as a law office were always stretched thin, and any substantial increase in trial work without additional help could cause us to hit a breaking point pretty quickly.

Sam continued, "The other thing I heard is that underwriting is going to get a big makeover, and they're going to be bringing in some heavy hitters with tons of commercial experience. I don't know about you, but I think our day as the company that's supposed to stand up for the little guy may be coming to an end."

Peter added, "If we're going heavy commercial, we'll probably have to get used to clients who are much less invested in the outcomes of the cases unless there's some risk that they're underinsured for the claim and might owe something out of pocket. I started in that end of the business, and the attitude was always 'I turned this over to my broker—why are you bothering me about this?'"

Well, I didn't know anybody in underwriting, so changes in personnel in that department were no big deal to me. But I did know that shifting into heavy commercial could be very risky for the company. Underwriting had to figure out whether or not Farmstead would insure a person or a business, and, even more importantly, how much to charge. Back in the day, when investments in safe assets paid returns of up to 10 percent per year, insurance companies could make money even if they took in less than they paid out, since they would typically put the money to work for a couple of years before they parted with it. Nowadays, with interest rates so low, either the company had to charge more than it paid out or make up the difference with riskier investments.

"Okay," Sam said, "the last order of business—trials and conflicts. Anyone up in the next few weeks? Anyone need help or coverage?"

"My Willows trial got bumped to September," I said. "So, I've got an open calendar in two weeks if someone needs it."

Peter, who had begun his work life in the building trades and still held a general contractor's license, looked up happily. "I'm double-set on expert depos in two construction defects cases here in town a couple of days that week. I'd love it if you could cover one for me." CD cases, as they are usually called, were not my cup of tea, as there was very little human element to them, but CD expert depositions were simply a matter of staying awake until the questions got around to the plumbing, the landscaping, or whatever other piece of the project our hero had worked on.

"You got it. Give Jocelyn the details."

Rather than going straight back to my office, I took a detour and headed over to the claims department to discuss my Boonville depos with Dave Fries, the adjuster on the case. Adjusters are assigned to the claims and take overall responsibility for the outcomes. Often, they are able to settle them without legal action, but Dave's caseload tended to include the more serious cases, which often required legal's involvement. He had a ton of experience, but always wanted to micromanage the attorneys handling his cases. In an operation like Farmstead's, which employs its lawyers directly instead of hiring a private firm, this can cause tension, as our clients' interests are not always the same as those of the company, especially when we defended cases where there might not be coverage under the insurance policy for some of the claims.

"Hey Dave—got a sec to talk about Adams?"

Dave swiveled his chair to face me. "Sure, how did it go? Have a seat."

I pulled over a nearby chair and sat down. "No real surprises, other than we almost had a knock-down, drag-out brawl between the two ladies. Adams says she warned the claimant about the holes like she did every year, and claimant denies that ever happened."

"So, where do you think we should go from here?"

"What I'd love to do is to find some older photos of the orchard, since I don't think it's any rattier now than it was years ago when the claimant started couch surfing with Adams. I asked Adams, but she doesn't have anything."

Dave tapped his foot a couple of times and gnawed on his lip. He had a mustache that twitched when he was thinking. "Hmm…" he began. "Here's a thought. This is kind of an unusual property. There's a chance that someone from risk management went out to look at it before we covered it. If they did, they probably took pictures. I can't tell from the file who the underwriter was back then, but they can look it up off the policy number."

"Well, it's probably worth a try," I replied, "but I hate dealing with underwriting. They always try to make me feel like the spendthrift child spending their hard-earned money, and I always feel like they were crazy to write the crappy business I'm stuck defending."

"I hear you," he laughed. "They're even harder on me."

I smiled as I got up from the chair. "I'll give it a shot. I'll let you know what I find out."

And so off to underwriting it was. They occupied the corner of the building all the way across from claims and legal and one floor below. Once upon a time, there were wide corridors running through the building, but the cube farm kept expanding and you could get lost if you weren't careful. I have a good sense of direction, but either I'd forgotten the way, or, more likely, things had been rearranged since my last visit. I started to think again about *Who Moved My Cheese*.

Rather than arriving at what passed for reception in underwriting, I found myself in the middle of the department before I realized it. My confusion must have been obvious, as a woman turned from her desk and asked if she could help me.

"Hi, I'm Jake Maxwell, one of the lawyers over in claims/legal," I said, "I'm looking for underwriting information on one of my cases."

"I'm Meg Vann. I'm on the risk assessment team. Maybe I can help you."

I knew most of the Farmstead staff by sight, but she didn't look familiar. She was about five years younger than I and had a wide smile.

"Well, I've got a policy number and I want to see if there were any photos taken of the property before the policy was written, or in connection with renewals, for that matter."

26

"Let me look it up. Won't take but a minute." I watched over her cubicle wall as she stared at the screen and typed in the information. She was wearing a green tunic top and slacks. Her hair was long and dark brown, with a few strands of grey, and was pulled on top of her head in some kind of complicated arrangement. She wore long earrings that swayed back and forth as she moved her head and very little makeup. Her work area seemed neater than most and had a colorful vase of daffodils in the corner. I didn't notice any photos or other personal items on her desk or wall. Almost involuntarily, I glanced at her hand, and noticed she wasn't wearing a wedding ring.

"Yes, here's the file." She paused while she skimmed the information. "Nope, this one was machine written, meaning the computer figured out the risk, so no one would have looked at it ahead of time. And there haven't been any subsequent inspections. What kind of a case is it?" She turned back to look at me.

"It's a fall in our insured's orchard," I said. "Totally bogus, but a bad injury to a fairly elderly lady."

Meg raised her eyebrows. "She's not running a U-pick operation, is she? That would make it a risk we wouldn't insure."

"Oh no, this was just some sort of friend of hers who was staying there for a few days. No money involved."

She turned back to her screen. "Wow, this property must be a long way from anywhere. The system shows the nearest fire station is twenty-five miles away from her. I don't think we would write this place today if it came in as new business."

"Well, I'd appreciate it if you didn't bring this to anyone's attention. I hate it when a client's policy gets non-renewed while I'm trying to defend them and need their cooperation."

She smiled. "Don't worry—it's not my account. My lips are sealed. Sorry I couldn't help."

"Well, thanks for trying. I owe you a cup of coffee next time I see you in the cafeteria."

"Sure," she said. "Nice meeting you."

Chapter 5

The rest of the week was a long road trip with appointments in Redding, Eureka, and Clearlake. The trip to Redding is straight north up the Sacramento Valley and is one of the dullest of the routes I follow, with no scenic alternative. With no stoplights, and moderate traffic, I set the cruise control at seventy-five and drove on autopilot. I had a chance to catch up on some podcasts and brought along a few of my favorite CDs. I had even brought along some continuing legal education CDs, but thought it best not to listen to them for fear of falling asleep. Interstate 5 is a highway which will be perfectly suited to driverless cars.

A large stretch of the Sacramento Valley is between two mountain ranges—the Coast Range to the west and the Sierra Nevada to the east. The day was clear, the sky a cloudless cerulean blue, and I could see for miles. Although the temperature was near eighty, I could still see snow on the Sierra. The freeway goes through large stretches of agricultural lands with a number of small towns and very occasional larger cities. Just north of Sacramento, the Sutter Buttes rise steeply out of the valley floor like an island rising in the middle of the ocean. The Buttes are said to be the smallest mountain range in the world. I've never been there, as they are privately owned, but I've heard you can visit on guided hikes.

As I passed Willows, about ninety minutes to the north, Mt. Shasta came into view. Seeing Mt. Shasta notch the horizon was always a highlight of the drive. On the southern end of the Cascade Range, Shasta rises over 14,000 feet above the valley floor to a peak covered with snow almost all year long. It is such a dramatic mountain that I can understand why there is so much lore surrounding it. Native American tribes have a legend that that it is inhabited by a great spirit. There are also people who believe that there's a city under the peak of the mountain inhabited by people from the lost continent of Lemuria. The legend lives on in Mt. Shasta City, at the base of the mountain, where new-age shops abound. The immense, dormant volcano dominated the horizon until I reached Red Bluff, sixty miles north of Willows, where the highway begins to run through hills, blocking the view.

When you finally get to Redding, there's not much there. It's the largest city between Sacramento and the Oregon border, and it's built along a highly scenic stretch of the Sacramento River. However, for many years, the city planners turned their back on the river, creating a totally uninspired downtown a mile away from it. The city now has a very nice park with river access, but it was way overdue.

The Red Lion Hotel was my home away from home whenever I was in Redding. I arrived after dark and grabbed a bite to eat at the hotel restaurant. My business this trip was pretty straightforward. I was there for a mediation to try to settle a run-of-the-mill auto accident case. Normally, I can size up a case and settle it over the phone, and the plaintiff's attorney in this case was generally reasonable with me (it probably helped that I had beaten him in a trial two years earlier). However, he told me that his client had overly high expectations of what he would get from his settlement, so we had to bring in a neutral party to try to make him see sense.

The mediator, Ron Jamison, was an old pro at this, having worked both as a plaintiff and as a defense attorney. His office was one of the few in town that took advantage of the river. The main conference room was three stories above the river bank, with a porch outside so close that a determined fisherman could probably get his hook in the water from there. During the salmon season, the river would be full of drift boats working the run. Ron's partner reputedly spent every lunch hour playing catch and release with the local trout.

Ron was near retirement and looked every inch the wise elder statesman. His grey hair was still thick, and he greeted each of us with a sincere, firm handshake. We sat around the conference table while he ran through his usual introduction with the plaintiff, his attorney, and me (although everyone but the plaintiff had heard it a dozen times). Once the preliminaries were done, he led me to a cubicle in the back of the office while he talked to the plaintiff. I didn't mind—I'd seen the river from the conference room many times, and being off by myself let me work on some other projects I had brought along. Like many lawyers, I found myself working on two cases at once and logging the hours to both files.

Ron came back to see me after being with the other side for about half an hour. One of the unwritten rules about mediation is that the mediator, who has just spent half an hour twisting the plaintiff's arm, has to then spend about as much time with me so that the plaintiff thinks my arm's being twisted just as hard as his had been. The truth is that Ron and I both knew what this case was worth, and if we'd written down estimates before we started, they would have been within 10 percent of each other. Usually we spent most of our meditation time together jawing about the Giants, but today Ron led off with something different.

"I hear Jim Scanlon is taking over Farmstead's claims department," he said. "I worked for him fifteen years ago, and God forbid I ever do something like that again." Ron looked for my reaction, then leaned back in his chair. "That man is toxic, unhinged, power-hungry, and—you'll love this—he has no use for house counsel." He seemed to enjoy giving me the bad news. "I hear Dan Casey's not long for this world either, and I'll lay you good odds that Scanlon will make a play to be put in charge of the legal department as well as claims."

This was maybe not surprising, but certainly demoralizing. House counsel is unpopular with many claims people. Claims would rather hire an outside firm to handle cases, even though the billing rates would be higher than what we charge internally, and the claims department would have less control over how many hours were spent on a case. At least one of the reasons for this preference became clear every Christmas, when the claims folk would be lucky if they got a card from the legal department, whereas the outside firms dealt in cases of wine and massive gift baskets. And don't get me started on the golf junkets.

"I hear Scanlon isn't much of a settler, either," I said. "Our long and happy relationship might be drying up if I have to take every little thing to trial."

"That's actually not exactly true," Ron replied. "He's just as glad to get a good settlement over a great trial verdict as the next person. No, what I've seen in the past is that management will bring him in when they want a wholesale makeover of a claims/legal operation, but don't want to fire people and have to pay severance. He'll reorganize and reprioritize everything so that no one can work effectively, and everyone will quit in frustration. Same goes for you guys in legal. He doesn't have to manage you out of existence. All he has to do is up your caseloads by squeezing down on settlement authority to the point where you can't see straight or get prepared for trial the way you need to."

"Well, you sure make it sound attractive." His news was certainly discouraging. "Anyway, back to business. What does the plaintiff want, and what do you need?"

"He's at 70 [meaning $70,000]. You gave him a low-ball offer of 25 last month, and that would only make sense if he's partially responsible for the accident. I know your argument, and you can probably get it to the jury if your expert holds up, but I think your chances of actually going anywhere with that are slim. I'll get him to 40, but he needs to stop someplace short of that first, so give me 35 and let's get the ball rolling."

Plaintiff being at 70 already was a good sign, as the demand a week before had been the 100 policy limits. I actually had 60 in settlement authority, but it wasn't my job to spend it if I didn't have to. So, the mediation wore its predictable course: I went up to 35, he came down to 50, I went to 37.5, and we did the deal at 40. Not the most scintillating morning I'd had in the past week, but that's the name of the game most days.

Chapter 6

The mediation finished just short of noon, which was pretty much what I had expected. The balance of the day would take me west over the Coast Range to Eureka on the Pacific Coast. The road, State Route 299, runs mostly through the Trinity River canyon, and has stunning views, although it is slow and one lane each way. Fortunately, I had driven the road often enough to know where all the passing lanes are, and I was in no particular hurry.

The Trinity is one of California's lesser-known rivers. It runs into the Klamath, which, in turn empties into the Pacific about forty miles south of the Oregon border. In the past, the Trinity supported one of the largest salmon runs in the state, but back in the 1950s, the federal Central Valley Water Project diverted 90 percent of its flow through a miles-long tunnel into the Central Valley. With the Trinity sucked dry, and with similar water diversions on the Klamath, the ocean salmon population off the northern coast of California crashed, leading to severe limitations in both the commercial and the sport fisheries. The Hoopa Valley and Yurok tribes, which live along the rivers, have also been heavily impacted. Nevertheless, despite the diversions, the river looked in pretty good shape on this trip, although too muddy to fish.

As I approached the coast, I could feel the temperature drop and the air become moister. I love going to the North Coast, and it's even nicer to get paid to do it. I think the attraction comes from growing up in Southern California, where rain is a rarity and the landscape is the color of an over-baked saltine more than half the year—not to mention how crowded everything is. By contrast, Eureka averages four times as much rain, and stays green even throughout the dry summers. Its population is low due to its isolation and lack of industry (both the timber and commercial fishing industries are shadows of their former selves), so there are miles of nearly empty beaches. And, of course, there are the redwoods. I always find a walk among them to be very soothing.

Although I was going to Eureka for work, I also planned to visit Drew. When I married Beth, I had no experience being a father (or a husband, for that matter) and, I have to admit, I had no idea what I was doing. I don't have siblings. My own father had been kind but rather distant. Coming on the scene with a kid in the mix who was old enough to have his own opinions was a challenge. Drew's father, who had remarried and moved to the Pacific Northwest, had been pretty much out of the picture.

I approached fatherhood the only way I knew how—I just spent time with Drew and saw what happened. On Sunday afternoons, we almost always did something together, either with Beth or not. Sometimes we took a drive or a hike. Occasionally we went to a Giants game. Mostly I took Drew fishing. We went to Lake Merced and fished for trout or to the pier in Pacifica when the fish were running. He was a quiet kid, and I spent many hours sitting next to him in silence, watching the bobbers on the end of our lines bounce up and down on the water. Sometimes he would invite a friend or one of his many cousins to come along, and I usually learned a bit more about what he was doing by listening in on those conversations than I did directly from him. As he got older, I would often take him to the site of the World War II-era coast defense batteries at the very northwest corner of San Francisco where he could skateboard while I worked on interrogatory answers in the car.

Drew shared my love of fishing and I was pleasantly surprised when he decided to major in fisheries science at Humboldt State. I considered him a friend and always tried to see him when on business in Eureka.

Around five o'clock I pulled into the parking lot at the Eureka Inn, a large, old-style establishment that was quiet and just a short walk from the courthouse. The slightly down-at-the-heels hotel had once hosted celebrities and heads of state. The lobby played up its former glamour with artwork and artifacts from its past. A number of portrait paintings filled the downstairs public spaces, boasting of the famous people who had stayed in the hotel during its prime, including Bobby Kennedy, Ronald Reagan, and Walt Disney.

The clerk was sitting idly when I arrived in the cavernous lobby to check in and told me that the elevator was out of service. "I can take you up in the service elevator if you want."

The hotel seemed empty and I could see keys in almost every room mailbox, yet for some reason, I was assigned a room on the third floor. I didn't mind the climb after the long trip in the car, so I declined the offer and carried my bags up the stairs. Once I got to my room, I checked my company email and voicemail, then called Drew.

"Hey, Drew, it's Jake."

"Hey yourself. How was your drive?"

"In one word, picturesque. We still on for tomorrow?"

"Yup. Meeting up at my place at noon still work for you?"

"I'll call if there's a problem."

"Okay, see you then."

I didn't expect a problem, as my deposition was of a local large-animal veterinarian, and we had scheduled it for seven o'clock in the morning in order to finish before he started seeing patients at eight. My client, who boarded horses as a side-line to his auto repair business, had been sued for not providing proper treatment for two thoroughbreds left in his care. Despite leaving her horses in such a casual setting, with no training for racing, the plaintiff was certain that one of them was going to be the next Triple Crown winner.

I left a little early the next morning, but found the vet's office easily. The deposition went well as far as I was concerned, with the vet testifying that the horses were no worse off after six months in my client's custody than they had been immediately before. I went back to the hotel, ate a late breakfast, dictated reports, and returned phone calls.

X⊙X⊙X

I checked out at eleven o'clock, and headed up to Drew's. As was my habit, I went the long way to Arcata, which took me west over a set of bridges that spanned the northern part of Humboldt Bay, and then north along the spit of sand separating the bay from the ocean, passing in and out of posted tsunami hazard zones. The sun was starting to break through the overcast sky. I got to Drew's a little early, so was glad to see that his truck was there. A little smart car painted in Grateful Dead psychedelic colors was parked next to the truck in front of the ancient doublewide that he and two or three roommates called home.

I had never met Drew's father, although I had seen pictures of him. He and Beth had met at a college mixer at San Francisco State. Beth had never said too much about their relationship. Drew had told me about some early memories, his parents fighting, and how sad he was when his dad left. In any event, he seemed to be enjoying college and doing well.

Drew answered the door looking like he'd just woken up. His hair was tousled and his clothes looked like they could use a wash. But it had been several months since my last visit and it was great to see him. He looked fit—much more muscular than he had been in high school—and I took that as a positive sign that he was getting enough to eat. I gave him a quick hug and a pat on the back. Two young men, who I assumed were his roommates, were sprawled across a couple of overstuffed chairs wearing earbuds and intently looking at their computers. I hadn't met his roommates, but no introductions were offered. I caught the eye of one of them and he gave me a nod.

"You want a cup of coffee?" Drew asked, looking toward an old Mr. Coffee surrounded by several unwashed mugs.

I appreciated the hospitality, but declined. "Thanks, I'm good. Maybe we should get going."

"So, ready for the big shark hunt?" he asked.

"Ready as I'll ever be. Let's go do it."

Drew's research project was under one of the fisheries faculty who was studying the shark population in Humboldt Bay, in particular the degree to which they traveled in and out of the harbor. To do this, it was necessary to tag the sharks with radio transmitters and with identifying bands which would be sent in by a fisherman who caught one. Drew, being the newest person in the project, was the stuckee when it came to tagging the sharks, and I was coming along to help. When we had made arrangements for this adventure, he had made it clear that we weren't going to catch any great whites or hammerheads. The biggest fish we were likely to tie into would be a cow shark, also known as a mud shark, or, more properly, a sevengill shark. Even so, it sounded intriguing.

We piled into his truck and headed back to Eureka, stopping at a marina south of town. The school's boat was on a trailer inside a fenced enclosure, and Drew hitched it up to his truck and put it in the water at a nearby boat ramp. The boat, an aluminum skiff about twelve feet long, had obviously seen better days. It looked like it might have been used at some time by someone studying the birdlife in the harbor, as it was painted in a dark green camouflage. The outboard motor, on the other hand, was relatively new, small and quiet.

We motored out into the bay, and went north under one of the highway bridges I had already been over once that day. When we got to the middle of Arcata Bay, Drew stopped the motor and threw out the anchor, tying a couple of plastic milk jugs painted bright red to the rope just above the water. "This is so I can find the anchor if we hook a good one," he said.

We prepared our gear—heavy bait-casting reels, heavy rods, fifty-pound-test monofilament line tied to wire two-way swivels, and two monster treble hooks at the end of each rig. We baited them up with a fairly ripe salmon head apiece, then cast the rigs into the water on either side of the boat.

"This isn't what I'd really call sport tackle," I observed.

"No sport about it. These sharks can get pretty big, and I'm not doing my job unless I can bring them in to tag them. If you want to fish with one of your precious fly rods, be my guest, but you'll have to do it on your own time. I'll be happy to give you some tags if you want to try that."

The weather was calm and the sun was warm, so sitting in the boat and chatting while waiting for some action was comfortable. The tide was dropping, and the shorebirds were congregating on the gradually revealed mudflats.

41

We left the reels with the drags set low and the clickers on. About thirty minutes in, Drew looked up and said "I think I've got business." Shortly after, a click, then a couple more, then another single click, came from his reel as the line was slowly pulled out. "Could be a bat ray, which really can't get a salmon head in its mouth. We'll see in a second." A couple more single clicks, a few more together, and then an almighty zing as the line tore off the reel. "Nope, it's a shark all right. Now comes the fun part. Pull in your line—the last thing we need is two fish on at the same time."

Drew stood up in the boat and raised the rod tip up as high as he could while the line continued to tear off the reel. He tightened the drag and let the rod tip be pulled until it was underwater, then put his back into it and heaved up on the rod.

About fifty yards out, a huge fish—probably six feet long—leapt out of the water and came down in an enormous splash. "Yup, shark all right. A big sevengill, it looks like. Probably a female—the males don't get that big." At Drew's direction, I untied the anchor line from the boat, leaving the milk jugs floating at the end. The shark proceeded to drag us around the bay as Drew reeled in the line. A marker on the line came into view, and Drew called out, "There's fifteen more feet of line still out. Take the rod and keep the tension on. Her mouth's so hard, the hooks aren't in for shit, so she'll get away if you go soft on her." I did as I was told, and Drew busied himself in the bottom of the boat. Then he called out, "Okay, I'm ready for the next step. Reel in and keep her head toward the back of the boat. Try to get her as close in as you can and keep her parallel to us." I complied, reeling in enough line that the shark's head came out of the water with its jaw opening and closing only a few feet from me. I could see that its mouth wasn't all that big, but it was full of nasty looking teeth and could obviously do serious harm if it got hold of a hand or a foot.

Drew tossed a rope with a loop on it into the water, and maneuvered it over the shark's tail. Giving a strong yank, he pulled the tail into the boat. "Keep her head out of the water," he called. Holding the rope with one hand, he grabbed a small tool and punched two holes in the shark's dorsal fin. He clipped a piece of gear on using one of the holes, then threaded a plastic line with markings along the side through the other hole, bringing it back and tying the ends together. "I've got the radio transmitter and tag attached. I'm going to slack the rope so its tail is free, and you need to let off the tension on its head at the same time. Okay, on three." We managed to let go more or less at the same time, and the shark jerked its head from side to side, spitting out the hooks. It immediately dove and disappeared.

"Well, there's one shark who's going to be swimming around wondering 'WTF?' for the next day or so," Drew smiled. "Where did we get to, anyway?" It turned out the shark had dragged us about half a mile on our Humboldt Bay version of a Nantucket sleigh ride. Drew's GPS led us back to the milk jugs, and we recovered the anchor line. "Want to go for two today?" he asked.

"No. I'm worn out and I've still got a three-hour drive to get to Lakeport," I laughed, wondering if he meant it. "Let's head for the barn."

"Suits me."

"A little more exciting than the trout at Lake Merced," I said as we motored back.

Drew smiled. "Yeah, just a little."

XOXOX

By the time we returned the boat to the yard and were back to Drew's, the adrenaline had evaporated. I would have liked to stay longer, but duty called. The drive to Lakeport was one which took a fair amount of attention, so I shortly said my farewells and headed down the road.

US 101 south of Eureka runs along the Eel River through the redwoods. The highway narrows down to one lane each way at Richardson Grove, a stand of huge old-growth trees that the department of transportation, Caltrans, is always threatening to cut back in order to widen the road. The grove features a chainsaw sculpture shop displaying a giant Bigfoot. Every highway bridge which crosses the river is named after someone. My favorite was the Elmer T. Hurlbut Memorial Bridge. Every time I passed over it, I made a mental note to check with Caltrans to see just who the heck he was.

As I left the redwoods around Piercy, the rounded hills, still green from the rains, opened up on both sides of the road. Bright yellow wild mustard grew in broad bands along the side of the road. Cows grazed in the fields and turkey vultures circled above looking for dinner. Just north of Ukiah, I turned onto State Route 20 and headed east.

I got to Lakeport before dark, and checked into the motel, which was on the shore of Clear Lake and had a nice view of the water. Clear Lake is a large, although rather shallow, body of water, and the Chamber of Commerce boosters brag that it's the largest naturally occurring body of fresh water entirely within California. That's maybe overdoing it on the qualifiers, but it is a very popular place for fishing and boating, particularly in the summer when the temperature is usually in the nineties.

I found a small restaurant within walking distance of the motel and finished off the new Walter Mosley book along with a pretty dry piece of chicken. Once back in my room, I called Claire to check on the dog. She assured me that Elwood was fine and had been no trouble. I was tired from the fishing trip and the drive, so I only watched a few minutes of baseball before falling into a deep sleep.

I got up early the next morning and went for a run down by the lake, showered and changed, and then headed over to the courthouse at nine. I met up with Jeff, the local Farmstead adjuster, who was standing in for the real claims handler who didn't want to make the trip from Sacramento. She was supposed to be at her desk, so we could reach her any time we needed more money, but I really hated having to convince two people to back my play instead of just one.

The case was a simple auto accident, but the damage claim had a twist. The plaintiff was a young woman from the area who had been studying at the San Francisco Conservancy of Music and playing bassoon in the San Francisco Youth Symphony. She had been home on break when my client had mistakenly turned in front of her. In addition to the usual neck and back complaints, she also claimed that her jaw muscles had been injured to the point that her career as a budding bassoonist had been ruined. How much does a symphony-level bassoonist make? Not that much, but like other loss of income claims, it adds up over time.

Not surprisingly, Jeff didn't think too much of the claim, and, fortunately, neither did the judge. She was able to use the fact that I had the deposition of the director of career development at the Conservancy of Music scheduled for the following week as a lever to convince the plaintiff that it was better to settle now rather than to hear what someone in the know really thought of her prospects when asked under oath. We settled for a reasonable sum, which generally means no one went away happy with the deal, and I was on my way back to Sactown before lunch.

Chapter 7

I pulled into the company parking lot about two-thirty and was wilting from the unusually hot weather by the time I reached the door. My immediate destination was the minifridge in the copy room, hoping to score a Diet Coke. Sadly, someone had violated the cardinal fridge rule that whoever drinks the last one buys the next batch, and all that was left were Sam's Dr. Peppers, which, not having grown up in the South as he did, is about the last thing I'd drink. Nothing to do then but to go down to the cafeteria and get one.

The cafeteria at Farmstead was adequate, nothing special. It had a salad bar, a few hot selections and the usual snack food and drinks. I got a Coke from the vending machine and was heading out when I saw Meg at a table in the corner texting on her phone.

"So, what's a nice girl like you doing in a place like this?" I ventured as I approached her table.

She looked up with a surprised glance, but it quickly turned into a 200-watt smile that I found encouraging. There was a half-empty cup of coffee and a brown paper sandwich bag next to her.

"Late lunch?" I asked.

"Yeah. It was busy today. Late lunch and catching up on some messages. My cousin's family has a new kitten and they're blowing up my Instagram with photos," she said with a grimace.

She was wearing black slacks and a beige V-neck top that crossed in a way that accented her breasts. Her hair was up in a different arrangement than it had been the other day, this time with a couple of clips stuck in for emphasis.

"Mind if I join you?" I asked.

"Please." She waved toward the empty chair and moved her phone into her purse.

"Thanks for your help the other day," I said. "I really appreciate it. By the way, I know that claims and underwriting are on different sides of the world, but I'm surprised that we haven't crossed paths before in the hall or at the company picnic."

"Well, it's probably because I've worked here for less than a year and, I have to admit, I took a pass on the picnic. The idea of spending a hot day at a waterslide park without kids and without a date just didn't appeal to me. Was it fun?"

"It was all right. I was in the same boat, but I've been here a while, so at least I knew a few people to talk to. The food was pretty bad even before it sat in the sun for a few hours." I smiled. "Have you worked in risk management for long?"

"For a few years. I worked in New York for a while before this job, but I missed California. I really wanted to move back."

"You grew up in Sacramento?"

"No. I grew up in Eureka but I came down to Sacramento State for college, so I know the area pretty well."

"Wow. I love it up there. I just got back from a business trip to Eureka. I always try to get the cases there so I have an excuse to go up north. What was it like to grow up there?"

"It had its good and bad points. Probably a lot like anywhere else. When you're a kid, you don't really know anything different."

"Do you know that little restaurant on the corner of Front and First Streets? They were one of my first clients at Farmstead."

"You mean Harry's? Of course. I went to school with their kids. They are super-nice people."

"I agree. They'd offer me meals whenever I was up there. I can't say that's always the case with my clients. The wineries I've represented in particular never seem very hospitable to their road-weary attorney. I was glad that everything worked out in that case. It was a slip and fall and not their fault at all. In fact, if I'm remembering it correctly, the plaintiff originally claimed the accident happened on a day when they weren't even open."

"Well, I'm glad it worked out for them, too." She looked at her watch and started gathering her things together. "Guess I'd better get back to work."

I tried to think of something to say to keep her from leaving, but nothing came quickly enough, so I simply said, "Me too. Nice to see you."

A couple of days passed and I was still thinking about Meg. I decided to take the next step. I chose email rather than text or phone so I wouldn't put her on the spot. Anyway, I figured it would be easier on me to be rejected in an email. I found her email address in the company directory.

In the heading I wrote: "Hi." Then, in the body, "I was wondering...." No, no, too passive. I deleted it.

"I still owe you a cup of coffee for your help the other day. Would you like to get together sometime this weekend? Jake." There. Simple, direct, and flexible. I left my email open on the computer screen to watch the feed.

Twenty minutes letter I saw a reply. "Sounds great. Would Saturday morning work for you? I have a commitment in the afternoon. Meg."

)O(O(

We arranged to meet at a Starbucks not far from my house. I arrived first and waited outside in the shade. I noticed her park and walk over to me. She was wearing jeans, sneakers, and a sleeveless shirt. She was carrying the large leather purse that seemed to be a regular part of her wardrobe. I wondered what she could find to put in there.

She gave a wave when she saw me. When I stood up to go inside, I was surprised to notice that she had a couple of inches on me. We ordered at the counter and then found a table. She had a latte and I had my usual large black coffee.

"So now that you know something about me," she said after we had exchanged a few pleasantries, "Tell me more about yourself. Are you from Sacramento?"

"No," I said. "I grew up in Orange County—not far from Disneyland, actually. I went to college down south, at Cal State Fullerton, and moved up to San Francisco with my then-girlfriend after we finished our undergraduate work. She was accepted for a graduate program at Mills College in Oakland, and I came along for the ride. Unfortunately, that ride didn't last too long. We split up after a few months, but I stayed in the city."

She nodded as if she understood. "Well, if you're going to be dumped, I guess San Francisco is as nice a place as any. Did you go to law school there?"

"Yes, at a small law school in the city; a night school. Very basic. The bar pass rate was pretty low, but fortunately I was able to make it through on the first try."

She took a sip of her drink and then scraped her spoon around the inside of the cup to get most of the foam.

"You have any kids?" she asked.

"Well, I guess it depends how you look at it. I was married to someone for a number of years. She had a kid when I met her. I think of him like a son. He's going to Humboldt State right now. How about you?"

"No. It never worked out for me. I was with someone for a long time, but it just wasn't in the cards."

She told me more about growing up in Eureka. Her parents were both teachers, and her father had a commercial fishing business on the side. "Fishing is his first love," she said, "But he didn't want the pressure and the risk of trying to make a full-time living at it. And anyway, he enjoys his day job as well."

We decided to take a walk, and drove to my house to get the dogs. I introduced her to Claire when I collected Abby. Claire and Meg really hit it off. Claire showed Meg a painting she was working on and was thrilled by

Meg's attention and admiration.

We walked along the river by Sacramento State. Meg pointed out some of the more memorable monuments to her years there. By mid-afternoon we were back at my house. The two dogs were lying on the grass and we sat on the deck. It was warm but pleasant in the shade. I showed Meg the small plot where I was planning to plant tomatoes, and we talked about the yard and the dogs.

As Meg drank the last of her iced tea, her phone chimed. She dug into her purse, pulled it out, and responded to a text. "I told a friend I would help her with some paperwork this afternoon," she said, "So I'd better get going."

"Sure I can't persuade you to stay?"

She smiled. "Maybe next time."

I walked Meg out to her car and then sat on the shady deck a little longer, thinking about her and how easy she was to be with. Before long the dogs began looking for attention. Elwood sat in front of me with his warm brown eyes staring into mine, his paw on my knee.

"Okay, boy," I said, patting his head. "I didn't forget you."

Elwood and I walked Abby next door. Claire was in her front yard repotting some succulents when we arrived.

"Thank you," she said. "I hope Abby wasn't any trouble."

"No, not at all. They do great together. Thanks again for watching Elwood."

Claire acknowledged the thanks with a nod. "Meg seems really nice," she said, wrestling a giant jade plant.

"I know it's none of my business, but I'd be happy for you if you met someone new. The dogs are great but we all need people around. And you can't work all the time."

"I know," I said, wondering why people say 'it's none of my business' before plowing ahead. "It can be hard meeting people."

"Well, you've got to get out there and live and not mope around—at least that's my philosophy." Claire looked at me with a smile. "Like Scoop Nisker used to say back when he was a DJ on KFAT, 'If you don't like the news, go out and make some of your own.'"

I laughed. "Words to live by, Claire; words to live by. Good night."

Chapter 8

Meg and I met for lunch in the cafeteria occasionally over the next few weeks and, from my point of view, things were going well. I wanted to move our relationship to the next level but felt a little rusty on just how to do that. Then, on Thursday afternoon, the claims and legal staff were told to drop whatever they had planned for Friday afternoon and to be in the large meeting room at two o'clock. As it happened, none of us was in trial that week, so with some kicking and screaming from the folks on the other side of our cases, we all managed to clear our calendars.

We knew before the meeting that it was going to involve some big news. Word travels at the speed of light in any business, particularly one where things were as up in the air as they were for us, and we knew that the meeting was going to involve both claims and legal. A joint meeting of the two departments was pretty rare, and nobody was expecting to hear that things were going to continue unchanged.

When I came into the room, I saw Dan talking to Anton and a couple of other suits I didn't recognize. One of them was a short, dark-complected fellow; the other was tall with over-coiffed white hair and a florid face.

Anton, the company president, was a fairly average-looking guy in his fifties with dark hair and a short beard. There were about forty-five people in the room and you could feel the tension in the air—there was very little chatting as we all found seats.

Anton was up first: "As you know, we're in the middle of some exciting changes here at Farmstead. Basically, Black Belt has decided to take us in a new direction, and while I know that change can be tough sometimes, we're bringing in a management team which I think will help make those changes as easy as possible. Fundamentally, we will be focusing much more on the commercial end of the insurance business, and shedding some of the smaller accounts. Although it will take a while to filter down to your end of the shop, I think you can expect to see a different level of exposure and a different mix of cases before long."

I was sitting next to Peter, who looked at me with a grimace.

"Now, before I take questions, I'd like to call on Dan Casey, from legal, who, as I think most of you know, will be leaving us."

We all expected this, but I don't think any of us in the room thought that the announcement would happen in quite this way. The Farmstead method of removing people from management was to have them clean out their desks in the dead of night, and then have personnel send out an email the next day letting people know that they had gone. Any going-away events would be strictly outside of the company realm, and attending one came with a certain career risk of being identified with someone on the outs with the higher-ups.

The fact that Casey was allowed to address us, rather than being shuffled off like most people, was probably due to the level of loyalty that existed between him and the legal team. The office was so tightly knit that there would have been a good chance of mass resignations if he had just been booted out on his ass.

Dan drew himself up at the lectern, and took a deep breath. "I'm happy to announce my retirement, effective at the end of the day. I've had a great run here at Farmstead, and I think we've done a great deal of good for an underserved sector of the state's economy. I'm going to miss you folks, but I'm not going far. Some of you know that I've been doing pro bono work for the Matthew's Promise homeless resource center, representing them in a disagreement with the city. They've invited me to open a law office on their campus to represent their guests in Social Security disability cases. So, if you're ever in the neighborhood, feel free to drop by. Once again, thanks for all the good times and interesting cases, and good luck in the future."

Dan hardly looked at the lawyers as his eyes moved over the gathering. I wondered if anyone in the office had known about his plans with Matthew's Promise. I sure hadn't seen that coming. I had heard of Matthew's Promise, but I didn't know much about them. From what I read in the paper, they had a pretty large operation, and were always at odds with the city and the county over homeless issues. Casey was known for having a soft spot for the underdog, but I had no idea how he expected to make this project work.

Anyway, after the applause, Anton was back up, and introduced the next speaker. "I'd now like to call on Jim Scanlon. Jim has been with a number of large property-casualty carriers, and, given this experience, Black Belt thought that he would be uniquely qualified to lead claims and legal into our new era."

Wait a minute—he said claims *and* legal? This did not bode well, although I had been warned that he might push for that authority. Compact and wiry, Scanlon was intense looking. He wore a suit that, to my experienced eye, didn't seem to quite fit. He had a confident manner, but I noticed that he seemed to be trying to avoid eye contact with anyone as he spoke.

"I'm happy to be here and to help in the process of turning Farmstead into a new and dynamic presence in the commercial insurance business. Doing this will involve a great many improvements in the way things are done here. In my opinion, Farmstead's been stuck in a comfortable rut for a long time and has not been generating the return on investment that it should. My job will be turning things around, which means shaking things up, and some of you may not like some of the changes. But trust me, if we want Farmstead to succeed in its new vision, that will have to happen. My door's always open to you if you have any ideas of changes that should be made.

"One change which I wanted to share with you right off the top, which will particularly affect legal, has to do with the geography of our caseload. As Anton said, Farmstead's moving away from covering small-time businesses and farms. Our underwriting will be increasingly focused on large risks and we will be moving more aggressively into urban counties. So, effective immediately, new cases in any county outside of a 100-mile radius of Sacramento will go to outside counsel. Cases you've already gotten underway won't be affected by this change, but we need legal to be where the action is, not spending ten hours on the road to take a two-hour deposition.

"Now, I want to introduce Mark McDowell. Mark's been hired as Dan's replacement. He was most recently head of the Business Risk Mutual house counsel office here in Sacramento, and I'm really looking forward to working with him."

I wasn't paying much attention as Mark, who turned out to be the tall guy, came up to the podium. I was busy texting Jocelyn, who was sitting across the room, to see if we had filed our response in the new Eureka case. If I wasn't going to get any more trips up there in the future, I was damned if I was going to give up my last shot. Fortunately, she texted back that it had been filed two days earlier.

I refocused on Mark: "So anyway, I agree with Dan that the big risks that we'll be insuring will require a whole different brand of lawyering than what Farmstead has needed up until now, and I hope that you'll be up to it. I'll be meeting with each of the lawyers in the next couple of weeks to discuss how you can help us meet this goal."

"Well, I'm sure we've given you a lot to think about," Anton said. "Are there any questions?" The room was like a ghost town after a hard winter, as everyone seemed to be reeling from the revelations. "Well, if there are none, I'll close the meeting, but feel free to come see me if anything occurs to you."

The suits left as a group, leaving Dan behind. There were lots of hugs and tears, some of each from me. Dan's leaving truly marked the end of an era. On the way back to the office, I fell in with Peter. "You know anything about this Mark McDowell guy?" I asked.

"Some. I had him as an arbitrator in one of my cases. He struck me as a legend in his own mind—a huge ego."

"Great," I said. "That's just what we need after someone like Dan, what with all the changes in the wind."

"Yeah, I think the one thing we can be sure of is that if corporate's trying to push legal in some direction or another, he's not going to be the one pushing back."

We headed to Dan's office, congratulating him on his retirement. The room was packed with well-wishers. He apologized for not telling us about the changes earlier, and seemed genuinely sad to be saying goodbye. I was sad as well, and we promised to meet for lunch when things settled down.

XOXOX

I was in something of a hurry to get back to my office, as I had noticed on my phone when I texted Jocelyn that Meg had sent a message. I opened it, finding a short message: "You free after work?"

"Sure," I texted back. "Meet downstairs in the lobby?"

"Call me."

I obliged, and she picked up on the first ring.

"Hi," she greeted me. "Can we meet someplace more private? Someplace off campus?"

I wasn't sure what to make of this, but asked, "Do you know El Gallito over on Northgate?" El Gallito is one of my local go-to Mexican places. It's close to the office, but in an older, much scruffier section of town, and not a place where I had ever seen a Farmsteader in five years of going there. Chips and salsa both rated an eight out of ten. Meg wasn't familiar with the restaurant, but I gave her directions, and we agreed to meet at five-thirty.

I got there first and got a booth in the back, ordering a beer. If she wanted privacy, we would have it. She walked in, looking distracted. Distracted looked good on her, but I figured so would most other emotions.

She sat down and ordered an iced tea. I told her about the meeting, about Dan's leaving, and about my worries for the future. She expressed concern but was unusually quiet.

"I'm sorry," I said. "Did you want to talk about something else?"

She came right to the point: "I think we have been hitting it off pretty well," she said, "but I'm afraid I may have given you the wrong impression. I'd like to see you again, but I'm really not in a place where I'm ready to start anything romantic with anyone." She had been looking at the table while she spoke, but now looked directly at me. Her dark brown eyes were intense. I have to admit I was disappointed, but I tried not to show it. At least she was being candid.

"All right. Sure," I said. "I've really enjoyed spending time with you, too. Are you seeing someone?"

"Actually, no," she said. "My last relationship was in New York, and it ended badly. I think I need to move more slowly."

I nodded. "That's fine. I don't know that I'm completely over my ex leaving me either. I hope I didn't do or say something wrong. My dating reflexes haven't been used in a long time, and I think they may have atrophied."

"You're sweet. It's not that."

"Well, can we still be friends? Just hang out? I don't really have much of a life beyond work and the dog. And Claire keeps asking me when you'll be over again. She really enjoyed meeting you the other day,"

"Sure, I'd like that. You seem to know the area pretty well, and I didn't have a car most of the time when I lived here before. Maybe we could go for a hike or something." She smiled. "And one other thing, I think I'd be more comfortable if we only met outside the office. You know, three people have asked me who I was with in the cafeteria the other day."

"Oh, jeeze," I said. "Office gossip is in a league of its own." I shook my head. "A hike would be great. This is a good time of year to get out of the city. I've got out-of-town cases that will jam up my weekends for the next couple of weeks, but maybe three weeks?"

"Sounds possible. I'll let you know." We chatted about work and her family for awhile and then went our separate ways.

Chapter 9

The office grapevine was buzzing. I learned that Dan had been thinking about this job change for a while, but that the decision to leave Farmstead was not his. He was told to leave or be fired. And the first impression of Scanlon was uniformly negative. The lawyers could see that the plan was to settle fewer cases, try more, and make our lives miserable. Ultimately, we suspected that the goal was to replace us with an outside firm. Time to polish the resume.

Given all that was happening at work, I was especially happy when Meg called a couple of weeks later about finding a time to get together. We arranged to take the dogs for a hike in the Sierra.

Bassi Falls is an easy but beautiful trail located past Placerville off State Route 50. I had been there once before, and I knew it would be a pleasant walk. Meg had offered to drive. I was happy to be a passenger for once and glad she didn't mind having the dogs in her car. I hadn't noticed her ride when we met at Starbucks, but it was a newish Accord with the more powerful V-6 engine than the standard model.

After nixing the idea of a romantic relationship, she seemed relaxed and comfortable as a friend. I was disappointed, but still hoped we could grow closer more slowly. As we headed east on Highway 50, I was impressed by her driving. She wasn't speeding or doing anything dangerous, but she seemed to be gaming out the traffic in all four lanes and anticipating peoples' moves before they were even aware that they were going to make them. As a result, we moved along quite quickly.

"You drive real smoothly," I commented.

"Thanks. I had to learn to think way ahead on the road at an early age. My high school car was my dad's '66 Volkswagen bus. Those things are so underpowered, you really have to drive defensively. God, dad loved that thing. He rebuilt everything from the front to the back, but never got around to cleaning up the body work, which was great, since I got a free pass on a couple of dents that way."

"Does he still have it?"

"No. We moved to a smaller house when I was in high school, and they didn't have room for it in the garage. With the fog and the salt air up in Eureka, a car like that would rust away in a hurry if it lived outside. It really hurt him to let it go, but he still has his '67 VW bug, which I think he wants to be buried in. It's pretty much showroom quality, and he's won a couple of awards with it."

"Sounds like fun. In my family, cars were just something that got you from place to place. We had about as much emotional attachment to them as we had to the dishwasher. That's just as well these days, as I run through a company car pretty quickly with all the driving I do."

"How much do you do? You certainly seem to be out of the office a lot."

"Probably 30,000 miles a year, not counting my commute. We're all road warriors in legal, but somehow I always wind up holding the record at the end of the year. Fortunately, there's a lot of nice scenery in this state, although there are some mind-numbingly dull places too."

We had been passing through one of those latter areas, which is the stretch between downtown Sacramento and Folsom, but our conversation had gotten us to the point where the road started up into the foothills and became more interesting. We passed through the grasslands (El Dorado Hills), the scrub brush (Cameron Park), the oak woodlands (Shingle Springs), and started hitting the pines at Placerville. From there to the turnoff, the forest was dense along the roadway.

"I've only been up this way a couple of times, going to South Lake Tahoe," Meg said. "I must have been in a hurry, because I really didn't notice how woodsy it is."

"It's woodsy right next to the road, but if you go off to the side for any distance, there's been a lot of clearcutting."

"Oh, yeah, and doesn't that sound familiar. Growing up in Eureka, it was noticeable how the logging companies tried to hide things. They called it 'protecting the viewshed,' but it really was to keep folks from seeing what they were doing."

About then, we hit the turnoff and headed up into the national forest. The area near the highway had been burned over about twelve years earlier, and the trees were growing back fairly nicely. Since they had all been planted at the same time, they were all the same height, which made it look like a Christmas tree farm gone feral, but I was impressed with the recovery. The Bassi Falls trailhead was about twenty winding miles up the paved forest service road, and then up another mile of dirt road from an unmarked junction.

When we got to the trailhead, the dogs jumped out of the car and started getting acquainted with the woodland smells and adding their own commentary. We rounded them up and headed off. It was an easy three-mile hike to the falls. A fair number of people passed us going the other way, with the highlight being a pack of off-road unicyclists. Bassi Falls always puts on a good show in the spring, and when we got there the water was flowing impressively.

The dogs headed into the pool at the base of the falls. I'm not much for swimming in cold water, so I knew I'd be giving it a pass. We pulled out our lunch and sat in the shade of the one pine that somehow survived the high waters next to the creek.

"I really don't want to talk work today," Meg said, "but are things getting as weird on your side of the building as they are in underwriting?"

"Why, how weird is it?"

"We've gotten a bunch of new people in the office, and several of the folks who had been with Farmstead forever have been let go. I don't think that's too surprising with a new owner taking over, but these new guys—and they're almost all guys, by the way—are kind of creepy. They spend a lot of time huddled in the conference room, and it's really unclear what they're talking about. And they seem to get along much better than you would expect, since they came from a bunch of different carriers. Don't get me wrong. They seem to know their stuff, even if they kind of sneer at the small-time business that Farmstead's written up until now. But something's going on, and I sure can't figure out what it is."

I kept my eyes on the dogs as they chased each other around the granite boulders. "Well, on our end, losing Dan Casey is huge. I don't have a feel for this McDowell guy who's replacing him, but the new claims guy, Jim Scanlon, is supposed to be a real bomb-thrower. It'll be a while before we see much change in our case mix, since there's a big lag between when new business gets written and when it starts generating lawsuits. But what really hurts for me at this point is losing any chance at new Eureka cases. Anyway, I'd rather enjoy the day than think about work."

"I agree. You're right. This really is too nice a place to talk about that stuff."

The dogs were finished with the pool, and came over to shake the water off into our faces. It was actually refreshing, if a little smelly. I got the frisbee out of my pack, and let them chase it over the rocks for a few minutes. Then another dip in the pool, a quick toweling down, and we were on our way back to the car.

Once we were back on the road, Meg thanked me for showing her the hike. "No problem. There're lots more places I can take you, although some, like most of the spots in the Coast Range, are too hot and dry in the summer to be much fun. I sometimes go with the Sierra Club. Should I let you know next time I'm planning an outing?"

"I'd like that."

We didn't talk much more on the way back, but when she dropped me and the dogs off, she said, "I really enjoyed spending today with you."

Of course, being as clueless as I am when it comes to these things, I didn't know how to take it, but saw it as a hopeful sign.

Chapter 10

There were further signs of what might be progress the following week, when Meg invited me to her house for dinner on Saturday. There were a few seconds when I thought that she might be signaling a move toward a closer relationship, until she added that the invitation included my neighbor, Claire. I tried not to show any disappointment when I accepted.

Claire and I arrived at Meg's place a few minutes after six. The dogs were invited too, so we brought them along. It was a condo, a few blocks from the state capitol in the Midtown section of Sacramento. Her unit was in a three-story brick building with outside stairs leading to the front door.

We rang the buzzer on the locked gate at the foot of the stairs, and Meg buzzed us in. The dogs bounded noisily up the steps, and I walked up more slowly with Claire. Although I had hoped for a romantic evening with Meg, I always enjoyed Claire's company. She was a lively and interesting person who was more forward-looking than most twenty-year-olds I've met. She was also a devout Catholic who had spent most of her years involved in efforts to improve life for others. More recently, as her age has started to slow her down, Claire has turned more and more to art, and has shown a remarkable talent in painting for someone picking it up on her own. But she also found time to distribute food in the park once a week to anyone who needed it.

When we arrived at the landing for Meg's apartment, the door was ajar. I could smell dinner cooking and could hear Meg talking sternly to the dogs before she turned to us.

"Welcome, welcome! Come on in," she greeted us.

"Smells delicious," Claire said. "Thank you so much for the invitation." Claire handed Meg a freshly baked apple pie. "I made it this morning."

"Yum! Thank you. So glad you could come."

I gave Meg a bottle of wine. "It's from one of the wineries we insure," I told her. "I had a complicated case with them a few years ago. Remind me to tell you about it sometime—bottles blowing up on store shelves, lots of excitement."

Meg explained her living arrangement. She rented a room from a high-level state government worker named Ginny Dolan, who lived and worked in Los Angeles but who needed a place in Sacramento about one week a month. The master bedroom was on the main floor. Meg's room, the owner's office, and a full bath were on the floor above. Meg had the condo to herself most of the time and, given its location and size, she never could have afforded to rent it on her own. It was also fully furnished, so she had been able to move in with little expense.

"So, this is what you come home to," I said, scanning the spacious living room. "It's nice."

"Yes. I was very lucky." Meg had poured a glass of wine for each of us. I took a seat in the corner of the couch and looked out the window at the restored Victorian-era home across the street.

"I don't want to dwell on work and bore Claire," I said, "but have you heard the latest? Jocelyn told me today about a new guy they hired to work directly under Anton. He's the special assistant to the president, whatever that means. His name's Charles Abercrombie."

"No, I didn't hear about that," Meg replied. "You're a lot more connected to the grapevine than I am. So let me get this straight—Anton stays on as president, the demon Jim Scanlon is top dog in claims and legal, and the mysterious Mark McDowell is now your immediate boss. 'Special assistant to the president'—is that a new position?"

"Yeah. I'd love to know what that's all about. You've got to figure that he's some kind of emissary from Black Belt to look out for its interests."

"God, what next?" Meg said with a classic eye roll. "I keep waiting for another shoe to drop—I think we're up to six or seven of them by now."

I glanced at Claire to apologize for all the shop talk. She was absently patting Elwood, who was now lying beside her. "Gosh, that name sounds familiar," she said. "I swear I've heard of him before. I just can't remember where."

"You are probably thinking of Abercrombie and Fitch," Meg said. "We'll have to see how well this guy dresses. Maybe he's related." Meg turned to me. "Have you met him yet?"

"I really doubt I'll be introduced any time soon," I said, "but Jocelyn pointed him out in the parking lot. I can tell you that he drives a late-model Cadillac Escalade, if that helps."

Meg just shook her head and invited us to come have dinner in the kitchen, which wasn't large, but had enough room for a small table covered with a red and white checkered tablecloth. A vase of flowers and a basket of warm bread filled the center of the table.

Meg brought the pot over from the stovetop. It smelled great—chicken stew with potatoes and artichokes. I can serve up a decent dinner when I have to, though I'm no great cook. But now that I live alone, it's harder to find the motivation to make anything complex. I'm more likely to fry up a couple of eggs or to buy something from the deli counter at the local market. Since I usually eat dinner by myself, tonight's combination of a good meal and good conversation was something I had been looking forward to.

"Jake was telling me on the way over that you grew up in Eureka," Claire said. "My daughter went to Humboldt State, so I've been up that way many times. It's so beautiful."

"Yeah. I miss it. My parents are still there, so I do have a reason to go up north and a place to stay when I do."

"Speaking of which," I said, "I'll be driving up on one of my cases in a few weeks. You want to come with me and visit your folks?"

"Possibly. I may need to go up there for work myself one of these days. Maybe we can coordinate our trips."

My always-hopeful heart skipped a beat. "That would be great."

"They've been giving me a bunch of larger commercial businesses to assess, and some of it is up that way," Meg said. "It seems like the type of businesses we insure is changing fast. In fact, I have to go to Southern California in a couple of weeks to look at some properties."

She offered more food to both of us. "I always liked the idea that Farmstead focused on small businesses. I'm not really all that comfortable with my skills with bigger commercial properties. People think my experience in New York qualifies me for that level of exposure, but it's not really true."

"Yes, lots of changes," I said.

"When my daughter was up at Humboldt State," Claire said, "she got really involved with Redwood Summer—I think it was 1990. She's been a tree-hugger since she was a kid, so it wasn't surprising. Do you remember that time?"

"I've heard of it," I said, "but I don't really know much about it. What happened?"

"Well, I sure remember it," Meg said emphatically. "I was just a kid living near ground zero. What I remember is feeling very scared about the standoffs between the loggers and sawmill workers on the one side and the rabble rousers like Judy Bari and Earth First! on the other. I was sure there were going to be people killed over it. The town was divided. I just wanted everyone to get along. I don't have good memories of that year."

Claire nodded her head and turned toward me. "There were a group of environmentalists, mostly college age, protesting the redwoods being cut. There was a lot of controversy, but the bottom line was they wanted to stop the destruction of the redwoods, particularly the old-growth trees.

"I remember there was this company—Pacific Lumber—up on the North Coast," she continued, looking at Meg. "From what I heard, it was a good little family company—responsible practices, good to its employees, etc., etc.—but it got bought out by a large corporation called Maxxam. This was in the days of Michael Milken, and Maxxam took on a huge junk bond debt to make the purchase. To pay off the debt, Maxxam decided to cut down as many redwoods as it could—clear-cut them—including some of the oldest trees on the planet."

"Yeah, 2000 years old," Meg said. "They also raided the Pacific Lumber pension fund," she added. "For some of my parent's friends, that was even worse. In my view, the whole thing was a big put-up job by Maxxam, which owned the land that people were fighting over. In the end, it sold the land to the government for way more than it was worth, because that way the environmentalists would get something and could declare that they won. The trees got saved, but the jobs didn't, and almost none of the money stayed in town."

Claire took another bite of chicken and continued. "Do you remember the bomb going off in Oakland in Judi Bari's car?" Claire turned to me. "She was one of the leaders of EarthFirst!"

"Yes, that I do remember," I said. "The FBI and the

Oakland Police Department said that she and her friend planted the bomb in their own car right under the driver's seat. The two of them sued, and as I recall, the jury awarded them millions."

"Right. I lived in Oakland back then and I followed the trial and the news fairly closely." Claire took another sip of wine. "Like I said, no question, EarthFirst! was controversial. Some of the other environmental groups didn't agree with them. But we always thought that some of the so-called environmental groups opposing them were FBI or timber company plants. My daughter called groups like that 'Astroturf,'" she smiled. "Have you heard that expression before?"

"I haven't," I said, "but I can guess what it means—a fake-grass roots organization, right?"

"Right," said Claire. "It was a very tense time."

We moved onto other topics of conversation, including Claire's family and Meg's recipe for dinner.

"Speaking of dinner," Meg said, rising to her feet, "let's have a piece of that pie before the dogs decide it belongs to them."

Claire and I raised our glasses. "Here, here," Claire said.

Chapter 11

The next time I ran into Meg was in the cafeteria a few days later. She was finishing up her soup and salad when I arrived.

"Hey, thanks again for dinner the other night," I said, dropping into the chair across from her.

"Glad you could make it. I enjoyed it."

"I will have to have you over to my place sometime. Maybe for pizza." I smiled. "You mentioned going to Southern California next week. What kind of property are you looking at?"

"Well, nothing I have any experience with at all," she said. "It's a collection of temples, owned by something called the Human Actualization Institute. It was founded by a famous Indian yogi in the 1920s, and they want a quote on property and liability coverage. I have to visit all their sites, so I'll be gone most of next week. I'm setting it up to fly into San Diego on Monday, then work my way north. I'll start at what I guess is the mother church somewhere north of San Diego in a place called Cardiff-by-the-Sea. If all goes according to plan, I'll fly home late Thursday from Los Angeles."

"The HAI? Cardiff? Heck, I know that place. It's right next to old Highway 101 on a bluff above the ocean with a spectacular view. When I was little, we used to occasionally drive to San Diego for a weekend, and we would always stop there for a mushroom burger. The architecture makes it look like something from a Hollywood back lot—very Taj Mahalish. There's a famous surf break just offshore called Swami's.

"I imagine the property coverage should be reasonably easy to figure out," I continued, "even if the structures are a little unique. I just hope whoever figures out the liability coverage is careful about what we do and don't cover. There was a guy in claims here who's now retired who had some pretty hair-raising stories about sexual exploitation claims he had to pay at his old company from a couple of new-agey places it insured over on the Central Coast."

Meg replied, "I think our policy exclusions are tighter now than what got written in the past, but I agree that a set-up like this could have those kinds of problems."

"So, you'll be in Cardiff next Monday, God willing?"

"That's the plan."

"Want to have lunch?"

"What? Are you going to be down there too? Are you flying?"

I smiled. "No, actually I'm driving. I'm scheduled to meet with an expert witness at UC San Diego Monday morning, and it's just a quick hop up the coast to Cardiff from there. Want to meet about one o'clock?"

"Well, I'm always ready for lunch, and I shouldn't have any trouble finishing my business, 'cause I'm taking the six a.m. flight down. Send me the details."

"Great. See you then if not before."

So, was I really already planning to be in San Diego a week from Monday? Well, no, but I could be. Oh, the expert witness was for real. So were the date and time for our meeting. It's just that I had planned to do the meeting by telephone rather than in person. Changing it to an in-person meeting required a good deal of drive time, but I had a Tuesday afternoon deposition in Modesto, so that would break up the return trip. And, it would be worth it if it got me some alone time with Meg.

)()()(

In general, business trips to Southern California were pretty rare. The few cases that Farmstead had in the south state went to local law firms, which was fine with me, but I didn't mind the occasional chance to go there and visit with the folks in the process. What I did mind was the drive. If I-5 north of Sacramento was flat, empty, and boring, I-5 south of Stockton was 250 miles of flat, empty, and boring on steroids. About the only point of interest was the enormous cattle feedlot next to the freeway about halfway between Sacramento and Los Angeles. The dog was usually my co-pilot on these trips, and long before I could smell anything, Elwood would pop up with an interested look on his face, his nose sniffing, as we approached it.

Elwood and I left home about ten on Sunday morning. The first couple of hours went smoothly, but then a cross-wind started to get up. It developed at about the same point in the trip when I started to see the signs along the freeway bemoaning a "Government-created Dust Bowl."

These were put up by the farmers in the irrigation districts on the west side of the valley, complaining about their reduced water allocations during the droughts, which have become more frequent. Water (or the lack of it) is a major problem in California. The state's water supplies are seriously over-subscribed, so even in an average rainfall year, someone—either residential customers, farmers, or fish—gets shortchanged. And the farmers had increased the pressure on the water supply by switching from annual crops like broccoli, where they could leave a field fallow in a year where there wasn't enough water, to orchards and vineyards, which had to be watered to protect their investments regardless of how much rain had fallen. Every time I drove this stretch, I wanted to buy a couple of acres next to the freeway where I could put up signs saying "Government-created Garden of Eden," or perhaps "Government-created Farmland." In any event, between the pesky cross-wind and the agricultural propaganda, I was not in the best frame of mind for the southern leg of the valley.

My spirits lifted, however, as I started up the Grapevine Pass into the Tehachapi Mountains. The rains had been as generous to Southern California as they had been to the north, and the poppies were in their full glory. The afternoon sun shone directly on the hillsides to the east of the freeway, returning a warm orange glow that I could almost feel on my cheek. Where the poppies weren't blooming, lupine and other blue flowers covered the ground, and the background shade was a deep green. Southern California is baked dry nine months of the year, so the contrast was especially sharp.

Soon enough, the road dropped from the sublime back to the ridiculous as I coasted down into Santa Clarita. From there on down to Garden Grove, it was freeways channelized by sound walls, much as the Los Angeles River is channelized by flood control structures. I always feel like a migrating salmon driving in Los Angeles. It being Sunday afternoon, it took less than another two hours to make it to the ancestral mansion (i.e., a fifty-year-old ranch home).

The house where I grew up looked unchanged from when I had left, other than a little stand with books in front of the house and a sign saying "Little Free Library." My mom was a librarian, so I figured she was bringing her work home. The old Bermuda grass lawn I used to unwillingly mow had been replaced by low-maintenance, drought-tolerant landscaping. The neighborhood seemed about the same, although the signs on the arterial street I had taken from the freeway were in an increasing variety of languages. When I parked in the driveway and let Elwood out, he immediately ran to the front door and began pawing it. My mother opened it before I could even knock, and he tore inside.

"I see he hasn't forgotten us," she said.

"No chance of that. Feed a dog bacon for breakfast, and he's yours for life."

"Well, I'm not allowed to spoil your father, and I don't have any grandchildren—at least yet—so I have to practice on someone."

She smiled and gave me a hug, as my father came up and joined us.

"I like the little library out front," I said. "That's new."

"Something I heard about recently," mom said. "Dad built the structure and the books seem to move pretty well. How was your drive?" she asked. "And what brings you to these parts?"

"The drive was okay—kind of breezy. I'll tell you about why I'm here, but I'd like to take Elwood for a walk. There was too much wind in the valley to do anything more than a minimal pee break. Want to come with me and we can chat?"

"Sure, just let me get a sweater."

The reason for my visit involved one of my more unusual cases. My client had turned in front of a car driven by a woman in her thirties. The ensuing T-bone collision was entirely his fault as far as anyone could see. She had probably been going twenty-five miles per hour when she hit him, and one wouldn't expect significant injuries from a relatively modest impact like that, especially as she had been wearing her three-point seatbelt. However, she had saline breast implants, and one of them had started leaking a week or two after the accident. She had had it replaced, opting for a larger size than the original, and had the other breast redone at the same time to match. Now she wanted us to pay for both surgeries, as well as the attendant pain, discomfort, and the cosmetic embarrassment while waiting for the surgery. I was on my way down to San Diego to consult with one of the leading experts in breast implant failure to see if we had a viable cross-complaint against the manufacturer.

I explained this to my folks as we walked over to the local park, where I knew there was a large dog area to run Elwood.

"Well, I suppose it all comes down to the physics of things," my father commented. "There are a lot of variables there, and I'd want to know a lot of information about her seat position and the manufacturer's specs for the seatbelt tensioner before I'd have anything like an accurate idea of the forces involved."

My father, always the engineer. He had worked for many years for an aerospace contractor. When the industry went in the toilet back in the 1990s, dad wound up working for a firm which helped lawyers analyze accidents and product failures. He was excellent at breaking down complicated concepts, so he served as an expert witness in a lot of trials. I still ask his advice when I have experts who can't figure out how to explain their findings in a way a jury will understand.

"I don't suppose her surgeon retained the ruptured implant?" my father asked.

"No such luck. I had our paralegal run a medical literature review on the issue, and it wasn't very useful. She also looked for jury verdicts with this injury. It turns out that there aren't that many, and the defense has won at least some of the cases."

"Well," my mother added, "at least this is a change from your usual run of whiplash cases and cows in the road."

We threw the ball to Elwood for about twenty minutes until he was good and panting, then headed back to the house. The Giants were playing the Dodgers on Sunday Night Baseball, so my mother and I watched the game while my father finished preparing dinner. He's the one in the family with the cooking gene, but it seems that it unfortunately skipped a generation when it comes to my skills at the stove.

We sat down to dinner, and I steeled myself for my mother's inevitable inquiries into my personal life. She started easy. "How are Beth and Drew? Do you see much of them?"

"Beth, no; Drew occasionally. In fact, I went shark fishing with him a few weeks back. From all I can tell, they're both doing fine."

"Another trip to Eureka," she said. "Have you been to the library yet? Eureka has the most beautiful public library I've ever seen—right on the water with huge windows and lots and lots of wood."

"I've been meaning to check it out." I said. My mother had mentioned the library before.

"And how about you?" my mother continued. "Anyone new in your life?"

"Well, maybe. I met a woman through work. Unfortunately, she just wants to be friends, but who knows. It could grow into something more."

"That's nice dear. I'm not getting any younger, and I'd sure like to have a grandbaby to play with."

"Whoa, whoa, whoa, slow down here. We're not even dating, let alone making decisions like that. I've heard your plea for grandchildren for years, and I'm not likely to forget about it. But you'll just have to wait until the time's right for me, even if the right time for you is last week."

"I know, honey, but you can't keep me from hoping." I imagined my mother and I having this same conversation when I was in my sixties and my mother in her eighties.

We returned to the living room and put the game back on. I was pretty tired, and went to bed shortly after the Giants won (much to my mother's dismay). My old room had, thankfully, been turned into an office rather than left as a shrine, so Elwood and I happily holed up in the guest bedroom.

Chapter 12

My meeting in San Diego was at eleven the next morning, so I didn't have to get up particularly early. Mom's library branch opened at ten, so she hung around and fed Elwood (bacon) and me (corn flakes). When I stepped outside and looked at the sky, it was that familiar tangy grey-brown mix of smog and marine layer clouds which has always said "home" to me. Not that it triggered any feelings of nostalgia. At one point, I had wanted to stay in Southern California but it's gotten increasingly crowded. There seems to be no way to build enough freeways to relieve the congestion, so it's just more concrete covered by more cars.

Fortunately, the guy I was going to see had his office on the north side of San Diego next to the university, so the ride wasn't as bad as it might have been. Jon Fitzpatrick, my expert, was an adjunct professor at the med school at University of California San Diego and a well-known reconstructive surgeon. He had first gotten involved in legal cases around silicone breast implants, and women's claims that leaking material from them had damaged their immune systems, and was very knowledge about saline implants as well. He was also pretty well known as a detractor of purely cosmetic surgery, which made him stand out in San Diego, which seems to be the state's epicenter for plastic surgery makeovers.

We sat down in his office, which was on the fifth floor of an office building with the windows facing east. From there, you could see the snow-covered San Bernardino Mountains, as well as the nearer Palomar and Cuyamaca ranges. "Great view," I said.

"Yes, at least when it's clear," he replied. "We need more rainy days to knock some of the crud out of the air, but I think we've pretty much come to the end of the string for this year. I hear you were pretty damp up north."

"No big floods, but plenty of near misses."

He nodded and then turned his eyes to the papers in front of him.

"Anyway," he said, "shall we get down to business?" He sorted through some of the pages.

"I've looked at the materials you've sent me. I don't think we need to get into the issue of her going up in size on the replacement augmentation and the cost doing the other breast as a result. I don't think a jury will buy that as anything other than a want rather than a need. It's pretty clear from her medical records that she was concerned with the cosmetics more than anything else. I noticed that she asked the surgeon several times how much cleavage her new look would show."

Jon flipped through a few more pages. "We don't have the ruptured implant, so I'll have to accept what the surgeon has to say about it. Since he did the original augmentation as well as the repair, we know the manufacturer and the batch number of the one that failed. There have been some reports of similar failures from this manufacturer, although none from anywhere near the batch number in this case, so we can probably rule out any production line problem. Of course, that doesn't rule out a bad implant—just not a bad batch of implants."

He finally looked up from his desk and addressed me directly. "So, we're down to three possibilities— either the failure was spontaneous and not related to the accident; the accident caused the failure, but a defect in the implant made it fail under less stress than it should have been able to withstand; or the forces involved in the accident were sufficiently extreme that even a properly produced implant would have failed. I can't quantify the forces myself, but when you look at how many women have implants and how many of them must be in similar accidents, you have to think there would be a lot more failures if they were that vulnerable."

"That makes sense," I said.

"My money is on the second possibility," he continued. "The accident caused the failure, but there was a defect which made it fail under less stress than it should have. I think you should have a valid cross-complaint. I will say, I'd like to have someone look at the physics before I testify to that, but I just don't see the failure happening in a good implant even if she had the chest strap right over the top of her breast."

I nodded. "I have an expert on the engineering/physics aspects of the case and I'll let you know what

---

she comes up with. Also, I haven't taken the claimant's deposition yet, or that of her doctor, so I'll get all the necessary parameters lined up before I do. Can I run down my deposition question checklist with you over the phone once I get it to make sure nothing's missing?"

"Sure. I'm looking forward to working on this one."

We went over a few more points in the case, then I collected my papers and got ready to leave. He rose from the chair and stretched out his hand. "Have a safe trip back," he said.

"Thank you. I'll try," I replied, shaking his hand.

The shoreline north of San Diego consists of small coastal cities perched on bluffs, separated by a series of brackish lagoons. Where it crosses the lagoons, old Highway 101 generally runs along the sand spits that have built up where they meet the ocean. At the south end of Cardiff, the spit is wide enough for restaurants on both sides of the road.

I met Meg at one of the ocean-side restaurants. From our window table, we could look north and see the ornate towers of the Human Actualization Institute up on the bluff. I asked her how her visit had gone.

"It went quite well," she said. "I was expecting the business end of the operation to be a little more touchy-feely than it was. In fact, the risk manager, who is responsible for all of their properties, struck me as having a lot on the ball. There wasn't much that I wanted that he didn't have ready for me." We had both ordered crab cakes and the server came with our food.

"I still have to look at the properties in Los Angeles," she said. "I hope I've factored in enough drive time for all my appointments. Unless traffic's worse than usual, I should be able to fly back when I planned. Oh, by the way, I asked about your mushroom burgers. He said the stand's been closed for years, but they're thinking of reviving it."

She smiled and dipped her crab cake into the aioli. "How about you?"

"It was good." I gave Meg a brief summary of the case. "We figured out what the best approach would be and I think we'll wind up working well together."

"That's a very personal loss," she said. "I can see the depositions being pretty awkward."

"Me, too," I said. "But it's just part of the job."

"The company I worked for in New York insured a sex toy manufacturer," Meg said.

I must have blushed because she started to laugh. "My God, talk about awkward," I said.

"Luckily, I wasn't involved in that part of the business," she continued. "From what I heard there were lots of discussions about the quality of latex."

"I think that's more information than I would want to know." I could think of a number of possible risk scenarios but decided to let the subject drop.

We talked about our respective experiences visiting Southern California for the rest of the meal. It turned out that Meg had only been south of Fresno a couple of times, so I was able to recommend some of the lesser-known attractions to her for her next visit. We said goodbye in the parking lot and headed off on our respective missions.

I hit the road, and made it back to Garden Grove in good time. I took the folks out for dinner at one of the many Vietnamese restaurants which had proliferated in the area since my time there, and went to bed early.

I was up at four o'clock and on the freeway shortly after that. I buzzed through Los Angeles and then took it easy from that point on, arriving in Modesto with plenty of time to get lunch before my deposition. Elwood was well-known by the court reporter whose conference room we were using. Her office was a converted bungalow in an older part of town. The backyard full of squirrels kept the dog occupied until it was time to head home.

Chapter 13

A s I arrived at the office the next day, I heard a din
of drills and hammering. Our deposition room was
under assault by a crew of drywallers. Charlene was the
only other lawyer in the shop. She was watching the
proceedings with a sour look on her face.

"What gives?" I asked.

"McDowell decided that Dan's office wasn't big
enough for him, so he decided to change the depo room
into his office," she replied. "Since it'll be twice as big as
any of our offices, I guess that means he must be twice as
something as the rest of us. Now we'll have to do depos
in the library, and God help us if we have to work on
a project in there where we need to spread out a lot of
documents."

It's true that most of our legal research these days
was done electronically, and the books in the library were
something of an anachronism. But Charlene was right
that there were cases where we needed the work space,
and having to continually bundle up our paperwork so
that someone could take a deposition was going to be a
pain.

"What's going to happen with Dan's old office?" I asked.

Charlene shrugged. "Maybe they'll turn it into the executive spa?" She smiled but then turned serious. "Something else I want to mention. Come in my office."

We went in, and she closed the door behind us. This alone was pretty unusual, as we generally kept them open while we worked.

"You know I've got some experience in online research, right?" This was an understatement. Charlene wasn't a hacker, but you could see it from there. She had gone to law school in hopes of being hired on as a special agent with the FBI in its cybercrimes unit. She was still on the waiting list, and everyone knew it was only a matter of time before she said *adios* to us. The only hope of our keeping her would be if the FBI decided they didn't want someone working there who had a sense of humor, something she had in good measure.

"You're head and shoulders above anyone else here," I said. "What's up?" I sat down in the chair across the desk from her.

"Have you ever looked at the Black Belt website?" she asked.

"Oh, sure. I've checked it out and read some of the resumes. I'm sure we all have."

She opened her laptop and typed a few characters. After a minute or so, she turned the laptop around so that I could see the screen.

I looked at the screen and saw the company website. "Is this what you saw?" she asked. I nodded.

"It's very generic," she continued. "But really, other

91

than window dressing, there is nothing there. Very little about what it does. All you can see is that it's a private equity fund, but there's nothing there about the ownership or the main investors. So, I went digging. Black Belt's registered in the Cayman Islands, which is one of those offshore tax havens. Turns out it's a shell company, owned by another shell company registered in the Isle of Man, owned by yet another company registered in Panama. I'm sure there're even more levels, but I haven't found my way past Panama yet."

"So, a shell inside a shell inside a shell, etcetera?" I asked.

"Looks like it," she continued. "I certainly haven't given up. And there's another thing, although they may not be connected. Over the weekend, I tried to research this new guy Black Belt dropped on us to babysit Anton."

"Yeah, Abercrombie, right? What did you find?"

"Other than a brief biography on the website, I found nothing. The dude doesn't cast a shadow online. Either that name's not real, or he's gone to great lengths to stay off the radar. I can't believe anyone can get that high up in a corporate structure like Black Belt without leaving some electronic footprints."

I headed back to my office in a reflective state of mind. When I got back, there was a note to call Dan Casey on my desk, and I hastened to phone him back.

"Hey Dan, how's the new gig?" I asked.

"More fun than I can imagine. I had forgotten how much I like being my own boss."

I sighed. "We liked having you as a boss as well."

Dan laughed. "Most of the people who work here

are either religious social justice people or formerly homeless themselves. I have to say, it is a much kinder group than the sharks where you are."

"It's only getting worse here," I said. "I'm really glad the change is good for you."

"Well, come on by when you can," he said. "How about late this afternoon? Want to come see my new digs?"

"Sure, I've got time. Just give me directions."

"You'll need them. Everyone who tries to get here using GPS gets lost."

><><><

I worked through my mail and straightened out my calendar, then left around four. I knew generally where Matthew's Promise was, but not how to get there by car. Casey's directions took me toward downtown, and then through a maze of surface streets. As I got closer to my destination, I began to see more and more people who appeared to be homeless walking or sitting along the streets with large packs, shopping carts, and dogs. As I rounded the corner by the Union Gospel Mission, a long line of people waited to get in. When I finally reached the resource center, I pulled up in front of an old bungalow under a huge black walnut tree. In the front was a sign: "Daniel Casey, Esq., Social Security Disability/SSI." Next to it were signs for a couple of other programs: "Youth Services" and "Jail Visitation." I walked up the few stairs to the front door and went inside. In the front room there was a line of chairs and I saw three older men sitting there, apparently waiting for someone or something. I walked down another hallway and found Dan at the back of the building.

The place was pretty bare. Dan's office furniture consisted of three filing cabinets and two old dining tables, one serving as his desk and the other as his credenza. He was never the neatest worker, and the credenza was piled high with what were obviously medical records. A small window in the back of the building let in a little light.

"Hey, Jake, good to see you." Dan got up and shook my hand.

"Good to see you as well," I said. "This is not the easiest place to find. Glad you mentioned the adult bookstore on the corner."

Dan laughed. "Yeah, Sadie's Boutique is a great landmark."

I sat down at the table and Dan brought in two mugs of coffee from a small kitchen next to his office. There was another room beyond that, which I assumed was one of the other programs. We talked for a while about Farmstead, and I brought him up to date on the changes as well as a few pieces of personal news concerning the other attorneys and the staff in the department.

"How are things going here?" I asked.

"Well, when I first got here, there was a lot of excitement among the guests. Everyone thought I was going to be the express train to the Big Rock Candy Mountain, and all they had to do was to sign up. It took awhile for it to sink in that they had to be clean and sober and in medical treatment for me to have a shot at winning their cases, and even if I took them on as clients, it could be two years before they saw any money."

"I suppose your background in medical and legal issues has been a big help," I commented.

"Less than you might think," Dan replied. "Of course, a lot of the orthopedic and neurological problems are really familiar, but I'm having to learn more than I realized about things like diabetes, hepatitis C, and cardiovascular issues. And mental health issues are a big deal, too."

An elderly man walked into the office and asked where the AA meeting was located. Dan got up and directed him down the street.

"It's a little hard to tease out the statistics from Social Security," he continued, "but it looks like my homeless clients have mental disabilities in their claims about twice as often as the overall average. Probably the most common thing I see is severe depression."

"Well, I can understand that," I responded. "Living on the streets would make me depressed, too."

"It's interesting that you say that," Dan said. "I think it's really more than that." He shook his head. "I don't know if psychiatrists would agree with me, but I'm coming to think that very depressed people would be depressed no matter what their circumstances. For them, depression is not the same thing it is for you and me. Not something that's caused by external events—someone dying or losing a job. Most people would get over those things in time."

"Huh. I never thought of it like that."

"Of course, their situation could aggravate the symptoms," Dan continued. "For example, one of the symptoms of depression is trouble sleeping. That is certainly harder if you're sleeping on the street."

"Sounds like you are learning a lot in this job," I said.

"That's interesting."

"Yeah, and a lot still to learn, that's for sure."

I took a sip of coffee from my mug, which had picture of two fish and a basket of bread. "So, who's Matthew, and what's his promise?" I asked.

"Well, the short version is that it's from the Gospel of Matthew, where Jesus tells his followers to feed the hungry, give the thirsty something to drink, clothe the naked, invite strangers into your house, take care of the sick, and visit prisoners in jail. That's where the part is about doing things like that for the least of us is the same as doing them for Jesus. The long version involves a nun and a priest who renounced their vows, got married, and ultimately started this show."

At this point, Casey was interrupted by what sounded like a pack of dogs barking right outside his window. "What's up with that?" I asked.

"Oh, that's just the kennel for the guests' dogs. You get used to it. I don't even hear it anymore."

"Kennel?"

"Yeah. The guests can't bring their dogs into the dining room, where lunch is served. And if they have to go for a medical appointment, a job interview, or to see their parole agent, they need someplace to park them. It's too late in the day to really show you how active things are down here, but they've got everything—showers, laundry facilities, mental health and physical health clinics, a school for homeless children. Even the pets get taken care of by a group of vet students from UC Davis. You'll have to come back for a tour." Dan smiled. He looked happier than I'd seen him look in a long time.

"Anyway, I called you because I wanted to tell you something else." Dan paused and took a long sip from his coffee mug. "You know I got eased out of my job as gently as ever happens in this business," he said. "And we both know why—if they'd just given me the heave ho, half of the legal department would have threatened to quit in sympathy."

"Very true, and not just threatened," I said, and I meant it.

"So, as a result, I'm not as toxic with the folks who are still there as some former Farmsteaders are. I just wanted to pass on to you what I heard in a very not-for-attribution kind of way."

"My lips are sealed."

"Well, what I hear is that last weekend, Jim Scanlon, this new suit from Black Belt—Abercrombie, I think his name is—and a couple of other minions from Los Angeles went through a ton of the claims files and dropped the reserves on all of them big time. We're talking several millions of dollars here. And you may not realize it, but cutting reserves instead of increasing them is really unusual in the context of new ownership. It's much more common to increase the reserves until you've had a reasonable chance to figure out just how good a job the previous administration did on setting them."

Dan had gotten my interest. Insurance companies set aside money, called "reserves," on claims based on a rough estimate of what the case will wind up costing. By reducing the reserves, the company could face a serious shortfall if things went south on the claims. Farmstead had never been overly liberal on setting reserves anyway, and they could be really inadequate after this.

Dan continued, "I think the message is not to buy any more company stock. I'm sure this is going to impact your cases and maybe even your job."

"That's discouraging," I said. "But thanks for the update."

"Well, if all else fails, maybe you can come down here and help me on my cases."

"More likely I'll sign up as a client, but thanks for the offer."

We spent a few more minutes talking about Dan's family, and how they were coping with his drop in income. As I left the office, the sky was getting dark. I noticed that many of the people I had seen along the road had disappeared.

On the way home, I tried to puzzle through what Dan had told me. Insurance regulators limit the amount of business carriers can write based on a percentage of their capital. Dropping the reserves on current claims translated into more earnings, which meant more capital, which meant more policies. It doesn't take a genius to make an insurance company look good in the short term by writing a ton of bad business on the cheap. But bad business has a way of turning into big claims, and big claims have a way of turning into big judgments. Farmstead could then find itself in a serious cash crunch if it was under-reserved on too many files. Just what was going on overall was entirely beyond me, but I could certainly see that the new philosophy on reserves could affect my work.

XOXOX

I got a quick lesson on its impact the following morning, when I grabbed the file for a mediation I had coming up on Friday and headed over to the claims department to talk strategy with the adjuster who had the claim. The case involved a traffic accident, a pretty typical case for our office. Our client, Harry Stone, was driving out in the country near Stockton. He started to turn left into a driveway without checking his rearview mirror, and was hit by a car trying to pass him.

I squeezed into the adjuster's cubicle, and he glanced at the papers in my hand. "Yeah, the Stone file. You're not going to like this, but all I can give you on that case is 15K."

"That's way not enough. The medical bills are almost 10. I know there's some question about liability, but our client's so nervous, the jury won't believe he's telling the truth when I ask him to state his name, let alone when we get into the facts of the accident."

"I know all that, and I agree with you personally, but this comes from way up the food chain. And I know I've been going to mediations to explain my position in the past, but I've been told that's another thing that's just not going to happen anymore."

"Wow. This really isn't a case we want to try, unless the demand stays way out of line."

"Again, I don't disagree, but I've got no say in the matter. Anything else I can help you with?"

So, on Friday, I headed down Interstate 5 for the one-hour trip to Stockton, which is located on the San Joaquin River in the middle of California's agricultural heartland. Despite being far from the coast, it has one of the larger ports in California. I've never particularly liked going to Stockton, as the trip is dull, and the area around the courthouse is seriously run-down, but I had even less of a taste for it that day, given that there was no way I could settle the case. Another detriment to doing Stockton cases was that I was (or so I had been told) a dead ringer for a criminal defense attorney who practiced there and who was not in good flavor with the judges. I had never met him, as the criminal and the civil courtrooms are on different floors, but it always seemed to me that whenever I had to interact with a court clerk or a bailiff, it took a minute or two for them to realize I wasn't the other guy and that I deserved a little better treatment than they initially were prepared to give me.

Stan Wilson, an attorney making a few extra bucks as a mediator, was someone I liked. Still, I bet it wouldn't take a few more cases like this one and he'd stop working with me altogether. We went through the same song and dance as always, then Stan caucused with the plaintiff and his lawyer. I worked on a medical summary on another file while they talked. Stan eventually came in. "I've got something like good news. They dropped the demand to 50, which I understand is the policy limit. I don't know how much more room they've got—I don't think it's very much—but what can you give me?"

"I'll give you everything I've got: 15K."

"What? That's way too low. What are you smoking and where can I get some?"

"It's not me, it's not the claims guy. We're in the middle of a big change in settlement philosophy, and this is my first experience with it. I know I'm not making your job any easier, but I have to ask you to give them my number."

"OK, but don't go anywhere. I bet I'll be back pretty quick."

And he was: "Plaintiff's attorney said he was insulted by your offer."

"If he's insulted by my offering him money, then he thinks our relationship is something different than it is. Anyway, I think we're done here."

"Reckon so. Maybe next time."

I drove home surrounded by big-rigs hauling their wares north. I wondered how long I could last at Farmstead the way things were going. Maybe it was time to figure out where I had put my resume.

Chapter 14

"You still interested in coordinating business trips to Eureka?" Meg asked. She was standing behind me in the cafeteria line at Farmstead. We had gone on two more weekend outings by then. We still made an effort not to be seen together at work, but she seemed to have grown somewhat more relaxed about it as time had passed. I looked around, and no one I knew was in hearing range.

"I'd love to," I said.

"I need to go up north—to New Aberdeen, actually, just south of Eureka —to look at an old hotel Farmstead wants to insure. Want to plan something at the same time?"

"Is that the Eel River Inn? What a beautiful old place." I remembered the hotel from my honeymoon trip up the coast. We had taken a break from camping and had spent a wonderfully romantic night at the inn.

"Yeah, it is. I guess they're remodeling it. Someone has decided to turn it into a five-star resort."

"Nice." The cashier was adding up my purchases. I usually stuck with a sandwich at the cafeteria, but today the pasta dish looked pretty good. "Want to sit with me?" I asked.

Meg was digging in her purse for change but stopped and looked up. "I have to get back to the office. The new boss is keeping a close eye on us. I'm looking at three weeks from Friday."

When I got back to my desk, I asked Jocelyn to set a deposition three weeks from Friday for the plaintiff in the case I had picked up a couple of months back. We represented the owners of the Sasquatch Minimart, a fairly prosperous little business on the main street in McKinleyville, a town about fifteen miles north of Eureka. The store was set back from the road. Between the road and the parking lot, there was a ditch about four feet deep parallel to the road. A culvert took the water from the ditch under a driveway that ran from the road to the store's parking lot and the gas pumps. The accident had happened on one of the brutally foggy nights they get up there every fall. Plaintiff, an eighteen-year-old woman, had driven off the road and into the culvert twenty feet before the edge of the market's property, and had sustained fairly serious injuries. My main question about the case was, "What on earth does this accident have to do with the minimart?" But, in order to ask that question in court, I had to spend some time getting all the facts.

Once Jocelyn confirmed the depo, I texted Meg: "All set for the 20th. Want to drive up together?"

She texted back: "Let's work out the details over drinks after work." The Mexican restaurant near the office had become our usual meeting place, so I didn't need to ask where. We were in there a least once a week.

Meg had already ordered some guacamole and a couple of beers by the time I arrived at the restaurant.

"Tell me more about your plans in Eureka. Do you want to drive up together?" I asked again.

"I think we'd better keep things separate," she said. "I don't want any questions about my expense report. And I'm thinking of spending some time with my folks."

I had hoped we would stay at the same hotel. "When you talked about 'coordinating' our trips, what did you have in mind?"

"Well, why don't I stay wherever you stay on Thursday night and then I'll stay with my parents Friday and Saturday nights. Their place is pretty small or I'd ask them if you could stay." She reached for a chip and took a scoop of guacamole. "I think I told you my dad loves to fish. He'll be out on the water most of the weekend going after rockfish. Would you like to join us?"

"You bet. I'd love to." I hadn't been deep-sea fishing in a long time, but anything involving a pole and a line was fine with me.

"Great. Make sure you have an up-to-date fishing license. We have plenty of extra gear."

"That sounds like a lot of fun. Getting a fishing license is a New Year's resolution I always keep. Say, tell me more about the site visit. How does this fit with Farmstead going into bigger commercial properties?"

"The place is going to be pretty big. When we talked about it at lunch today, it sounded like you're familiar with the hotel."

"I am. It was gorgeous—nestled in the redwoods along the river—right near the coast."

"Location, location, location. It's definitely got that," she laughed. "New Aberdeen was a company town, with a lot of mill workers. The hotel was mostly for big shots visiting the company on business. Eventually, the highway came through town, and tourists starting coming up from San Francisco to look at the redwoods. Over the years it gradually changed to a tourist inn. A company called Clearheart Lumber owns it now—they bought the whole operation from Coast Lumber—the mill and the hotel as well, although the hotel is a separate corporate entity."

"I do remember hearing that it was a popular get-away for the rich and famous back in the day. It was beautiful when I stayed there, with all the trimmings— claw-foot tubs, redwood moldings, and a fireplace in every room—but maybe a little tired around the edges."

"I'm not sure what they have in mind for it now," Meg said. "From what I've seen, they want to expand the hotel and build lots of gardens—something very grand."

"No golf course? Of course, a golf course would mean clearcutting a bunch of redwoods."

"Well, since they own it all, they could do that—cut down the trees and put in a golf course. It's all second- or third-growth trees anyway. But that's not in the plan as far as I know."

"So, what do you look for on the site visit?" I asked. "Risk? Seems like there is a lot of natural risks here— earthquakes, floods, fires...."

"I think they've probably experienced all of those things at one time or another, not that we necessarily cover all that," she smiled. "But, the more risk, the higher the premium. And whichever way you slice it, hope that you're not the one holding the bag when there's a disaster. Like I said the other day, the large commercial properties are a little out of my range of experience, but hopefully I can get a good reading on the values and the exposure."

"I'm sure you can do it. Do you want me to make a reservation for both of us for Thursday night? I was thinking of staying in Redding to break up the drive."

"That works, but I'll have my assistant make my arrangements," Meg said. "I don't want to raise any eyebrows. Just let me know where."

Chapter 15

The Thursday of our drive to Eureka was cooler than the weather had been for a while. Meg and I had continued to discuss whether to take one car or two, but Meg insisted on two. We planned to meet in Redding, three hours north on Interstate 5.

We had both left Sacramento around four-thirty, so we pulled into Redding a little after seven. We met for dinner at Duff's, one of the few old-time Redding institutions still around. Duff's had excellent steaks, and I would usually hit it at least once if I was trying a case up there, but its one drawback, at least until I started downloading books onto my tablet, was that it was too dark to read.

We had a quiet dinner. When the check came, I grabbed it. "I forgot to tell them to split the check. This one will have to be on me instead of on Farmstead."

"Well, let me pay my share at least," Meg replied. "This isn't a date or anything, right?"

"No, don't worry," I replied.

We headed over to the Red Lion. There were two lines at the reception counter, and I got my room key before

Meg did. I waited in the lobby until she was checked in. "Thanks for dinner," she said. "Maybe I'll see you in the morning. I'll probably just get up early and go."

I went up to my room and turned on the end of the Giants game, which beat what passed for nightlife in Redding. I tried unsuccessfully to call Drew.

About twenty minutes later, there was a knock on my door. I checked the peephole, and there was Meg.

"What's up? Everything okay?"

"I'm fine—just wanted to know if you could use some company." She had changed out of her work clothes into jeans and a sweatshirt, so it looked like she wasn't going anywhere that night. Her hair was up in a ponytail.

"Of course, come on in—or we could go down to the bar if you'd prefer."

"I'm not much of one for hotel bars when I'm out on the road. Too much chance of meeting Mr. Wrong. Not to say that would apply if we went together, but I find those scenes depressing, if not downright desperate."

"Sure. Make yourself at home." She sat down in the desk chair while I sat on the bed. She looked over at my open computer. "So, you play Candy Crush?"

"One of my minor vices," I said, a little embarrassed. "It's pretty mindless, but it helps me get over white-line fever before I go to bed. Otherwise, I'm dodging trucks in my sleep as well as during the day, and I really don't need that."

"You definitely are a road warrior."

"It comes—or at least it came—with the Farmstead package, but I've figured out how to work in a little fly fishing or birding along with the travel, so it's not all bad.

And I'm at least part way toward completing my research on the definitive guide to rural Mexican restaurants of Northern California."

She looked at me for a moment with an unreadable expression. "Would you mind it if I came over there and kissed you?"

Well, this was a surprise, especially after an explicitly non-date evening at dinner. "I'd be honored if you did."

We embraced and kissed tentatively. I had never been close enough to her to notice it before, but she smelled really nice. It wasn't scent or cosmetics—just her natural self. She was as sweet as freshly baked bread or new-mown grass, without being anything like either of those, or any other aroma I could put a name to.

She kicked off her shoes, pulled off her sweatshirt and took off her jeans. She was wearing a silky black push-up bra and tiny black panties. I wondered if this was what had been under her work clothes, though I doubted it.

"Um, you know, I didn't bring any condoms with me—I don't plan on getting lucky on my road trips."

"Relax ace, I've got it handled."

Jerry Seinfeld supposedly said that a date is like a job interview that lasts all night. I think I did okay on the interview, especially since I got a call-back in the wee hours of the morning. As I drifted off to sleep after making love a second time, I was thinking how much I had missed sharing my bed.

XOXOX

My phone woke me at six. Meg and her clothes were gone, and a note was on the desk saying she'd text me once she was done with her inspection. I washed up, grabbed a quick bite in the coffee shop, and hit Highway 299 at seven-thirty—exactly enough time to make it to Eureka for a ten o'clock deposition.

I pulled into the parking lot at the office of the plaintiff's attorney with about ten minutes to spare. The lawyer, Phil Stevens, and I went back a ways, and we each respected the other's skills. But even a good lawyer can't make bad facts into good ones. As I had suspected, the plaintiff, who had only been driving for about two years on her own, claimed that she had been heading for the minimart when the accident happened. She wasn't in the process of making a turn—she had just wandered off the right-hand side of the road while trying to spot the turn in the fog. Her car went into the ditch and struck the end of the culvert that ran under the actual entry into the parking lot.

After the depo, I stayed and talked with Phil. "What's your theory of the case?" I asked. "I know you alleged that the end of the culvert's on the minimart's property, but it's not. I have Frank Jamison doing a survey right now to establish that fact, but I'll bet you twenty dollars that the culvert is more than fifteen feet from the nearest point my hero owns."

"No takers on the bet," he said, "but you and I both know that commercial establishments have some duty to ensure safe passage of patrons onto their premises even where they don't own the route. And I don't think there's any real question that my lady was on her way to the minimart instead of somewhere further down the street."

"Well, she is—or anyway was—a regular customer. My guy admits that. I have to say that I'm curious whether

her claim that she was going to Sasquatch would hold up if I had someone out there asking questions, but I don't know that this case merits that expense."

Phil was generally right about the law, but I thought I had a good shot on a motion for summary judgment (or an MSJ, as we call it)—and I planned to file one. If there's no real dispute over the facts, an MSJ is a way to see if the plaintiff's legal theory can hold up—in other words, do they really have a case?

The problem was that there were three judges in Eureka who could wind up hearing the motion. I felt secure in my chances of winning in front of two of them. The other one was likely to be much more sympathetic to Phil's client. I knew from many conversations with local attorneys that there was just no way to game the system to get the judge you wanted. Still, two-to-one put the odds in my favor, and even if I lost, there'd be more trips to Eureka. Since this was probably the last case I'd have up there, I wanted to make the most of it.

As I left my meeting around noon, I checked my phone, and there was a text from Meg suggesting that we meet at one o'clock at The Reef, an old-time place a little south of downtown. The food's average, but I always feel young when I eat there, as it really attracts the older set.

As I walked into the restaurant, I saw Meg sitting in a booth in the back, reading the menu. I felt both nervous and excited, and wondered how she felt. I slid into the booth across from her. She looked up and smiled. "Hi," she said. "How was your drive from Redding?"

"Nice. I was in a particularly good mood this morning."

The waitress was at our table and asked if we needed more time. Meg asked for a cup of coffee while we decided.

I reached across the table and took Meg's hand. "I had a real nice time last night," I said.

"I did too," she replied. There was a couple of seconds of silence, then she exclaimed, "I'm starving."

We talked about our mornings. She said that the hotel was in the final stages of renovation, with a grand opening planned in a few months.

"The hotel as a job site was really clean," she said. "I don't think there are any occupational safety or health issues with the way things are set up. I certainly didn't notice anything. That's not what I'm really looking for. But, ultimately we will be insuring the finished product, and I couldn't get into most of the rooms, the kitchen, or the ballroom."

Our food arrived and smelled heavenly. I had ordered a fish sandwich and fries, and Meg had the crab louie. I offered Meg some fries before dousing them with ketchup.

"Most of that beautiful redwood trim we talked about was off the walls and on the floor being refinished," she continued. "The same went for those claw-foot tubs— they're being re-glazed on site. The only corrective action I recommended was that their external security fence seemed a little sketchy, and there's some nice stuff in there, not to mention tools and whatnot. What bothers me is that they want to insure it now on the basis of what it will be worth once the project is finished, and that's not how we usually do it. Plus, if there is damage that is severe enough that it can't be repaired, they want to be able to take a cash payout rather than Farmstead paying the cost of a reconstruction.

"Well, that's ultimately the underwriter's call, isn't it?"

"Yeah, and he's one of the new ones, so I've got no idea what he'll think of all this." She mixed the crab into her salad and took a bite. "So how was your deposition?"

"Pretty much what I expected. I think I managed to plant a seed in the head of the plaintiff's lawyer that claimant's story about where she was heading that night might not hold up under a rigorous investigation. I'll probably be back up here on a motion in a couple of months. Maybe you'll have another inspection around the same time."

"I might, but I've decided I'd like to spend more time with you in Sacramento too if that's okay. I really liked last night, especially how you cuddled afterwards." She smiled and took my hand across the table.

I got up and slid onto the bench next to her. "I'll cuddle with you anytime you want," I said, putting my arm around her shoulder and drawing her closer. "I love spooning and if I wind up on top of the wet spot, so be it."

She laughed. "Yes, so be it," she said and gave me a kiss. "And, now that we've established that we both had fun last night, would you still like to meet my parents? It's Friday, and neither of them have afterschool activities today. I have to warn you, all they know is that you're someone I know from work. I haven't admitted to any romantic involvement at all, but that won't keep them from assessing you as possible boyfriend material."

"Sure. I'd love to," I said. "And I'll try to hold up my end of things."

Chapter 16

We drove to the Eureka Hotel so I could check in and then I followed Meg to her parents' house, a mile or so east of downtown. It was a neighborhood of mostly mid-century houses, with the exception of a Victorian—probably an old farmhouse—about every other corner. Meg's parents' house was in the middle of the block, with a patch of huckleberries in the front yard instead of a lawn. Two unremarkable sedans were parked under a carport in front of the garage.

"Isn't this near the zoo?" I asked as we got out of the car.

"Yeah, about three blocks over that way," she gestured. "I never had to set my clock, because the animals get noisy around dawn. Plenty of weird shrieks and hoots. Anyway, they're both home," she continued. "Hope this goes well."

She rang the bell, and it quickly opened, revealing a woman with clear skin, bright blue eyes and short white hair. She grabbed Meg and hugged her, calling, "Don, Meg's here." She then turned to me and shook my hand, saying "Welcome, Jake. I'm Judy. And here's Don." Don, tall and skinny with a droopy moustache, shook my hand and gave Meg a big hug. "Good to see you both," said Don. "Please come in. Judy's made some of her famous cookies."

We went into the kitchen and sat down around the table. Don and Judy spent the first twenty minutes bringing Meg up to date on family and friends. Then they turned their attention to me.

"So, you work with Meg?" Don asked.

"Well, we both work for Farmstead," I said, "but in different departments. She was there for months before we crossed paths, and even then it was just by accident." I glanced over at her and smiled.

"What kind of work do you do?" Judy asked.

"I work in the legal department. We defend claims brought against Farmstead's insureds. Meg's department decides who Farmstead insures and how much they have to pay for their coverage. If they could do their job perfectly, there'd be no need for my department, because no one would have a claim brought against them. Obviously, the real world isn't that predictable." Judy passed the cookies, a delicious blend of chocolate and nuts, and I took another.

"So how did you get into law?" Don asked.

I explained that my father's work as a legal expert had gotten me interested in the law. "And, since I didn't have a head for math, I didn't see any chance of a career in a technical field. I'd like to think I have some of my dad's communication skills, which help with juries, so law was a good fit."

"How about you?" I said. "I hear you're both teachers." I helped myself to some more tea.

Don spoke first. "I teach advanced placement math at the high school."

"That's great," I said, taking a sip of the tea. "You do have a head for math."

Judy added, "And I do special education with junior high kids."

"How do you like teaching?" I asked them both.

"I'm pretty good at it, but it's sometimes a little disheartening," said Don. "A good many of my students go off to college, and they're mostly well-prepared, so they often do well there. But whether they go locally to community college, Humboldt State, or go out of town, there's very little work here in the county for anyone with a STEM degree, so they migrate out."

I nodded. It's a common story in rural counties.

"As for me, special ed is its own reward." said Judy. "It's awfully tough sometimes, but when you break through with someone, it's exciting. And, since no one wants to do it, there're always jobs. I was able to take time off when each of the kids was born, and then go back to work when I wanted to."

Meg chimed in, "My parents are great teachers. The kids adore them."

"Meg tells me that she has two brothers. What do they do?" I asked.

"Yes," said Don. "Meg's in the middle. Bob, the oldest, is career Air Force. Mike, the youngest, lives in New York and works as a salesman for a craft beer distributor. Bob's got his twenty years in, and thinks he might move back here once he figures out where to go after the service, but I don't expect we'll ever see Meg or

Mike coming home."

"Well dad, like you just said, there aren't many jobs here. If you could export the view, and charge for it, this would be the richest county in the state. Even the weed industry is probably going to go downhill once it's legal to grow it anywhere."

"It's true. It's beautiful up here, but that doesn't pay the light bill," Don said.

Wanting to change the subject a little, I turned to Meg. "So, what was it like growing up between two brothers?"

She started to respond, but Judy jumped in. "She was tougher than either of them," she said with a laugh. "We were living further out in the country back when the kids were growing up. She could out-shoot, out-fish, out-wrestle, and out-punch either of them any day or both of them on a good day. I think she really intimidated the boys in high school. But don't get me wrong. She could handle the girlie stuff too. It's just that she could turn it on and off, and no one really knew what to expect."

"Oh mom, you know I've mellowed out quite a bit since then."

"Sure hon, but you still can be a little aggressive at times."

Darn right, I thought, not that that's always a bad thing. "Meg's also told me about helping work on your Volkswagens."

"Oh yes," said Don. "We had several when she was little, but by the time she was driving age, we had a '66 bus and a '67 bug. I made Meg work with me rebuilding the bus. She got really good at it. I'll bet she still knows what the sparkplug gap is when you do a tune-up."

".024 inches, if anyone cares," Meg replied. "Do you want to know the dwell angle as well?" She looked at her father and they said in chorus, "50 degrees."

"I loved that bus," Judy said. "That huge steering wheel and sitting so close to the front. Driving it was just such a different experience. Of course, it was scary dangerous, and thank God none of us was in an accident. But once we had it rebuilt it never let us down or stranded us, which isn't something I could say for the American cars we've had over the years."

Don added, "Now all we're left with is the '67 bug. You like cars? Would you like to see it?"

Sure I did. I was happy to stretch my legs and move around. Meg continued talking with her mother and waved goodbye to me. We went out the front and over to the garage. Don hit the door opener, revealing an older pickup with a couple of crab pots in the bed, and a surprisingly small dust shroud next to it. Pulling it aside, the bug was revealed.

It was a light blue and had obviously been carefully waxed in the recent past. There was no pitting in any of the chrome, or any dents or distortions in the body. Dan popped open the rear lid, pointing out the features: "This is the original engine, so it matches the chassis VIN number. It's a stock 1500 cc engine, which is probably the best engine VW ever made. In fact, what makes this really special is that it's completely stock, meaning there are no aftermarket parts in it at all. Not every part is the original, of course, but all of them came from boxes marked "VW" instead of being made by someone else. So, it's really exactly like what you would have seen on the sales lot back in 1967."

Don circled the car as he spoke and I followed. "The only changes I made are radial tires instead of the bias ply tires that came with it, three-point seatbelts instead of the stock lap belts, and a passenger side rearview mirror. And I swap those out for the originals when I show it in competition."

"It's impressive," I said, looking through the window. "I can see you take a lot of pride in it."

"I wish we had room for another project car, but what with work and my fishing, if I did, Judy would never see me and I wouldn't want her to forget what I look like." Don had a nice smile and an enthusiastic and friendly manner. I could see why his students liked him. "Would you like to go for a spin?" he asked. "I need to gas it up. It's so cold and wet up here all the time, you'll get a lot of water condensation in the tank if you leave it nearly empty. And I haven't found a car that runs on water yet."

"Sure, I'd love to," I replied.

We drove down to Highway 101, pulled into a gas station, and got out. Don opened up the front hood to access the gas cap. "I had forgotten that's where the gas goes in these babies" I said. "The only one I ever rode in belonged to a roommate of mine when I was in college. It had a fuel door on the side by the front fender."

"That means it was a '68 or newer. That was the year that the Environmental Protection Agency and the Highway Safety Administration really started cracking down on VW, and they had to make a whole bunch of changes in the basic concept of the car, which really ruined things. So, 1967 is the purest expression of what a VW was meant to be. Hey, want to hear a VW joke?"

"Sure." How could I say no?

"Well, I first heard this as a blonde joke, but I guess they're not politically correct these days. So, anyway, these two Humboldt County hippies show up at the same gas station in their bugs, both of them seriously baked. One pops open the front hood and goes, 'Oh man, someone's stolen my engine.' The other one replies, 'Don't worry, man, I've got a spare in the back of mine.'" I actually had heard it before, but I groaned appropriately.

As he hung up the gas nozzle, Don offered to let me drive. "You do know how to use a stick, don't you?"

"Yeah, my car in high school and college was an old Volvo four-speed my father bought in his never-ending search for the 500,000 mile car. I suppose it might have made the grade if I hadn't taken it over, but as it was, it died at about 300K."

As I maneuvered the VW through the streets, I was surprised how much pep it had, and mentioned that to Don. "Sure, this thing is so light that it doesn't take very many horses to push it around. But you have to spend the time to keep it happy with tune-ups and carburetor adjustments, and you really have to know its limits."

"Well, I can see why you enjoy it. Meg says she thinks you'll be buried in it."

"Oh, yeah? Actually, I'm thinking Viking funeral," he laughed. "Nah. It would be a sin not to pass this on to someone else who'll do right by it."

As we were covering the bug in the garage, I brought up the fishing trip. "Meg tells me you're going after rockfish tomorrow. Okay if I join you?"

"Sure. Would love to have you along."

"I've got a sport license. I don't know what I'll do with the fish if we hit them good, but tell me where the boat is docked and what time to meet you there. I brought my foul-weather gear and my boots, so I think that covers it."

"Don't worry—once your friends hear you've got fresh rockfish, they'll be all over you. Let's go inside and make plans."

Once we had the arrangements worked out, it was time for me to head off to the hotel for the night. Sleeping alone while Meg was a mile away felt lonely, but at least our time together was increasing, so life was still good.

Chapter 17

Don had set five-thirty a.m. as our meet-up time at the dock, explaining that the earlier we got out on the water, the better our chances of getting back before the wind made things really uncomfortable. When I got to the parking lot, it was still dark, but the dock and the boats were lit up like it was a movie set. The morning was cold, and I was glad for my gloves and warm jacket.

I found Don's slip. I could see the boat's name—*School's Out*—on the stern. It was a twenty-five-foot diesel-powered commercial boat with a wheelhouse in the front and a small cabin underneath. Judy and Meg were already there, along with a younger guy who looked a lot like Don. He was wearing a Mariners cap and a thick hooded sweatshirt. Meg introduced him as her cousin, Ike.

"Hi," he said, extending his hand. "So, I hear you work with my cuz."

We settled into the boat's bench. "Yup. How about you? What line are you in?"

"I work for Clearheart in their mill as a grader."

"A grader? What's that?"

"I figure out how to cut up each log that comes into the mill in order to get the most value out of it. Not long ago, it was tape measures, chalk and eyeballs, but now it's all computers and lasers. But someone's got to be there to tell the computer when it's full of shit."

"By the way, how's business?" Judy asked.

"We're going gangbusters—running two shifts. I don't know where they're getting all the trees. Our deck at the mill is stacked up solid, but we don't have that much space there. I haven't had any call to go out to the satellite yards, so I don't know if they're empty or what, but I'll take the work while I've got it and won't ask questions."

Meg was sitting in the back, and chimed in, "You know I came up here to look at the Eel River Inn, right? Do you hear anything about that job?"

"Not really," said Ike. "I just wonder what boy genius came up with the idea that a five-star hotel and a lumber mill across the street will make good neighbors. I guess since they're basically both part of the same company, it doesn't matter so much. But I wouldn't stay there even if I could afford it. Too noisy and too smelly if there's a night shift running.

"Actually, that reminds me of one interesting thing I heard," said Ike. "The historical society—we all call it the 'hysterical society' around here—made a big deal about all the redwood detail work in the inn, and Clearheart agreed to refinish it using the same methods that were used when it was first put in. That means they're using some really nasty chemicals for the process, and they had to cut a special deal with the Air Resources Board to put in a new scrubber at the mill a year ahead of schedule."

"That's funny. No one mentioned that to me yesterday," Meg said. "Oh well, it won't make any difference once it's up and running."

Don showed up with a pushcart loaded with poles and tackle boxes. We tossed them in and got the boat headed for the harbor entrance. Don steered and I sat in back next to Meg. The shoreline became more distinct, and we could see an ocean-going freighter moored alongside a dock taking on a load of logs. Soon we passed the Coast Guard station near the mouth of the bay and moved out into the open sea. There was very little breeze, so the water outside the jetty was flat, although there was a strong swell. We turned south and headed down past the Eel River toward Cape Mendocino, about a ninety-minute ride.

The noise from the diesel and the waves slapping on the side of the boat made it tough to do much talking. Meg pointed out a couple of Dall's porpoises heading in the opposite direction from us, looking for all the world like miniature killer whales. Don passed back a thermos of coffee and Ike took the wheel.

I took a quick trip through the wheelhouse and the cabin, which was pretty spartan, with two benches and a table between them. I noticed a bolt-action 30-06 and a 12-gauge shotgun clipped to the wall, and asked Don, who was now sitting at the table, whether pirates were a problem.

"There's certainly an element out here that wouldn't say no to poaching from someone's crab pots, but we're generally pretty peaceable. In case Fish and Game asks, those are our 'shark guns,'" he said with air quotes. "Used to be, we could take a shot at the sea lions if they were going after our salmon. Now, with the Marine Mammal Protection Act, we're not allowed to, but I've concluded that a warning shot with blank ammo will scare off at least some of them." Right about then, I felt the boat slow and knew it was time to get down to business.

After much discussion between Don and Ike, with frequent reference to the depth gauge and the direction of the wind, we finally arrived at the preferred spot. Don killed the engine, and we made our first casts of the day.

Rockfishing is strenuous work, as you have to put a pretty heavy weight on the line to get it down to the fish, and you have to keep bouncing it along the bottom so you don't get stuck. Once you hook them, the smaller rockfish don't put up much of a fight, but you still have to reel in a lot of line against more than some resistance to get them into the boat. On the other hand, ling cod, the top predators on the reefs, can get quite big and put up a good struggle.

We had reasonable luck. Meg and Judy each landed ten-pound lings and the rest of us brought in limits of brightly colored rock cod. We headed back to the harbor around eleven, and the fish were all filleted and packed in ice by the time we got to the dock.

As we were unloading the boat, Dan asked if I could drive his truck back to the house. "Meg doesn't like driving it," he said. "I need to get something for the boat, and I need to use Ike's truck for that, as mine has those crab pots in it. You okay driving it? It's got three on the tree and Armstrong."

"Say what?"

"Oh, sorry—mechanics' shorthand. I mean it's got a three-speed column shift and no power steering. Get it? 'Armstrong?'" He raised his eyebrows and smiled.

"My uncle's truck was set up that way, and I was driving it when I was fourteen, so I should be able to manage." I turned to Meg and tossed her my car keys. "See you at the house," I said.

We had gotten such an early start, there was plenty of day left once we got back to her parents' house. Meg asked if I wanted to go further up the coast to Patrick's Point, and I happily agreed. "One condition, though," I said. "We have to drive through McKinleyville and look at the Sasquatch Minimart and see if there's anything else I should know about the accident there."

"No problem here," said Meg.

We took my car and headed north. The drive by the minimart was a short detour. It was a small grocery with a carved Bigfoot statue in front. I was able to see the layout of the property and the surrounding streets, which matched the photos I had gotten when claims sent the file over.

Patrick's Point is a beautiful spot—a rock headland and a long sand beach to the north of it. Meg told me that the beach was a good place to look for agates, but the tide was in, so we didn't find any. Not that the walk wasn't just fine without the agates. However, it was less peaceful than it might have been, since the Coast Guard was running a drill with its helicopters, simulating a rescue from the point.

"I'm going to stay over again at my parents' place tonight," Meg said, somewhat wistfully.

"Sure you can't sneak out?"

"Actually, I'm sure I could. That was one of my specialties in high school. I imagine I'd enjoy the thrill, but I really don't see my family enough as it is. This is the first time I've gotten up here in a long time, so I want to make the most of it."

"Well, I'll be thinking of you."

"Likewise."

I dropped Meg off, kissed her goodbye, and headed back to the inn. It had been a long day. I read a few chapters of a recent Dewey Lambdin sea story and turned in early.

ХОХОХ

Meg and I headed back to Sacramento the next morning. We stayed in sight of each other most of the way. Wanting to extend our time together a little longer, I suggested we stop near the Avenue of the Giants for a walk in Redwood State Park. Finding a short trail, we walked beneath the towering trees taking in the cool, moist air.

"I really had fun," I said, taking Meg's hand. "I like your parents. They seem like old hippies." I smiled.

"What gave it away?" she laughed. "Was it my mom waxing poetic about driving the '66 VW bus?"

"That was a clue," I said.

"I had fun, too," she said. "Particularly at the Red Lion." She smiled flirtatiously.

"Me too."

Sunlight was beginning to filter through the fog in the dense canopy, falling on a tangle of green ferns and vines. Trees in various stages of decay covered the forest floor creating the rich soil for new life.

127

"I'm so glad you want to spend more time together," I said as we reached the cars. I pulled a couple of Diet Cokes out of the cooler and handed one to Meg. She snapped it open and took a sip.

"Would you like to come over to my place tonight?" I asked.

"I can't tonight," she said. "I've really got to do a wash and get organized for work. But soon."

I kissed her softly and my lips tingled—possibly from the carbonation of her drink, but probably not. "Yes, I support that idea," I said. "Let's look at the calendar when we get home and we can set a date."

Chapter 18

A nd so, Meg and I began a relationship. We were still careful not to couple up at work, but we spent two or three nights a week together either at her house or at mine. Claire and the dogs were happy with the new addition to their lives. I was happy, too. I realized, in retrospect, that I had been pretty lonely since my divorce.

The week that followed our Eureka trip was uneventful—actually kind of quiet, other than the construction going on in the office. By Friday, I had worked through almost everything pending on my cases, and started preparing for a jury trial in Willows, which was scheduled to start a week from that coming Monday. Until lately, even though Farmstead tried more cases than most carriers, most of them still settled. I supposed that I should get used to the new normal. I didn't mind trying cases, although I tended to be uncomfortably wound up for a week or so after they finished. Farmstead never sent two lawyers to trial where one would do, so I never had the luxury of being the second briefcase. Once in a great while I could take our paralegal with me, which was a huge help, but I had to share her with five other lawyers, and she wasn't coming with me on this outing.

I hadn't realized how late it was getting until Jocelyn knocked on my door frame and asked if I needed anything before she went home.

"Whoa, don't tell me it's five already. I really lost track of time. I'll be leaving in a sec. This stuff has been ready to go since the last time it was set, and nothing's changed that I can see."

She stepped into my office and lowered her voice. "Can I ask you something personal?"

"I guess," I responded. "What's up?"

"Are you seeing someone? You seem much happier the past month or so and you're not working quite as hard as you have been since your ex left."

"Well, you're right, I am seeing someone," I said. "And don't let this get out, but she works here in underwriting."

"Get out of town!" She smiled.

"I'm surprised you noticed, but I suppose I'm going to be the last person to realize that I'm happier."

"I'm glad for you. As far as keeping it quiet, Jocelyn sees all, knows all, tells no one anything. You know you can count on that."

I wasn't sure that I could, but I said I did. "Have a good weekend."

At that moment, my cell chimed with an incoming text. I saw it was from Meg, and excused myself from Jocelyn. I opened it: "El Gallito. Soonest." I texted back "OK" and was out the door in seconds.

I saw her car in the parking lot as I pulled in, and

headed to what had become "our" booth in the back. She hadn't ordered anything, which was unusual, and, even more unusually, she looked extremely troubled. Usually, Meg radiated self-assurance, and I could not recall ever having seen her this out of sorts.

"What's up?"

"You won't believe this. I'm not even sure I can believe it. Jill—the new underwriting VP, called me in to her office. First, she told me that she had looked at the report I had done on the Eel River Inn, and that it was a good job. Then she mentioned that she had heard that I was troubled because I hadn't been able to access all of the spaces, which is not something I told anyone at Farmstead or put in the report. All I said was that I didn't see everything—not how I felt about it. Anyway, she told me not to worry, that everything would be okay, and that the inn looked like the kind of risk the new management wanted to write."

The waiter came to the table and Meg asked him to come back in a minute.

She watched him leave and turned back to me. "After that, she did an 'oh by the way,' and said that she'd also heard that I was seeing someone from the legal department. I was already kind of floored, but this was way too much way too fast."

I quickly tried to think of who might know we were seeing each other. I hadn't mentioned it to anyone but Jocelyn.

"Anyway," she continued, "she said that there was nothing wrong with intra-office romance as long as it didn't involve people at different levels in the same department, but then she brought up the confidentiality agreement that we all signed when we started here, and made it very clear that it extended to talking with fellow employees about company business where there wasn't a need to know.

"How on earth she knew about us is beyond me," Meg continued. "I've never sent you an email using the company server. I don't use the company phone to call or text you. I haven't told anyone anything about us. The only thing I did was look up your profile on the company website after we met the first time, and even then I was at home, so I used my own computer. All I know is that I really don't like this. I feel really intimidated, and that's not a comfortable feeling for me."

I shook my head and tried to think. "I looked up your profile too. I was home, but it was probably on my work computer. The only person in the company who knows anything about us is Jocelyn, my assistant, and she's probably the only person with the people skills necessary to figure it out. She would never tell anyone, and anyway, I only told her about our relationship half an hour ago when she asked why I was so happy all of a sudden. What do you think this all means?"

"I don't know, but I think it's a pretty clear signal that I'm not supposed to tell you what's going on in underwriting. This has me really upset. Someone has to be spying on us, and I can't think why either of us would matter even if there was some scheme being hatched."

"Me either. But you know me. If there is something going on, I'm probably going to be the last one to know."

"Well, anyway, I've got girl's night tonight, like I told you. I'm going to make sure I'm not the designated driver this time, that's for damn sure."

"Sounds good. Call me whenever, especially if you want to talk more about this."

"Thanks." She kissed me and headed out the door. She seemed to have regained her usual composure, but I doubted that it was real.

Chapter 19

I was keeping my calendar clear to work on preparing for trial. All I had out of town the next week was one late afternoon deposition. The morning of the depo, Meg and I were doing our getting-dressed dance, trying to stay out of each other's way as we got ready for work. For a mercy, neither of us had a pre-work "breakfast meeting," which had become something of a hallmark at Farmstead lately. Even the best fruit plate (not that we usually got that good a spread) couldn't balance out having to show up at seven to hear some suit natter on about some new corporate initiative.

Meg was humming a rock song from the 1970s that I couldn't quite place while she was putting her hair up. "Just how many different ways do you have of wearing your hair to work?" I asked.

"Don't know," she responded. "I've never counted. Does it count twice if I start left over right one time and right over left the next?"

I started singing, mostly under my breath, "50 Ways to Put Your Hair Up" to the tune of the Paul Simon song, *50 Ways to Leave Your Lover.*

"Oh, please don't sing that song," she said forcefully. "It's so sad. I mean, Paul Simon sings it all jaunty, but really, all the ways he mentions of dumping someone are pretty cruel. Besides, it was in rotation on the classic rock station my parents used to listen to in the car back during high school when I was going through my first break up, so I've got bad memories on top of that."

"Were you the dumper or the dumpee?" I asked.

"Oh, the dumpee, most definitely," she replied. "I think I was too much for his sense of masculinity, but probably the kicker was the fact that I was a good four inches taller than him. Which reminds me—I've never asked if you mind my being taller than you."

"Not at all. I mean, you're only noticeably taller when you have your heels on, and, anyway, I know just how tall you are when I get you down to my level." Meg elbowed me in the ribs and asked, "You sure?"

"Sure I'm sure. You know, when I was in college, there was this seriously cute girl in our circle who I think was interested in me, but she was quite a bit taller than me and I was just intimidated enough by that that I never asked her out. So, I guess I can appreciate your high school boy-friend's dilemma a little. Well, if Paul Simon doesn't do it for you, how about a little Willie Dixon?" I started singing, "I got twenty-nine ways just to get to my baby's door, and if she needs me bad, I can find about two or three more."

"Is that one of your old blues songs? I remember you playing it in the car the other day. How did you get into that music, anyway? It seems like an acquired taste."

"I had a good friend in high school who was a guitar wizard, and all he wanted to play was blues. He got a band together, but needed a drummer. As you may have noticed, I can't carry a tune in a sack, and I've got no aptitude for any instrument, but I could keep pretty good time, and that's about all you need to be able to play drums in a blues band at our level. We did just enough rock covers to fill up a demo CD, but usually we ran out of stuff that wasn't blues toward the end of the first set. As a result, we didn't get invited back for another gig by most of the places where we played, since all they wanted to hear was rock."

"So you're not named after one of the Blues Brothers?"

"That would be pretty difficult, since I was born well before the movie came out. No, I'm named after my uncle—my mother's brother. He's the stereotypical weird uncle. He moved out of Orange County thirty years ago because it was getting too liberal for him. He bought some acreage out in the high desert east of Los Angeles and started raising emus."

"Emus—you mean the birds?"

"No shit. There's a market for the eggs and the meat, but it's not as good a one as he thought it was going to be. He still has a few birds so he can file a farming tax return and deduct a bunch of stuff, but now he's the manager of a tire shop in Palmdale. Anyway, visiting Uncle Jake was always what my family did for spring break, since it was way cheap. That's where I learned how to shoot, ride a horse, drive a feed truck—all sorts of things that were totally useless in Orange County, but were fun up there.

"By the way, we were speaking of getting you down to my level a minute ago. Are you free tonight?" I asked.

"I'm not sure. I'll have to get back to you," she replied.

The deposition was in Manteca, which is about fifteen miles south of Stockton. Forty years ago, when my deponent, Franklin Smith, MD, opened his medical practice there, it was a sleepy farm town. Now it's a fast-growing bedroom community, mostly housing folks who commute forty to seventy miles to the west to work in the greater Bay Area. Their commute, and the brutal traffic on the Altamont Pass, is the price they pay for something approaching reasonable housing prices. The other price they have to pay is living in a town whose name, translated from Spanish, means "lard."

For many years, Dr. Smith had been the only orthopedist practicing between Stockton and Modesto. As a result, he was familiar to our office, since orthopedic injuries are common in our area of the law. And, like many doctors, he was well-known as a prickly witness, even on a good day.

Lawyers and doctors get along as well as cats and dogs. I've never really figured out why. Certainly, every physician is always, at least subconsciously, looking in the rear-view mirror for a malpractice lawsuit. And while such suits are actually not all that common, every physician sued has shared his or her (probably exaggerated and distorted) tale of woe with dozens of colleagues. But I have a theory that the core of the tension is the difference in our training, both in school and on the job. Lawyers are trained to see things in shades of grey—physicians and other science-based professionals in black and white. We're taught in law school that a competent lawyer can argue either side of a case with equal sincerity, although the reality is that most of us find ourselves more comfortable on one side than on the other. Law pushes us in the direction of uncertainty, whereas medicine, at least on the surface, pushes for certainties. This means that when you start asking hard questions about just why a physician (or engineer or crop scientist or whatever) holds a particular view, their back immediately goes up, since you're challenging their ability to hold a definitive position. Put another way, once a physician has completed residency training, he or she is simply unused to having to defend a diagnosis or a treatment plan.

As I had learned before the deposition, Dr. Smith was also well-known in our office for another reason. In orthopedic medicine, there are a couple of dozen tests that are commonly used to diagnose certain injuries and conditions. Most of them have a proper name attached, acknowledging the physician who first popularized the test. Others, like the "Beer Can Test," which tests for shoulder injuries by asking the patient to hold out an arm and rotate it as if pouring a drink, have more prosaic origin stories. In any event, I'd learned most of the tests by heart and could easily look up any that I didn't remember or that were new to me. However, in getting ready for this deposition, I noticed that Dr. Smith had recorded positive findings on something called the "Lucas Test."

I couldn't find anything about a test by that name online or in any of the medical texts in our library. Peter had happened by the library as I was going through the books and asked what was up, since it was rare for us to be cracking them. I explained about Dr. Smith and the Lucas Test, and he laughed. "Ah yes, Dr. Smith. I took a depo from him about ten years ago, and had the same question. I asked him, under oath and on the record, about the test and what a positive finding meant. He refused to answer. Then, after the depo, he told me that it was his shorthand for a case where the complaints didn't match the symptoms, and that "Lucas" referred to George Lucas, as in *Star Wars*, meaning that there was a great deal of fantasy involved on the part of the patient. So, if you've got a positive finding in your case, I think you'll find his testimony helpful."

This put me in somewhat of a tactical dilemma when it came to the deposition. Specifically, whether I wanted to force Dr. Smith to explain the "test" on the record, alerting the other side, or to save it for when I was cross-examining him at trial. As it turned out, the plaintiff was represented by a young lawyer from Sacramento who had never met the good doctor before, so I contented myself with highlighting all of the inconsistencies in the records without mentioning the "test." I doubted that the case would find its way in front of a jury, but the prospect, even if unlikely, of a true Perry Mason moment was too sweet to pass up.

After coming home, I took Elwood and Abby for a long walk around the neighborhood. When we were done, Claire invited me in. "How are things going for you?" she asked.

"Could be better," I said. "The changes at the office are piling up, and none of us worker bees have any idea where things are going to wind up. I kind of wish they would do it all at once and be done with it, but that doesn't seem to be their style. I'm beginning to think about looking for something else."

"That would be a shame. You've been there what—five years?"

"A little more than that, but longevity and institutional memory won't mean anything if we're doing things in a whole new way for a whole new set of clients."

"Well, I'm sure you'll land on your feet if things don't work out there."

"Maybe, but I don't want to leave the area. One of the funny things about Farmstead—at least up to now—is that we don't have all that many cases here in town. I'm much better known in Redding, for instance, than I am here in Sacramento."

"And, how's Meg?" she asked.

"Well, I guess we're a for-real item," I smiled. "Things are good on that front. She is a rising star in her department so she's out of town more than I'd like, but it's all good."

Chapter 20

The changes to the deposition room must have been finalized while I was in Manteca, because when I got into work the next day, Mark McDowell was already in residence. The previous week, I had noticed that he'd gotten a parking space assigned to him (something no one else in legal had ever had), and had occupied it with what had to be the world's largest SUV. He was talking with a woman I didn't recognize as I passed by, so I simply waved and headed to my office.

A few minutes later, he came to my door, still accompanied by the woman. "Jake, this is Emily— Emily, Jake. Emily came over with me from Business Mutual, and she'll be in charge of the legal support staff from this point on. I'll let her brief you on our new plans for her end of the department."

Emily smiled and shook hands. She was pretty and either nervous, tightly wrapped, or both. "We're rationalizing the support staff to make more efficient use of their skills," she said. "I'll be sending out a memo. No one's going to have a legal assistant to call their own. Cherise will handle everyone's calendars. Jocelyn and

Marty will do production keyboarding. And Linda will do phones, reception, and filing. I think by doing this we'll get rid of redundancies and allow everyone to specialize in certain tasks, and everyone will be responsible for the quality of all of our work."

I was a little gob-smacked by this. Although Jocelyn didn't work exclusively with me, she and I had worked together for almost five years. Losing her daily input on my cases was going to be a big blow. And from what I had heard from people in other offices where this had been tried, making everyone responsible for everything actually meant that no one was responsible for anything.

"Well, I'll be sorry to not to be working closely with Jocelyn," I said, "but I know we've got a good crew here. I hope it works out." I hoped my insincerity didn't show.

Mark piped up, "Are you in tomorrow? I need to go over everyone's pending trials, motions, appeals, and that sort of thing as soon as I can." I resisted the temptation to refer him to Cherise, since she was now in charge of our calendars.

"Sure. Is ten o'clock okay?"

"Works for me."

I spent the rest of the day prepping for the trial. Getting up to speed on a case more than once is something of a drag, and I had to force myself to go over depositions I'd already read several times. But such is the life of a Farmstead lawyer out in what the local judges called the "cow counties." All it took was one meth dealer not taking the plea of the week, and there was nothing to do but to bump my civil case.

The next day, I sat down with Mark. "So, give me the highlights on your cases over the next few months," he said.

"Well, I've got a trial next week in Willows, an MSJ up in Eureka which is coming up fairly soon, and an argument in the third circuit a couple of months after that on a writ from another MSJ I won in Sacramento. I've got a couple of trials set still further out than that if you want to hear about them."

"No, that's all right," he responded. "I should be up to speed on everyone's cases by then. I just don't want any surprises in the meantime. Tell me about your Willows case. Who's the plaintiff's attorney?"

"Hal Robbins out of Chico. You know him?"

"Ah yes, there's someone I haven't thought of in awhile. He can try a case, though. You ready for him?"

Hal certainly could try a case, but while he was a good attorney, he thought he was a great one. I'm a good attorney who knows he's never going to be better than good. Hal had shot himself in the foot a couple of times when I'd gone up against him, but he'd beaten me a couple of times as well.

"I think we've got a good case. Our hero is a local contractor who built a new store for the independent grocer in town. Plaintiff claims that the concrete apron between the store and the parking lot was too slick and she fell. We claim no defect, and no notice, so no chance to remedy the defect if there was one. The store's settled out, and we dismissed our cross-complaint against it."

"What are the injuries?"

"Here's where it gets a little weird. Plaintiff claims

143

that she developed traumatically induced fibromyalgia, but she wasn't diagnosed with anything more than a soft-tissue strain/sprain for about eight months. And fibro cases are hard for a jury to get a hold on, since by definition there aren't any findings on X-rays or blood work. I've got a medical expert who will say that her big problem is that her treating doc has been way over-prescribing Vicodin, and she's become addicted. I've also subpoenaed the orthopedist who saw her shortly after the fall, and he'll say he would not have expected her to have developed fibromyalgia from the accident. As far as liability is concerned, our guy did get called in after the accident and roughened up the concrete, even though he didn't think it needed it, so no one has any objective measurement of coefficients of friction or any of that good stuff as of the time of the accident."

"What have the settlement discussions been?" he asked.

"The store settled out for 100K. We've offered 60, but Robbins wants 100 from us as well. I suspect he'll ask the jury for over 500. I'll argue for a defense verdict or, failing that, giving her 15 for her soft tissue injuries."

"Sounds like you've got it set up. Mind if I sit in on closing argument?" he asked.

Well, not my preference, but, "Sure. That will likely be Thursday afternoon. I'll let you know," I responded.

)(*)(*)(

The trial in Willows went pretty much as I had expected, although the plaintiff's attorney had asked the jury for 750K rather than 500K. It lasted four days. The judge was one I knew fairly well and whom I considered fair. The jury, though not ideal from my point of view, was good. We had a mix of small business owners, a casino worker, a teacher, a student, a couple of farmers and a few others. I stayed at the Wagon Wheel motel, an old, locally owned place filled with dark wood and still smelling vaguely of smoke despite an established no-smoking policy.

As he had warned me, Mark was there on the last day of trial. My closing went well and Mark left once closing arguments were finished. After the judge had given his instructions and the jurors filed out into the jury room, I began to organize and box my files. I was going to have to make at least two trips to the car and had just returned when the bailiff walked in and announced that there was a verdict. Robbins' comment, not unreasonable since the jury had been out a maximum of twenty minutes, was "Oh shit," and, indeed, they came back with a unanimous verdict in favor of my client.

My drive home was pleasant, but I knew I'd have a bunch of work piled up for me at the office on Friday, since I couldn't focus on anything else while I tried a case. I hoped I could get together with Meg over the weekend, although I was worried that I might be a little too manic for her. She had never seen me in the aftermath of a trial, and I knew it would take me a while to get back to being my usual self. Well, maybe she'd like the manic me. We would have to see.

Chapter 21

That weekend, rather than going on our usual walk somewhere in Sacramento, Meg and I decided to take the dogs to an off-leash park in Davis. We loaded them into my company car. Having both Elwood and Abby in the car can be a challenge, but luckily traffic on I-80 was light and the ride was short.

The dog park was just off the freeway, between the highway and the train tracks—a fairly barren couple of acres—but it was filled with dogs of all sizes and colors. There was a separate fenced-off area for small dogs. I opened the back door, and Elwood and Abby leaped from the car and joined the party. It was our plan to tire them out—something that is not easy with border collies—and we had brought some tennis balls along to help.

We found a small piece of shade and sat watching as the dogs sniffed and ran in packs around the grassy area. Despite being late afternoon, the weather was warm and the shade was welcome. A lot of the people at the park seemed to know each other, and groups of dog owners clustered together in conversation.

"Let me give them a run," Meg said, getting up and grabbing a couple of tennis balls. She called the dogs and they came running. "Go get it!" she cried and threw the ball. Both dogs ran in a sprint toward the bouncing ball. Abby even brought the ball back to Meg, which was uncommon. I usually had to chase the dogs to retrieve the ball. As I watched, I thought back to what Meg's parents had said about her growing up with two brothers. She didn't throw like a girl, that was certain. I mentally calculated how far she was tossing the ball, and hoped I could match the distance when it was my turn.

After we had been at the park for about forty minutes, the dogs began to slow down. I was also slowing down, and my arm was worn out from throwing the ball as far and as strongly as I possibly could. I started to walk back toward where Meg was sitting. She was looking intently at her phone, a concerned look on her face.

"Ready to go? Looks like we've managed to tire these guys out." She didn't look up from her phone. "What's up?"

She briefly looked up from her phone. "There's been a fire. I got a text from my dad. The Eel River Inn burned down last night."

I felt my stomach sink. "What does he say?"

"He sent me an article from the Eureka paper about the fire. Let me see . . . 'Last night at approximately 2:30 a.m....blah, blah, blah...the hotel was totally destroyed....' Oh, God...someone was killed. 'The charred body of a man was found.'" She looked up at me. "My dad said they could see the smoke up in Eureka." She continued to look at the phone in silence. When she was done, she sighed deeply and put her face in her hands. I sat down next to her and put my arm around her. "Can I see?" I asked. She handed me her phone and I read the short article.

On Saturday night, at approximately 2:30 a.m., police and firefighters were called to a fire at the historic Eel River Inn located on the Clearheart Lumber property south of Eureka. According to Police Chief Daniel Campos, the historic hotel was totally destroyed by the fire, and the charred body of a white male was found at the site. The man has not been identified by police.

Reached for comment, Stanley Black, a representative of Clearheart Lumber, said "We are deeply saddened by the fire and loss of life on the property of the historic Eel River Inn. We are grateful for the help that police and fire agencies throughout the county provided to our local fire brigade, and we will cooperate fully with the investigation of the fire."

There were a few more details about the hotel but nothing more about the fire.

I looked back at Meg who still had her head in her hands. "I feel responsible," she said, looking up. "I should have looked more thoroughly when I was there. I should have been more forceful in making them show me everything. I'm sure they had tons of refinishing chemicals in there. Oh, God. And now someone is dead."

"Well, it could be that the person who died is the one who started the fire."

"Even so," she said. "That shouldn't have happened. He shouldn't have been able to get onto the property. I should have been sure anything flammable was stored safely."

"Don't blame yourself," I said.

"I do," she said. And then as if it were a second thought, she added "Oh God, I don't want to talk to Jill on Monday. Do you think I'll lose my job?"

I rubbed her back. "No, I don't. They knew all that and they approved the risk. You just did your job."

"You know how things go at work. They're always looking to blame someone no matter what happens." I couldn't argue with that.

After a few more minutes, we walked slowly back to the car. The day which had started so brightly had turned dark. We drove in silence back to Sacramento.

"I'd like to just go home," Meg said. "I don't think I'm very good company."

"Do you want me to stay with you at your place for a while?"

"No. I'm fine. I just need some time alone."

When we got to her condo, I parked the car and leaned over and gave her a kiss.

"Call me if you want," I said. "If I don't hear from you today, I'll call you tomorrow."

"Thanks." She grabbed her things and walked toward the apartment without looking back.

That night, I was able to learn some more details about the fire from the website of one of the Eureka television stations. Some camping and cooking equipment had been found near the body, and, as Meg had foreseen, the fire department blamed the wood refinishing chemicals for accelerating the flames.

Chapter 22

Meg called me the next day to let me know that she was feeling better. She promised to call me after she spoke to her boss on Monday. When I hadn't heard from her by eleven on Monday, I called her and we arranged to meet in a small pocket park on the far side of the building at noon.

Meg was there when I arrived, but otherwise the park was empty. We sat on a bench next to a small grassy area under one of the few remaining live oak trees in the area.

"So, how did it go?" I asked.

"Surprisingly, it appears to be a non-event," she said. Despite the reassuring words, she nervously clasped her hands together. "No one even mentioned it until I raised it."

"Had they heard about it?" I asked.

"Yes, they knew but seemed surprised that I knew. I told them my parents live in Eureka and had sent me the article." I took her hand.

"I guess Jill didn't know that I grew up in Eureka. Honestly, that seemed to surprise her more than the fire." Meg shook her head, squeezed my hand, and then resumed nervously clasping her own hands. She smiled weakly.

"Well, I guess that is good news," I said. "Sounds like it won't cause you any trouble with your job."

She shrugged. "We'll see."

"Want to get some lunch?"

She shook her head. "Not today. I have some errands to run."

She got up, gave me a quick kiss, and walked toward her car. As I watched her walk away, she turned and waved.

I bought a sandwich at the cafeteria and as I brought it upstairs to my office I saw Jocelyn eating at her desk. "So, what's your thinking about this change in assignments for the support staff?" I asked, sitting down next to her.

"No one is happy with it," she said. She was reading a Louise Penny mystery, which she closed and lay on the desk. "We really won't have nearly as much involvement in the cases. The chances that we'll catch something before it jumps up and bites us will be a lot less."

I nodded. "I think we're at about the first dozen of the death of a thousand cuts. It's only going to get worse."

"You're probably right. I worked on my resume this weekend. Will you give me a recommendation?"

"You know I will. I've never worked with someone as devoted to the job as you are."

"Thanks. By the way, I just saw an email from HR asking everyone to update their personnel files. You probably got it, too. If not, let me know and I'll forward it to you."

"Okay, but I think they have all my current info," I said. "I haven't moved or anything."

She leaned back in her chair. "I don't remember what all was asked when I was hired, but they seem to want more—more background information, more emergency contacts, and so on."

I sighed and stood up. "Whatever. If they wait awhile, most of us will be gone anyway."

She smiled and turned back to her lunch. "And by the way," she said. "Mark was looking for you. He wants to see you after lunch."

I went to my office and ate my lunch while working the crossword puzzle in the *Sacramento Bee*. Before I had finished, my interoffice line buzzed. It was Mark.

"Can you come over to my office and bring your current case list with you?" he asked. I looked at the clock and saw that it was one o'clock straight up. I put aside the crossword and walked the three doors down to his.

"Close the door," he said as I knocked on his doorframe. I sat down in the chair across from him. His desktop was extremely neat and practically bare.

"First off," he began. "That was a good job you did up in Willows. Thanks for calling me right away with the outcome."

"Sure."

"I've been looking at our office's statistics over the weekend, and I'm troubled by what I'm seeing in your breakdown. The company expects its attorneys to bill 2000 hours a year to specific claim files, and I think that's a reasonable figure. None of you are on pace to hit that, and you're the farthest behind of everyone. It's going to be tough for you to make things up in what's left of the year."

"Dan and I had that discussion more than once," I responded. "If you look at the average time a case is on my desk from when I get it to when it closes, you'll see that I'm turning things over much more quickly than the office average. He didn't mind if I didn't hit the billable number, since I was clearly doing things efficiently."

"Look, let me explain this, and I'm sorry if Dan never made this clear to you. Case turnover is not a metric that we're concerned with. The bean counters know how much the legal division costs the company, so that's more or less a fixed number. They also know how much we pay to outside counsel, how many hours they bill us for, and what that works out to as an hourly rate. So, the more hours in-house legal bills, the more hours there are to get divided into that fixed amount, so our effective hourly rate goes down. If we want to keep our jobs, we have to prove we're cheaper than outside counsel."

"So, you mean the less efficient we are, the better we look?"

"I'm not sure I would put it that way, but in any event, I doubt I'll be able to recommend you for any year-end bonus money unless a miracle happens and you get your numbers up. Any questions?"

Well, at least he got to the point quickly. I could feel my face growing red. "Nope. Guess I'll go work a couple of those files."

Well, that sucked. Billable hours had been something of a joke in our office up until now. Being slammed for working efficiently and not wasting time on a case, or for not billing two hours to a task which only took one, was galling, to say the least. I was going to have to talk to Peter, who was the only lawyer in the office who had experience working in a large private firm. He always seemed to coast along fine without breaking a sweat over hours, so there must be some tricks he could share.

As luck would have it, he was in that afternoon. I sat down and explained my dilemma. Peter was sympathetic, but it turned out he had his own problems: "You got reamed out for being too efficient—I got yelled at because I've been billing more discovery preparation and reporting time than the company guidelines allow. I never paid much attention to them, but I guess we're supposed to take no more than an hour to summarize 200 pages of medical records. The nimrod who came up with that standard certainly never had to wade through one of those monster files we get from Kaiser or UC Davis."

"Well, I guess we're going to be trying more cases, so maybe I'll just bill trial prep every time I think about a case."

"Hey, that's how we did it at my old firm. Just sharpen up your pencil. There were lawyers there who could routinely bill more than twenty-four hours in a day."

"I don't know if they want me to have a sharp pencil in my hand if they start riding me about getting things done quickly."

I decided to head home on what was for me the early side. I felt much better than I usually did after a trial, but I still had some nervous energy that I had to get out of my system. I changed into my running gear and leashed the dogs up. I had been running Elwood and Abby together for about a year now, and they kept mostly to business. They probably suspected that we would finish things off at the dog park behind the local community center, and they were right. We were all good and tired when we got home, and I was ready to veg out in front of the television.

Before I could, I saw that there was a message on my phone from Dan Casey. I called him back.

"Hey Jake," he greeted me. "How're things?"

"Work things suck; everything else is the best it's been in a long time. How about you?"

"Can't complain. This Social Security thing is taking off real fast. There's a lot of unmet need, because the other lawyers in town have trouble keeping in touch with homeless clients, so they don't tend to take their cases. Since I'm at Matthew's all the time, clients can drop by, or, if I need to see them and they don't have a phone, I can leave a message at the service desk where they pick up their tickets for lunch. I wasn't joking when I said that I might be able to use you down here."

"And I wasn't joking when I said I might be seeing you as a prospective client rather than a prospective employee. You've probably heard some through the grapevine about the changes in legal, but they are not fun."

"Actually, it's strange, but my sources on the inside have been drying up at a remarkable rate. The only people I've heard from in the last two weeks are a couple of the old-timers in claims and the folks in legal. Anyway, the reason I called wasn't to talk shop. I'm hosting a party at my house, two Fridays from now. There'll be some of the old crew as well as some of the people I've met at Matthew's. Bring a guest or two and a bottle or two of something, and come any time after eight."

"Sounds good, as long as my intended guest doesn't have other plans."

"Oh, so you've got someone in mind? This sounds promising."

"It is. I think you'll like her."

Chapter 23

O n the night of the party, we arrived at Dan's house when it was already in full swing. Meg and I were dressed casually. She was wearing flats, which was a departure from the heels she usually wore at work. I was struck once again by how she carried herself like she was two inches taller than she actually was, regardless of what she had on her feet.

"Hey Jake, how's it going?" said Dan, as we came through the door. "Who's this with you?"

"Dan, this is Meg. Meg, Dan."

"Nice to meet you. How did you two meet?"

"I actually work in underwriting at Farmstead," Meg said.

"No kidding! I bet you're a breath of fresh air in that group. Is Mack still the VP?"

"No, we have a new VP from Black Belt and a bunch of the underwriters are new to us as well, although they all seem to have big company experience."

Dan's attention was drawn to a new group of people arriving and he turned to greet them.

"Well, enough shop talk," he said, putting his hand on my shoulder. "Enjoy yourselves."

I introduced Meg to a few more people and then went and got a couple of beers from the bar. Meg was talking to someone I didn't know, so I gave her a beer and decided to circulate myself. To my surprise, I bumped into Carlos. Carlos was not much for parties. At work, he was Farmstead's in-house expert on insurance coverage, and he was also involved in rewriting policy language to make sure that Farmstead didn't accidentally cover some risk that it didn't get a premium for. He lived a sort of monastic existence in corporate legal, but he actually reported directly to Anton and others in the corporate president's office.

We talked for a few minutes before turning to work. "Have you been impacted by the changes?" I asked.

"Well, I've got plenty of work, and with these big commercial risks starting to come in, we're writing policies that are much more customized, which can be interesting if you're in to that sort of thing. I'm doing all right, but it's Anton who's got me worried.

"How so?"

"Well, all the VP and division manager slots have been filled with people either directly from Black Belt or hired by them from other carriers. And they're not letting Anton manage them. Any intra-office beefs get handled at Black Belt. So, Anton doesn't have upper management to keep under control, he doesn't have stockholders to keep happy, since Black Belt pretty much runs the board of directors, and pretty soon he won't have sales agents to care and feed, since almost all our business will be coming from brokers. He's nothing more than a symbol somehow demonstrating that not everything's changed at Farmstead, which anyone there can tell you isn't true. One of these days he's going to get tired of smiling and pack it in."

"I had no idea it was that dire, but what you're telling me certainly fits with what I've been seeing. I have the feeling that our house counsel operation is on its way out."

"Could be. It's not going to get better."

We talked for a few minutes longer until music started coming from the back. I excused myself, found Meg, and invited her to dance. Not to my surprise, she was a great dancer who kept excellent time to the music. I did my best to keep up, and felt like I was doing a reasonably good job. The music changed from rock to salsa, and I excused myself while Meg went looking for someone who knew the steps. I could see that the wine on the drinks table was mostly gone. I had another bottle in my car, so I went to get it. Instead of going through the house, I went down the side yard, through the gate, and into an area next to the garage which was overgrown with foliage and quite dark.

When I reached the driveway, I saw someone walking around the cars parked on the street with a cell phone in his hand. I couldn't see what he was doing for sure, but it looked to me like he was photographing vehicle license plates. I walked up toward him, and, before he noticed me, asked loudly, "Are you here for the party?"

He jumped and stared at me. "Ah, no," he said, slipping his cell phone into his pocket. "This street seems to be a hotspot for Pokémon Go, and I'm trying to catch some." Now this guy did not look young enough to be a Pokémon player out at ten o'clock in a residential area, but, since I knew almost nothing about the game and his answer had the tiniest ring of possibility, I didn't make a big deal of it.

"I've never heard of there being any Pokémon on this street. Maybe they're in the park around the corner."

"That's a good idea. I'll try over there." He spun on his heels and walked quickly away.

I went back inside and found Dan. "Can you think of an innocent explanation for why anyone would be interested in knowing who's attending your party?" I described what I had just seen out in the street.

"Well, I suppose it depends on how paranoid the Black Belt folks are. I mean, there're plenty of people here tonight who still work there, and it wouldn't be odd for someone to ask about it at work. Hell, I even invited some of the Black Belt people themselves, although none of them showed. But, I have a feeling that for some reason they think I'm leading the "resistance," whatever that would be. Maybe they think I want revenge. If you really wanted to make a complete list of the enemy, I suppose license plates are one way to go."

I decided to keep this from Meg, as she was already jumpy enough. We enjoyed ourselves well enough that we lost track of time and wound up helping Dan start the clean-up.

The highlight of the night came as we were driving home. Meg turned to me and said, "You are a really good dancer. I think your past musical experience shows."

Wow. Complementing a near-geek like me on his dancing was certainly one way to win my heart.

Chapter 24

I spent most of the next week working on the motion for summary judgment in the Eureka case. My surveyor had confirmed my expectations that the plaintiff had never gotten within twenty feet of my client's property before coming to an abrupt stop against the end of the culvert. The facts seemed straightforward, but an MSJ has a great many moving parts, and every part has to fit together without any conflicts or omissions, so I had to be very careful in putting it together.

The brightest spot in the week came when I got a letter from Annie Adams up in Boonville with some conventional photographs and negatives which showed her "friend" Leslie standing in the orchard wearing a sweatshirt from the Giants' 2012 World Series championship. The note that came with the photos explained that Annie had forgotten that there was half a roll of film in her camera, and she had just had it developed. Actually, I didn't know where one went to get film developed these days, but I was glad Annie was so resourceful. It was clear that the picture had been taken with Leslie standing in exactly the same area where she fell, and the gopher mounds and holes sure looked identical to the ones which she said had caused her fall. I took some time out from the MSJ to draft some sharp written discovery questions to plaintiff's attorney, hoping that this new evidence might bring an element of reasonableness into settlement discussions.

Meg had asked me to find out what was going on with the Eel River Inn claim, since it seemed that everyone else in underwriting had already forgotten about it and had moved on to other things. I decided to sound out Phil Silas, who was one of a handful of senior claims adjusters left over from pre-Black Belt days and the only one who still took a regular break. I knew I could probably find him in the cafeteria at ten-thirty with his coffee and crossword puzzle.

"Hey, Phil, how goes the battle?"

"Well, other than dealing with the usual fraud, deception and just plain overreaching by claimants, now we have to try to settle cases with way too little authority. And just wait until that starts hitting our metrics come salary review time. How about you—sounds like no more fishing trips disguised as depositions."

"Actually, there's plenty of good fishing even in our smaller bailiwick, but I am going to be sad to give up the Eureka cases. Speaking of Eureka, do you have any idea how bad that fire loss up there is going to be?"

"Well, everyone who was paying attention heard about the loss. You can't have something that big hit so quickly after you write such a large policy without it sending some sort of ripple through the system. But since then, I haven't heard anything. I assume Ann Baxter, the new first-party commercial risks adjuster, has the file, but that's only because she was hired to work those kinds of claims. Anyway, good luck getting anything out of her. She takes need-to-know very seriously. If there's anything fishy with the claim, the only people besides her who would know are Scanlon and Abercrombie. God knows she spends enough time closeted with them."

"So, the short answer is 'I don't know?'"

"Yup, and if you want my two cents, it's not a good way to do business. We're all getting so far out of the loop compared to the way things were before Black Belt that it's not funny." Phil drained his coffee cup with a flourish.

"Ditto on that from my side of the shop," I said. "Need any help on the crossword puzzle before I go?"

"Yeah—what's a six-letter word for 'Hillary aide?'"

"How about 'sherpa.'"

"Ouch. I think you're right."

Well, it certainly didn't look as if inquiring from within was going to produce anything. I didn't like the idea of telling Meg I'd hit a dead end, but I didn't have any plausible business excuse to ask Ann Baxter about it. When I got back to my office there was a text from Meg on my phone with a link to an article in the Eureka paper:

The coroner's office announced yesterday that it had identified the individual found dead following the fire at the Eel River Inn as Frank Lyman, also known as "Buzzard." Mr. Lyman was a native of Eureka and had continued to visit his family here from time to time, although he apparently spent much of his time living in a homeless shelter in

Sacramento in recent years. The cause of death was given as smoke inhalation, although a high level of opiates was found in his blood. An employee of the New Aberdeen fire department, who asked not to be identified due to the ongoing nature of the investigation, stated that it appeared that Mr. Lyman had been camping for some time in the basement of the inn while it was under renovation, and that he had fallen asleep with his camp stove lit, igniting the blaze.

I texted Meg back, asking her what she thought. She replied almost as soon as I had hit send: "I think this is a set-up."

My heart sank. It was bad enough that Meg wasn't giving up on following the Eel River Inn story. It was even worse that she kept dragging me into her investigations. But now, for her to go full-tilt boogie conspiracy theory on this was just too much. Only one thing to do—El Gallito.

We met right after work. She was looking as distressed as I had ever seen her. "What's up? Why do you think there's something wrong with the picture?" I asked.

"Well, what I didn't tell you—because I didn't want to leave an electronic footprint somewhere—is that my mother knows Frank Lyman. He was one of her students about fifteen years ago, and she always considered him one of her success stories. I think he had drug issues a while back, but she ran into him at the mall in Eureka this spring, and he seemed to be doing okay. He even mentioned that someone was fixing him up with a job in the area, although he didn't give any more details. He still had family in the area, and they always let him couch surf, so mom can't think of any reason why he'd be camping in some basement somewhere."

"That's not much to go on," I said. "A lot can happen in few months, especially for folks on the bottom rung of the economic ladder."

"Maybe you're right, but it still feels wrong somehow. Anyway, the paper said he was staying in a homeless shelter in Sacramento. I wonder if your friend Dan might know someone who knows about Frank. Do you think you could ask him?"

As much as I wished Meg would drop it, I figured that Dan's information would likely be innocuous, and that might get her off the conspiracy path. "Sure. I'll set something up with him."

Chapter 25

I was away from the office for most of the next week, first heading to Redding for a settlement conference and then over to Weaverville for a deposition on another case. I stayed overnight in Redding at the Red Lion and was assigned the same room as the one I had been in with Meg. Sadly, the stay was not nearly as memorable.

Weaverville is just over the hill from Redding in the direction of Eureka. It's not much more than a wide spot in the road, but it is the seat of government for Trinity County. My client this time, Missy Evans, had the unhappy distinction of breaking a trifecta of traffic laws by driving into an elderly pedestrian with a white cane in a marked crosswalk, resulting in serious injuries. To make matters worse, she wasn't driving her own car, but rather one owned by the couple for whom she worked as a caregiver. The wife worked out of the home, and Missy took care of the husband, who was in a fairly advanced state of dementia. The day of the accident had been a sunny one, and even though she hadn't been told to do this, and hadn't ever been told that she was allowed to use the family car, she decided that what the husband needed was a drive in the country. Naturally, there was a huge fight as to which insurance, if any, covered the accident. Missy's policy with Farmstead had only the minimum legal limit of coverage, while the family's coverage on its car, which was with another company, was substantial.

The accident had happened down in Sonoma County, and Missy had more or less fled in embarrassment to Trinity County. The law about how far you can force someone to travel to attend a deposition is pretty clear, and so we had to come to her rather than do it somewhere more convenient for the attorneys. I met Missy for breakfast ahead of the ten o'clock deposition, and spent the whole hour trying to calm her down, as she was sure the sky was going to fall on her because of the case. The court reporter's office was right next door to the diner, so we eased in about ten minutes early. Plaintiff's attorney, who I knew pretty well, was there already, but the deposition had been noticed by the attorney for the family, so we certainly had to wait for them.

With a substantial policy limit on the line, the insurance carrier for the family had hired a large, well-known Sacramento office. Unlike most mega-law firms in Northern California, it got its hands dirty doing a little personal injury defense along with its business and regulatory work. I expected someone to show up who was a little uncomfortable in a setting as rural as Weaverville, maybe giving me a subtle leg up. What I didn't expect was to see two attorneys climbing out of Weaverville's only cab, evidently having gotten to town by air taxi. The second briefcase was an attractive blond woman wearing a slightly too-short navy skirt and jacket and heels; first briefcase was wearing a suit which I knew from my days at Macy's probably went out the door for at least $1800. That might be how they rolled in the halls of power, but their ensembles were totally out of place in Trinity County.

The deposition was 90 percent on the question of whether Missy had any reasonable belief that she had permission to use the family car, with only 10 percent on the accident itself. This made sense, since I couldn't think of an accident with facts less sympathetic to the defendant. Missy, for all her nervousness, actually paid attention to my pre-deposition coaching and remembered her basic points—namely that she hadn't been specifically told that she couldn't drive the car, and that if she had to transport the husband due to some sort of emergency, her own car was too small and too unfamiliar to the husband to have any chance of getting him into it. After what seemed like an all-day exercise, although it really only lasted until two o'clock with a break for lunch, first briefcase and second briefcase took the taxi back to the airport and were probably on the ground in Sacramento before I had finished debriefing Missy and had gotten as far as Redding. I hated to think how much the family's lawyers charged the insurance carrier that had hired them, but it wasn't my job to look out for its interests.

I reached Sacramento a little after six. There was no pressing reason to stop at the office, so I went straight home. I had texted Meg from the road, but hadn't heard back from her before I arrived. While I was feeding Elwood, I got a call from her.

"Hey, would you like to come over tonight?"

"Always, but can I bring Elwood with me? He's got a hot date with the groomer tomorrow, and I have to drop him off before work."

"That would be fine. Can you come by around eight?"

"Sure. See you then."

One drawback to Meg's condo was the absence of visitor parking. I had to park a couple of blocks away because of the street cleaning schedule. Meg buzzed me up. She was looking very tired and worn, and did not want to break her hug with me until Elwood started getting pushy and whiney for a pat of his own.

"What's wrong?" I asked.

Meg ran her fingers through her hair, sighed deeply, and sat down on the couch. "What do you think—the goddamn Eel River Inn is what's wrong. I know you think I'm overreacting, and half the time I think you're right and these are all just innocent coincidences, but other times—like today—another shoe drops."

I sat down next to her and put my hand on her knee. "So, what happened?"

"Jill brought me into the conference room for a call on the speakerphone with the guy from the fire department investigating things. She made it very clear that the only thing the investigator wanted to hear about was the gap in the fence I had noted in my inspection. He had a copy of the inspection report, and I told him just what I had said in it—that it looked like someone could have used it as a way into the building. But at the end, I added that I had some information about the guy they found in the remains. As I started to tell them about

170

him, Jill motioned to me to stop. The investigator said they were still looking into that, but didn't see anything inconsistent with their initial impression, and he'd follow up if it seemed necessary. What was weird, though, was Jill's reaction to what I'd said. I'm sure her blood pressure was through the roof. She just snapped, 'OK. Thanks. That's all.' And, after the call, she asked me in great detail about my mom's relationship to Lyman."

Though it seemed to me that she was overreacting, I tried to be sympathetic. "Meg, I really don't like how all this is affecting you. You're right that there are some odd things about this case, but if there's some sort of conspiracy to intentionally torch the place that also involves people within Farmstead, I can't see where the gain is. I don't do arson cases, but isn't the most likely time to burn a place down when it's having a run of bad luck? It can't possibly be right before the grand re-opening, after all the investment has been made."

"What if it turns out that the investments weren't actually made? What if all that redwood trim shows up on the market some time down the road? Remember, the fire was hotter than usual because of the chemicals, so someone who really knew what they were doing could have substituted cheap shit for the high-end fixtures we're paying for and no one would be the wiser for it because so little was left. What if Buzzard was some sort of patsy, or even drugged and dumped where he'd be blamed for the fire?"

"I see your point, but I'm just not sure. Can we just chill for awhile and talk about something else. We both need to get our minds off of work."

"Sure, but I'm not feeling real sexy tonight."

"Well, I'm a little worn down from the road myself, although you may be interested to know that I got room 226 at the Red Lion for the second time in a row."

"Aw, how cute. Did you have as much fun this time?"

"What do you think?"

We went to bed relatively early. It wasn't unusually cool, and I was comfortable in my boxers and t-shirt, but Meg put on a pair of heavy flannel PJs and spent the first half hour shivering in bed. I cuddled as closely to her as I could and stroked her hair until she finally dozed off. As I fell asleep myself, I realized that whether there was anything to Meg's suspicions or not, the Eel River Inn was definitely getting in the way of my love life. I tried to match my breathing with her steady, slow breath, and dozed off to sleep.

The next thing I knew, there was a tremendous crash downstairs and Elwood ran out of the bedroom barking hysterically. My first thought was that the dog had knocked something over and frightened himself. The clock showed 2:40 a.m. Meg jumped out of bed and looked down the stairs to where she could see the front door.

"Fuck, the door is open." She opened up the bottom drawer in her nightstand and pulled out two automatics. She took the smaller one, pulled back its slide and handed it to me. "It's hot. The safety's off and there's a bullet in the chamber. Stay up here." She grabbed the larger gun and worked the slide as well, then went out the bedroom door in a low crouch.

I felt a little superfluous standing in the bedroom, but at least I knew the basics of using a handgun from my visits with my uncle. I didn't have a gun at home anymore, figuring I would be better off with the Louisville Slugger in my bedroom closet. Anyway, I was sure that the last place I wanted to be was someplace Meg didn't expect me to be, so I stayed put.

A minute later, she called up the stairs. "The place is clear. Leave the gun upstairs and come down." When I got to the door, I could see that the lock had held and the door was intact, but the door framing had splintered into a dozen pieces.

"What the hell was that all about?" Meg asked.

"Beats me. This sure doesn't look like someone was drunk and got mad because their key didn't fit your door. Let's call the cops."

Meg called 911, and two units responded quite quickly. The officers asked all the usual questions about who might have done this, mostly getting nothing from us since there was nothing to give. Two of their questions got me thinking, however. The first was how whoever had done this had gotten to the landing of Meg's front door, since her front gate was intact. The other was a little more personal. Once they had established that Elwood and I lived elsewhere, the officer speaking with me asked whether anyone else knew the dog and I were going to be there that night. I told her no, but held back the fact that someone who knew my car would not have seen it that night, as I had parked on another block. The cops were mystified, and told us this was hardly the usual precursor to a residential burglary.

After they left, I drove Meg and Elwood over to my house and put them to bed. I went back to her apartment about four-thirty and called the emergency board-up company I knew Farmstead used. Playing the company card got a few strings pulled, and they were out quickly. The lead guy on the truck seemed as baffled as the cops had been, but sagely observed, "Momma always said nothing good ever happens after closing time."

By the time I got back from Meg's, the sun was already up. She woke as soon as I came in the house. "Things are fine at your place. You'll need a new door frame, but your door and the lock will work well enough for now and you actually can't see any damage from the outside."

"Thanks for doing that," she said. "I sure don't like the thought of having to explain all this to Ginny, since it's really her door. And anyway, who do you think did this, and why? I'm really scared to think I've touched something off and that this was a not-too-subtle way of sending me a message. But the only message I can think of is to get off my Eel River Inn kick."

I sat down next to Meg on the bed and took her hand. We were both silent for a minute and then I said, "I know you think there's something more going on with the Eel River Inn." I paused to think of the best way to proceed. "But we have both seen a lot of claims. Fire and other shit happen. In fact, that's why we have our jobs."

Meg sat quietly without looking at me.

"Break-ins happen all the time, too," I said. "I know it is so scary when it happens to you, but I'm worried that you are getting too wrapped up in this work thing and seeing monsters where they don't exist."

I paused for a moment, but she didn't say anything.

"There have been so many changes at work," I continued. "I think everyone is on edge. But I think all this crap at work is just life in the dog-eat-dog world of corporate America. All that matters is the rich getting richer."

Meg continued to sit silently. "Maybe you should take a few days off," I said.

When Meg finally looked at me, her eyes were sharp. She took her hand from under mine and rubbed her hands together as if she were cold.

"I'm sorry you don't believe me," she said in a soft voice. "I thought that we had something going and could trust each other, but I guess I was wrong."

She started to get out of bed. "I do trust you," I said. "And we do have something here. I'm just worried about you."

"Well, don't worry about me," she said. "I'm sorry I can't count on you, but I need to get to the bottom of this."

"Please, listen to me, Meg. I know you are upset. Let's take a day to relax and get the door fixed and talk about all this again later."

She continued to gather her things, including the things she generally kept at my house. "I need a ride home," she said. "Can you drop me off?"

"Of course. Do you want me to arrange to get the door fixed?"

"Don't bother," she said. "I'll talk to Ginny and take care of it."

We drove to her house in silence. As she got out of the car, she said "I'm going to take some vacation time. I think it would be best if we also took a break from each other for awhile."

"Meg, please," I started, turning to her. "Let's talk this out." She got out of the car quickly. I watched sadly as she climbed the stairs to her apartment.

Chapter 26

I took the breakup with Meg pretty hard. I tried to reach her by text, phone, and email but she wasn't returning my messages. I felt like I was just going through the motions of life. It was hard to focus and I was having trouble sleeping.

A few days after Meg left, I decided it might be good for my emotional state to take a trip to Matthew's Promise. At least it would help me appreciate having a job and a roof over my head. Although I doubted it would amount to much, Meg's suggestion to inquire about Buzzard also gave me an excuse for the trip.

Last time I had visited, Dan had told me to come in the morning when things were hopping, so I stopped there around eight-thirty on my way into work. The street in front of his bungalow was quite a bit more crowded than it had been in the afternoon when I had been there before. I dodged around the shopping carts and the bike trailers, and parked under the black walnut which cast a deep shade at this hour.

Dan was alone in the back of the bungalow and luckily wasn't dressed for court, so I figured I could steal a little of his time.

"Jake! What brings you down here? You ready to file your disability claim?"

I shrugged as we shook hands. "Not just yet," I said. We drank some coffee and I brought Dan up to date on the news from Farmstead.

"Actually, I'm here on a mission from God. My friend Meg, who you met at your party, wanted to see if I could get the story on someone you may know here. He passed away up in Eureka, and apparently Meg's mother knew him up there. His name was Frank Lyman, but I guess his street name was Buzzard. He supposedly spent a lot of his time in Sacramento."

"Buzzard? I don't know anyone by that name, or Frank Lyman either, but there're about 600 people who cycle through here every day, so that's no surprise. We need to go up to the park and talk to some of the staff who know the guests on a day-to-day basis. I've got some time, so let's go. I just need to lock up."

We walked up the street while Dan acted as my tour guide. We passed several buildings with large, hand-painted signs. "Here's the health clinic, which takes case of minor injuries and chronic conditions like asthma and diabetes. Here's our temporary school for homeless children where they can go until their folks can get a permanent address and enroll them with the school district. Here's the washhouse for showers and clean clothes. Here's our day shelter for women and children." He pointed to each building as we passed. "Over there is our mental health counseling program, and next to it is the office for our clean and sober project." We were approaching a large, fenced-in area. "And here's the park," he said, "where the elite meet to greet."

We turned off the street into the lot, which featured a number of small kiosk-like huts, benches, and gazebos. I could see rows of lockers and a coffee urn with a cup for donations. Trees shaded most of the park, a necessity in Sacramento, where summer temperatures can reach 110 degrees. A large blackboard had a few messages posted: "Today's temperature—82." "Bus vouchers now available in the dining hall" and a couple of others. It appeared to be a cool and welcoming spot. An ice machine and a couple of pay phones stood under a shade structure. Casey walked up to an unmarked door and knocked confidently.

"This is where Jordan hangs out when he's not in the park. He's the park director. Since I didn't see him out there, he's probably inside." The door was opened by a fresh-faced college-age woman in a green sweatshirt.

"Hi, Lisa, this is my buddy Jake," Dan said, introducing us to each other. "Is Jordan in?"

"Sure. He's here and I think he's free. You know the way." She motioned down the hall.

Dan led me back through a maze of small rooms crowded with desks and gear. "Lisa just graduated from college," he said, "and is working as a volunteer this year."

We entered the office at the end of the corridor where a man about my age looked up from his computer and greeted Dan warmly. "Jordan, this is Jake, who I used to work with. He's trying to track down information on a former guest who's joined the great majority, and I thought you might be able to help."

Jordan stood up and shook my hand. He had an athletic build and a kind face.

"Sure, if I know anything," Jordan responded.

"I appreciate it," I said. "Quite an operation you have here."

"Did Dan give you a tour?"

"Yes. The services are impressive. Have you been working here long?"

Jordan had returned to his seat and leaned back in his chair. Dan and I sat on the other side of the desk. Like Dan's office, the furniture in the office was old and unmatched. "I've been park director for about six years," he said. "But I was a guest here for awhile myself so it's been longer than that. Helps my job to know what it's like on the other side."

I nodded. "I was wondering if you have ever met someone named Frank Lyman. I think he might have been known around these parts as Buzzard. Does that ring any bells?" I asked.

"Buzzard? Sure, I know him. You say he's dead?" Jordan shook his head sadly. "That's a shame. He got his name because his hair and his eyes were so dark and he was always hunched over. He actually was one of the nicest of our guests. He'd always lend a hand if it was needed. How'd he die?"

"Apparently, he was killed in a fire up near Eureka."

"Eureka? That sounds right. I remember he came from there. He was always trying to find some way of moving back up there permanently." Jordan looked out his window, his attention drawn by two men speaking loudly.

"It's a touchy subject," I continued, "And obviously I would understand if you don't want to answer, but did he have some sort of drug issues when you knew him?"

Jordan turned back from the window and laughed. "Hah! If you had asked me that awhile back, I would have said 'boy howdy.' He was one of our big-time tweekers back in the day. But he got sick and tired of being sick and tired and got into our clean and sober project. He got his two-year coin about six months ago, which is the last time I remember seeing him. Sad that he passed when he was just starting to get his life back together."

"You say he used to use meth—how about opiates or heroin?"

"Buzzard? Not a chance. Why do you ask?"

"The coroner says there were opiates in his system when he died."

Jordan shook his head. "I'm sorry, I just can't believe that. For one thing, it's pretty rare for a tweeker to switch over to opiates, and for another, Buzzard had a brother who OD'ed on heroin. He was deathly scared of that shit." I let that sink in as Dan asked Jordan about a client he was trying to reach.

"Well, thanks for your time," I said to Jordan when it looked like they were done.

"If I find out anything more, I'll let Dan know so he can pass it on."

"I'd appreciate that."

"If you need it," Jordan added, "I could probably put you in touch with some of the people he used to run with back in the day, and the clean and sober people probably know who his porch buddies were when he was in that program." Jordan looked at Dan. "We'll have to add Buzzard's name to our memorial wall," he said. "We have a memorial for all our guests who pass," he said, turning to me. "It's quite a long list, and it gets longer every time I blink."

After leaving the park, I thanked Dan and drove to the office thinking about what Jordan had told us. I really wanted to find a way to get Meg off of her kick, but what I just had learned wasn't going to give her any reason to think that she was wrong.

Chapter 27

The rainy season started off strong with a series of storms in late September. Rain is always a good thing in drought-prone Northern California and after the rain the air was crisp and fresh. Even though the showers had revealed a small leak in my roof, I still enjoyed the weather and the changing colors, particularly the bright yellow Ginkgo trees near my house. I hadn't heard from Meg in a couple of weeks. I had seen her car in the parking lot but wanted to let her make the first move.

One Saturday, after taking the dogs on a long walk, I saw Claire raking leaves in her front yard. Our area has a dense urban forest, which is lovely six months out of the year but creates something of a nuisance for parking in the fall when the curbs disappear under piles of fallen leaves.

I hadn't told Claire about the break-in and Meg's departure but today she seemed to want to talk and invited me to stay for some wine. She rubbed her hands on an old towel and poured a couple of glasses of generic red.

"I think everything just got to be too much," I said, as I told her about Meg. "Everyone at work feels like we are chum for the sharks." I sighed and shook my head. "And then, the fire and the break-in."

"I'm sorry," she said. "But once things quiet down maybe you two can figure it out."

"I hope so."

The dogs were tired and lay on the floor between us. Claire's house was comfortable and always several degrees warmer than mine. Her furniture was well worn and her artwork, along with family pictures, adorned the walls.

Claire rested her foot on Abby's back. "Do you remember when we had dinner at Meg's I said that Abercrombie's name sounded familiar?"

"Vaguely," I said, "but I think that was about the time he started, so we may have been talking about him."

Claire took a sip of her wine. "Well, you probably remember that we talked about Redwood Summer and I said my daughter Katie was involved in the protests."

I nodded. "Yes, I do remember."

"I was talking to her the other day and she remembered someone named Chaz Abercrombie from those days. She thinks that he was involved in one of those pseudo-environmental groups. It was called "Redwood Forest Action Committee," or something like that."

"That would be interesting," I said. I took out my phone. "Let's see if we can find anything on Google," I said. "Charles. . . Chaz. . . let's see. . . a missing man from Ohio, lots of people in the white pages, some historical figures."

"Of course, all of this took place before the internet," Claire said.

"Let's try Redwood Forest Action Committee," I said, entering the name into Google. "There is no website, but it looks like it is mentioned in an article. . . yes. It says that it was an organization formed by the timber industry to promote efficient and productive management of natural resources."

Claire hmphed: "Astroturf."

"Did Katie say anything else? Did she describe what he looked like?"

"I didn't ask her," Claire said, "but I will next time I talk to her."

"That would be great. Nice to dig up some dirt on the higher ups." I smiled.

Like clockwork, the dogs began to let us know they were ready for dinner. I thanked Claire for the wine, and Elwood and I headed for the door.

"Good luck with Meg," Claire said. "You two seem to be a good match."

I waved from the front porch. "Thanks. I think so, too."

)O(O(O(

Later that evening, as I was settling in to watch the baseball playoffs, Claire called.

"I talked to my daughter," she said, "and I wanted to let you know what she said about Abercrombie."

"Sure." I muted the sound on the television.

"She found an old clipping she had in a box of college things showing one of the protests she was in. He isn't mentioned by name, but she circled the person she remembers as Chaz Abercrombie.

185

"Wow, that's great. Can you send the photo to me?"

"Will do. Don't forget, this was twenty-five years ago, so I expect, if it is him, he looks different now."

"Of course. Thanks, Claire. And please thank your daughter."

I went back to the game and saw that Houston was ahead, though struggling against the Yankees. I watched for Claire's email and saw it arrive.

The clipping was a large photo with the caption, "Protesters block logging equipment from gaining access to old-growth grove." In the picture, there were approximately 10 people, mostly young, standing arm-in-arm across a dirt road. In the foreground, facing them, was a bulldozer with an older man in a hard hat standing beside it, his back to the camera. A few other people looked on from the sidelines, including the young man Claire's daughter had circled with a marker.

I expanded the picture as much as I could and studied it. The man was probably in his mid-20's. He was facing the camera and was tall with brown hair pulled back in a ponytail. He wore jeans and a denim work shirt and boots. With the newsprint enlarged, it was difficult to make out more details. Since I had only seen him once or twice, it was hard to tell if this was our guy.

I phoned Claire and asked for Katie's phone number. She gave it to me and assured me that it wasn't too late to call.

The call was picked up on the second ring. I introduced myself and thanked Katie.

"What was your impression of Abercrombie?" I asked.

"We didn't trust him," she said. "He seemed to be on our side, but even at the time we knew that his group was funded by timber."

"Did you know him very well?"

"Not well, but I saw him a lot. He seemed to show up when the cameras were there and seemed more interested in his personal role, rather than the trees. A trust-fund kid, if I had to guess."

"Are you in this picture?"

"I am," she said. "That's me. . . second from the left on the road." I looked at the photo and saw a young woman with a fierce expression and long sandy hair held back with a bandana.

"Do you still have contacts in the environmental movement up north?"

"Not really," she said. "I've been in Santa Cruz now for twenty years so I'm more involved down here."

"Well, thanks again. Let me know if you remember anything else about Abercrombie."

I wasn't sure what to make of this connection, but at least the new information gave me another reason to talk to Meg.

Chapter 28

I waited until the next day to contact Meg. I had an early morning "pre-work" breakfast meeting (no fruit plate; donuts only) and, before calling Meg, I decided to stop in and see Charlene.

Charlene's office door was open and she sat at her computer behind a pile of open files.

"Can I interrupt you a minute?" I asked

"Sure, come on in." I entered her office and shut the door behind me.

"I found something about Abercrombie," I said. "It may help you find out more about him." I pulled out my phone and scrolled to the photo Katie had sent me.

"This is a photo of a protest to protect the redwoods. It was taken around 1990 up in Humboldt County and, evidently, the person circled here," I pointed to the photo, "is named Chaz Abercrombie."

She raised her eyebrows. "Wow. Where did you get this?"

"I'd chalk it up to skill if I thought I could pull it off, but it was just chance that his name came up with

someone I know whose daughter was also at this protest
and had kept the clipping."

Charlene strained to see the small photo. "I've only
met him once," she said. "Mark introduced me to him
in the cafeteria." She turned the photo to another angle.
"Hard to tell from this, but it could be him in his younger
days. He doesn't seem like someone who would take a
stand for the environment."

"Evidently, the group Charles, or Chaz, was working
with was trying to discredit the environmentalists while
pretending to care," I said. "I think it was called Redwood
Forest Action Committee. This is all pretty much pre-
internet, but maybe it could help your research."

"I'll check it out," Charlene said. "On another topic,
you going to Peter's show Friday night?"

I had forgotten that our resident attorney-comedian
(or comedian-attorney) had invited the office to come to
his stand-up show at a nearby club. "I'm going to try to,"
I said.

She nodded. "Hope to see you there."

I went back to my office in a reflective state of mind
and sat for a few minutes before trying to contact Meg.
There were some strange coincidences, I had to admit. It
seemed that something was going on, but I was not ready
to embrace the idea of a full-blown conspiracy.

I got a cup of coffee and took out my phone. "Hi,"
I texted to Meg. "I'd like to talk to you. I have some
information and want to help. Can I call you?"

A few minutes later I received a text: "OK."

I phoned Meg and she picked up right away. As we
exchanged small talk, she sounded distant but at least she

answered my call this time, which was a good start. As I told her about what I had found out about Buzzard and Charles, she began to sound like her old self.

"I have to admit, Meg, I think you might be onto something," I said. "Something fishy is going on."

"I'm glad you agree," she said. "I thought I was going crazy."

"Well, if you are," I replied, "I guess I'm going along for the ride."

She laughed and I felt more relaxed than I had since she had cut things off.

I told her about the photo and my talk with Katie. Meg had taken a trip to Eureka to attempt to get more information about Buzzard and the fire. Her family had a lot of ties in the area and, since both her parents were teachers, their contacts crossed two or three generations.

"I tried to visit the site," she said, "but no-go. The whole area is locked down with security. They're in the process of demolishing the old place."

"I'm not surprised," I said. "Does your cousin Ike have any insight? Since he works in the mill, I thought he might."

"Not really. The inn was fairly separate from the mill. He seems to believe the company story. I did learn a little more about Buzzard, though. It sounds like he was like a lot of kids, just getting by and growing up with few prospects. I had a chance to talk to one of the homeless advocates up there. It's her feeling that he was set up, maybe killed and brought to the site to make it look like an accident."

"Why does she think that?"

"She wouldn't say. I tried to press her, but she said it was just a feeling."

"Do you think she could have some inside information?"

"She could. Her name is Pat and she is well-known up here for her work. If you think my parents know a lot of people, Pat knows just about everyone and she has a lot of ties with the local police. She knew that Buzzard had been in Sacramento and had heard that he had gotten clean. He showed up back in Eureka last spring for a while, but then disappeared again."

"Sounds like he does more traveling than I do. And without the benefit of a company car."

"Very funny," she said. "He showed up again just a few weeks before the fire. She said that she had noticed that he actually seemed tan—not his usual pale self— and he had some money. He was staying in a flea-bag hotel downtown."

"Too bad he wasn't staying there the night of the fire."

"I don't know how much cash he had. He may have run out. The rumor was that he had a field job trimming in one of the marijuana farms. That might explain the tan, since the growers tend to locate outside the fog zone."

"I guess that is one job opportunity in the 'emerald triangle.'"

"As weed becomes more legal and widespread, we'll see how the 'emerald triangle' does. I'm not sure if weed grows particularly well in that climate or if it's just grown there because of the isolation. I guess time will tell."

"I miss you," I said. "I want us to be together."

"I miss you, too," she said. "I'm out on a job right now, but I'll be back Friday morning. Let's find a time to get together."

"I can't wait." I said. "By the way, did I ever tell you that Peter, from my office, does stand-up comedy? He's invited the office to come to his show Friday night."

"Wow. I would never have guessed. Sure. Sounds like fun. I have an invitation for you, too. My dad says you should come up again during crab season. It'll be sport season, so there's a bag limit, but it should be fun. Maybe you could fit it in with your court appearance up here."

"Ah, yes. I know how that works. The more people on the boat the better. I think I can make that fly—the court hears those motions on Friday mornings."

"Great. See you soon."

"Stay safe," I said.

"As you've been known to say, it's mostly out of my control."

As we hung up, I breathed a sigh of relief and forwarded Katie's photo to Meg.

XOXOX

I went to Peter's office to check on the plans for the show, but paused as I noticed that he was resting his head on his desk in what looked like serious discomfort. This was concerning, as he was always one of the most upbeat people in the shop.

I stuck my head in the door, and asked, "You look like you just got some bad news. What's the deal?"

"Oh, you'll love this," he responded as he looked up. "Since you were out of the office yesterday, you missed our claims-legal meeting. Scanlon is rolling out another new initiative. He's signed the company up with some data-wranglers who claim they can predict the settlement value of a case with just a few easy keystrokes to enter the information. From now on, the claims adjusters can't authorize a deal in excess of whatever number the system spits out."

"Well, it's hardly as if we don't try to do the same thing ourselves every day," I replied. "The only issue is whether it gives us a fair reading on a case."

"That's what concerns me," said Peter. "The salesman who was demonstrating the system plugged a couple of real cases from claims into the matrix, and what came back was jaw-droppingly low. I could tell from the muttering that the claims folks thought the numbers were bogus, too. And then we started asking questions about methodology. Turns out it's a complete black box. I asked about how the system comes up with its numbers, including where they get the data to compare with the inputs, and he claimed it was proprietary and he couldn't reveal that. So, we have to trust some artificial intelligence that we can't understand to tell us how to do our jobs."

"Sounds like another reason we're going to be trying more cases," I sighed. "And another metric they'll use against us when the verdicts come in above where the computer tells them they're supposed to be. You know, I can remember when I enjoyed coming in to work. At this point I think they're just trying to get us to quit."

"I hear that," Peter responded. "Well, I for one am not taking this shit lying down. Luckily, I'm still working on my stand-up, so I'll have something to fall back on." I could tell from his expression that his humor had returned.

"In fact," I said, "that's what I came to ask you about. Tell me about your set on Friday. I'd like to come."

"Great! You can cheer me on. It's a ten-minute slot in the Friday Showcase over at The Dock. I go on at 9:20, and it's pass the basket with no cover, no minimum."

"Sounds good. Have you met my friend Meg? I think she'll be coming with me."

Peter raised his eyebrows. "As in a date?"

"Yep."

"Well, it's about time you started circulating. It's been a long time since Beth left."

"I suppose it could have happened sooner, but it may be more a case of when the student is ready, the teacher will appear. Anyway, we plan to be there."

Chapter 29

I phoned Meg on Friday to make plans for the evening. I had been out in a deposition all morning and decided to work at home in the afternoon rather than go into the office. I arranged to pick her up around seven for dinner before the show. Where things would go from there, I wasn't sure.

"By the way," she said. "In the photo you sent me from Claire's daughter, did you notice the woman standing next to Abercrombie?"

"I didn't notice," I said. "Let me look." I pulled out my phone and scrolled to find the picture. Even when it was enlarged, it was hard to make out much detail. The woman next to Chaz stood in profile to the camera and appeared to be talking to the protesters.

"The short woman with curly hair and glasses?" I asked.

"Yes. Doesn't she look like my boss, Jill?

It was hard for me to tell. "Maybe, a little." I honestly couldn't say.

"I should have realized something was weird with Jill," Meg continued. "She didn't know that I was from

Eureka and her whole demeanor changed when she found out. Now the things she asked me about make sense."

"What do you mean?"

"She asked me a lot of questions about my background, my connections in Eureka, my feelings about the environment, and my family. But really, she seemed to know the answers before I told her."

"What about Chaz Abercrombie?" I asked. "Do you think that could be the same guy?"

"I do," she said. "He's been in our office a lot lately talking to Jill and some other people and I'm pretty certain that's a young version of him. I'd recognize that long face anywhere."

"Well, ok. Let me call Katie again," I said. "I'll see if she knows anything about this woman.

"Ok. Let me know." said Meg.

I phoned Katie and asked her if she knew the woman in the picture.

Katie had deleted the photo from her phone so it took a few minutes for her to find the clipping. "Yes. Chaz's girlfriend," she said.

"Do you happen to remember her name or anything about her?"

"I knew her better than I knew Chaz," Katie said. "Her name was Jill. Jill something. . . Ford or Chevy. . . it was the name of a car."

I felt my stomach drop. "Was it Dodge?" I asked.

"Yes, that was it," she said.

Jill Dodge. Meg's boss at Farmstead.

"Wow," I said. "I think she is working with Charles now. Do you know anything else about her?"

"No. That was a lifetime ago. I don't really remember."

"Thanks, Katie." I said, before ending the call. "Let me know if you remember anything more."

I texted Meg: "Yes, it is Jill. Let's talk more tonight."

That evening, Meg and I went to a Thai restaurant not far from the club where Peter was performing. At first, it was a little awkward being together, but fairly soon we both relaxed. Sharing a bottle of wine didn't hurt. She took my hand during dinner and nodded when I invited her over to my house after the show.

When we arrived at the club, I saw several people from the office at a table in the front, including Jocelyn and her husband, Charlene, and Larry.

The Dock is one of several bar/restaurants in town built on barges floating in the Sacramento River. They range in scale and price, with The Dock being firmly at the lower end. This may explain why its barge had a bad habit of sinking when no one was watching.

We saw Peter at a table in the back working on a Perrier. I introduced him to Meg. The room was about two-thirds full, and the crowd seemed to be enjoying the evening.

"Is your time slot a good one?" Meg asked.

"Generally, it's one of the best, unless one of the earlier acts does a big-time face plant," Peter replied. "I've been doing sets here for a couple of years, and one of the owners describes himself as a recovering attorney, so they tend to be pretty nice to me."

We found a seat next to Charlene at the Farmstead table, ordered drinks, and I introduced Meg around the table. Just then, we saw the emcee get up, and we turned our attention to the stage.

"Now folks," he said. "Please give your attention to a very funny man. He is a regular at The Dock. Mr. Peter Penna."

There was modest applause with a few whistles and hoots coming from our table.

Peter jumped up on stage, holding an acoustic guitar in one hand, and grabbed the mic. "Good evening, ladies and gentlemen. And thanks to the kind people at The Dock for making this time available to me." He gave a nod to the emcee. Peter's wide eyes and dark eyebrows gave him an expressive look, not unlike Groucho Marx. His facial expressions alone brought laughter from the audience.

He started the set with a song and had a surprisingly good voice. "This is an old Jim Stafford song," he said, "called *Don't Pet the Dog*. As the song warns, 'he gets it confused with romance.'" The audience laughed and Peter started singing. By the time he was finished, the audience was warmed up, laughing, and singing along.

"I've been coming here for a couple of years now," he said, putting his guitar down, "and like most of the other performers who are here on the weekends, I have a day job. I'm a lawyer. Okay, go ahead, get it out of your systems." There was loud booing and catcalls, including some from our table.

"Thanks," Peter said, bowing deeply. "Now, some lawyer jokes. I've heard them all. I think I wrote some of them."

Rapid fire:

"Why do some scientists use lawyers instead of lab rats in their experiments? The grad students don't get attached to the lawyers. Boom.

"Why won't a shark attack a swimming lawyer? Professional courtesy. Boom.

"How many lawyer jokes are there? Three. All the rest are true stories. Boom.

"What's the difference between a dead skunk in the middle of the road and a dead lawyer in the middle of the road? Skid marks in front of the skunk. Boom.

"Here's a quote attributed to Winston Churchill: Lawyers occasionally stumble over the truth, but most of them pick themselves up and hurry off as if nothing happened. Boom.

"And here's a poem written by a lady named Alice Murray, who I know nothing about:

"'I've practiced law for almost 40 years
Practice makes perfect?
Why, after practicing years
Am I not perfect?'"

The crowd gave some groans, some half-hearted applause and a few laughs.

"Any fans of the NPR show *Car Talk* in the house?" Peter asked. (Smattering of applause.) "Well, as you may know, they always end their show with shout-outs to their staff, including their attorney, Huey Louis Dewey from the fictional law firm of Dewey, Cheatem & Howe. Well, there are real-life firms here in California that put Dewey, Cheatem & Howe to shame. In fact, I've litigated cases against all of them. For instance, if you were hurt in an accident in the Bay Area and sued for money damages, you might wind up against the law firm of Low, Ball & Lynch. If you had a similar case in Fresno, the other side might be represented by Stammer, McKnight, Barnum & Bailey. And if you had a big-time beef against your landlord anywhere in the state, his lawyer might be from the firm of Dicker & Dicker. Just goes to show that truth can be at least as amusing as fiction.

"I'd like to give props to the other lawyers in my office who are here tonight. Let's hear it for Jake and his friend Meg. (Very scattered applause.) Jake knows this is a true story, because it happened at work. I've got a very good friend—we'll call him Rob—who used to live up here but moved to Southern California about a year ago. A couple of weeks back, I got a text from a mutual friend saying she had just heard that Rob had passed away. I was shocked. I had talked to him recently, and he hadn't said anything about his health. I texted back and tried calling her, but she didn't pick up. I was really bummed out, and found myself wandering aimlessly around the office. I saw Jake and I kind of dumped my distress in his lap. He gave me what support he could. I went back to my office and sent a text to Rob's wife expressing my sympathies. About ten minutes later, my phone rang. The caller ID said the call was from Rob's phone, and I figured it must be his wife using his phone for some reason. When I answered, it was Rob. He told me he was fine and that he didn't know why our friend had thought something had happened to him. To paraphrase Mark Twain, rumors of his death were greatly exaggerated. Just at that moment, Jake walked past my office door. I called out to him, 'Hey, want to talk to my friend who I thought was dead?' Jake looked at me and replied, 'I don't know. Where's he calling from?'"

(Scattered applause and a few laughs.) Peter finished with another old song and, once again, the club was in stitches.

He took a bow. "Thank you very much ladies and gentlemen. I'm Peter Penna. Ask for me by name."

When the applause died down, Peter came to the table and was welcomed by the Farmstead folks with back slaps, fist bumps, and some good-natured ribbing.

"How did you end up with us?" Larry asked. "You should be on the stage."

"As a matter of fact," said Peter, "that's what that industrial psychologist was wondering, too." Farmstead had hired an industrial psychologist who had us spend a half-day earlier in the week taking the Myers-Briggs Personality Test. I found the questionnaire for the test difficult, as there is no definite answer for many of the questions and no way to give a nuanced answer.

"He told me he rarely saw test results like mine for someone in the legal profession." Peter continued.

"What's that supposed to mean?" asked Jocelyn.

"Beats me. He said it's much more common in the 'caring professions' like teaching, social work, healthcare."

"I always knew you had a soft heart," said Larry, placing his hands on his chest.

We laughed. "We can't have that in the legal profession," said Charlene. "No caring," she admonished, wagging her finger at Peter.

"So, I asked him, 'Does that mean I shouldn't be a lawyer?'"

"And what did he say?" I asked.

"He said that I seem to have made a successful adaptation to the job," Peter said.

"Well, that's debatable," I laughed.

"And then he said that if he had seen those scores before I started law school, he probably would have advised me that I wouldn't be happy in the field."

"Well, I think he got that right," said Larry, "particularly given the changes we are going though at work in this hellscape of late-stage capitalism."

"Did you mention your second job as a musician and comic?" asked Jocelyn.

"Hell, no," said Peter. "I try to say as little as possible to anyone coming from corporate."

"Well, I wouldn't worry about it," said Charlene. "Myers-Briggs is something of a blunt instrument."

"Even so, I could just see filling out papers in the unemployment office and stating the reason for my being canned from Farmstead as 'incompatible test scores' or 'fired for caring,'" said Peter, laughing.

After a while, we noticed people starting to leave the bar. Larry had just started talking about his work for the Bernie Sanders for President campaign when Jocelyn looked at her watch. "Well, our babysitter is going to be calling soon if we don't get home. Thanks everyone," she said as she and her husband got up. "Great show, Peter."

The rest of the table began finding their coats and purses and saying good night. Meg left to go to the restroom and I waited for her near the door. Charlene was putting on her coat when I took her aside.

"Did you find out anything on Abercrombie?" I asked.

She nodded slightly. "Best not to talk about it here, but yes, I think he is the guy in the picture."

"Interesting. I have some information for you, too," I said.

She looked over at the others and then turned toward me and spoke in a low voice. "Come by my office on Monday."

I waved goodbye to the others, and Meg and I headed to my house. Elwood was as happy to see her as I was.

Chapter 30

Early Monday morning, I found myself in Charlene's office, telling her about what Meg had discovered in Eureka.

"I think it's Abercrombie in that photo," Charlene said. "And I say that because I believe from some things I've learned that he's heavily invested in timber. It's really only a guess on my part, but when redwood became protected and the industry declined, several small companies were purchased by a group called Conch Global. And, though it's difficult to verify, he seems to have a large stake in that company."

"Interesting," I said. "Well, here is another lead for you. Look at the picture again." I pulled the photo up on my phone. "The woman next to Abercrombie in that picture is Jill Dodge. She was his girlfriend back then and now she's here and is the VP for underwriting."

Charlene, raising her eyebrows. "Very interesting."

I told Charlene our suspicions about the fire and Farmstead's seeming reluctance to investigate or do anything other than pay the claim as soon as possible. Over the weekend, Meg and I had tried to think of ways to get more information on the Eel River Inn loss and similar claims. I thought Charlene might be able to help.

"I think the key might be either with Jill in underwriting or in claims, probably with Ann Baxter, the new adjuster for the big first-party claims," I said. "If I can't read their minds, I'd sure like to read their files on the loss."

"Hmm," Charlene said, "have you thought about going to Frick and Frack with the fraud allegations?" Frick and Frack were the in-office nicknames of Joe D'Angelo and Jim Marshall, two retired law enforcement officers who comprised Farmstead's special investigations unit. They were responsible for ferreting out fraudulent claims and referring them to the authorities for criminal prosecution. They were also nominally in charge of internal security. I say nominally, because that was rarely a problem. In fact, the only big-time internal fraud during my time—a claims manager who discovered he could write checks for his kids' preschool tuition off of closed auto property damage cases—was uncovered not by them but by one of the clerical staff who put her job on the line by taking the matter straight to the top.

"Well, I think this is probably over their pay grade," I said. "What I'm really unclear about is how high up this goes, and whether there's some kind of Black Belt involvement in the whole thing. On the other hand, I suppose all the change that we're seeing up close and personal might have knocked me off center to the point where I'm making connections where there aren't any."

Charlene leaned back in her chair. "Obviously, the best way to find things out would be to look at the files themselves. You probably didn't notice this, but remember when Black Belt first came in and we had to reset all our passwords? That coincided with a big upgrade in the company's computer security. I didn't try getting into the system, although I bet I could do it and not leave any footprints, but the electronic walls are a lot higher than they were. And, if there's something criminal going on, we probably don't want to do anything illegal that could result in our evidence being tossed out. So, we'll have to find another way of doing this."

Oh, yeah. Constitutional law. Fourth amendment. Search and seizure. Fruits of poisonous trees. All that good stuff I hadn't had reason to think about since I took the bar. "Well, let's think about this. There's got to be a way somehow."

※※※

I went back to my office and started going through a stack of medical records. About five minutes into this, my interoffice line pinged, and I picked it up, thinking that it was Charlene changing her mind about helping. Instead, it was Mark, who wanted me in his office right away.

My adrenaline was pumping like mad as I walked down the hall, thinking Charlene had ratted me out and wondering how many boxes I needed from the supply room to clean out my desk. I knocked on his door frame, and he gestured me to sit down while he finished up a phone call. "You don't look too good," he said as he hung up. "Is everything all right?" This didn't sound like the start of what I was expecting, so I perked up a little. "Nothing I can't cure with a walk along the river at lunchtime."

"I'll have to get over there sometime," Mark replied. "Anyway, starting now, I'm taking over assigning cases, so there'll be no more of this wheeling and dealing around who gets what. And I've got a new one for you which just might solve the problem with your billable hours.

"This is a first notice lawsuit against our insureds, who run a farm equipment repair shop up in Butte County outside Oroville. It looks like the guy they bought the business from a few years back used to build equipment as well as repair it, and one of the units he built bit someone bad. We're talking a leg off at the hip. One question is going to be whether the new owners are liable for the old owner's equipment. Another question comes up because the accident happened in Arizona. It's possible there are some defenses under Arizona state law that we don't have in California. You'll have to figure out if we can apply them in our defense. I'll give Jocelyn the file before the end of the day so she can open it. Any questions?"

Wow. This case sounded like a bad law school exam question. I knew the law on successor liability, which was pretty much a matter of running down a checklist. But the issue of which laws of which state would apply took me all the way back to law school.

"Well, I took conflicts of law in school, but I sure haven't had any need for it in more than ten years of practice. I guess there's a first time for everything. I'll let you know if I have any questions after I've read the file. Thanks for the case."

207

Thanks for nothing, I thought as I headed back to my office. Mark was probably right about the impact a monster like this might have on my billable hours, but I recognized that this would be one of those sadly non-mythical cases that eat your brain. Plus, it was probably going to involve multiple trips to Arizona, and since getting together with Meg, I'd lost much of my interest in out-of-town travel by myself.

I hadn't been kidding about a walk by the river to calm me down, because it never fails to work. Today, there was a belted kingfisher working over the water and scoring big time on what looked like salmon smolts on their way out to the ocean. I wished the smolts luck, in the hopes that I might have a chance of catching them three years down the road when they were fully grown and returned to fresh water to spawn.

I had turned off my phone while I went on the walk. When I got back and turned it on, there was a text from Meg: "Big News! CU at EG 5:15."

I got to El Gallito a little late, and Meg already had the chips, salsa, guacamole, and beer on the table. She seemed excited and maybe a little smug.

"What's up?" I asked.

"Well, I have three pieces of news for you," she said.

"I'm all ears."

"So, first off, you've said before that it might help if we had an idea of how claims were being settled. It took a little thought, but I found a way to get some of that information. Underwriting gets statistical information on claims, and if you know how to read it, you can see some details of how fast a claim was paid and for how much. I don't regularly get these printouts, but I can access them if I need to. Anyway, the woman who wrangles the data—the statistical clerk—sees it all as it comes through. The rest of the underwriters treat her like she's a piece of the furniture, but I've gotten to know her, and we've gone to lunch a time or two. My parents taught me that the most important people in the schools where they worked were the secretaries and administrative assistants, and I've always lived by that rule." Meg dipped a chip in the guacamole. "Anyway, Zoe knew how badly I was broken up over the Eel River loss, so it wasn't a big stretch for me to ask if there were other claims with a similar pattern. And guess what? Besides Eel River, she dug up at least six claims, all handled by Ann Baxter, paid really fast and for close to the full amount of the reserve. And the reports had enough information on the insureds that I could look them up on line and see that they were all owned by other corporations which I bet are offshore entities. I bet if Charlene did some digging, she could trace these back, and it wouldn't shock me if they all ended up at the same place."

"Wow. Just wow. There really is a pattern," I said. Meg smiled and took a couple of sips of her beer. "So, what else do you have?" I asked.

"I hope you don't mind my trolling the waters of my past relationships, but one of my high school sweeties works for the fire department in Fortuna. I figured that they must have rolled all their equipment on the fire, and, sure enough, he had been on duty that night. He said that he had seen plenty of commercial and industrial fires in his time, but neither he nor anyone else had ever seen one burn as hot as the one at the inn. Since the lead on the investigation is being handled by the county, his department doesn't see any of the information from it other than what they themselves generate, BUT a friend of his who works with Humboldt Bay Fire told him that the amount of carbon monoxide in Buzzard's blood and the amount of soot particles in his lungs shown in the coroner's report were really marginal for assigning smoke inhalation as the cause of death."

"Very interesting," I said.

"On the other hand," Meg continued, "the amount of opiates in his blood was plenty enough to kill someone who didn't already have a tolerance, and there wasn't enough left of Buzzard to see if he had needle tracks or any other evidence that he had been using recently. His friend also told him that the word was out to keep the investigation on the down low and to do everything possible to avoid cheesing off Clearheart."

"Of course," I said, rolling my eyes. "I guess when you're one of the biggest industrial employers in the county, you have friends you don't even know about." I sat for a moment thinking about what Meg had said. "Poor guy," I said. "I guess that means he was either taking drugs or was injected with the drugs against his will. I wonder if the lack of soot particles means he was dead, or almost dead, before the fire started."

"I don't know," said Meg. "But it is getting curiouser and curiouser."

"You said you had three pieces of news. What's number three?"

"Well, out of the blue, I got a raise and a promotion today. I mean a big raise, as in a $12,000 a year raise. I'm now an underwriter III instead of an underwriter II. So that's the good news."

"Congratulations. That's a big promotion. Is there bad news to go with it? Let me guess—they're opening an office in Los Angeles and you're moving there."

"No, not that. It's not really bad news, but it's certainly weird news. They are sending me out on a number of big accounts, including Clearheart—mill, warehouses, docks, the whole nine yards. Management wants a policy written, and they want it in the next month. They want it by the end of November."

"Jeepers. I can't think why they'd toss that to you, after the ruckus you kicked up over the inn."

"Neither can I, unless there's something similar going on with the mill, and I'm really being set up to be the patsy."

"When are you thinking of scheduling the Clearheart job? I hate to have you leave town again so soon."

"I would prefer not to, too. Let me schedule this job and another job in Crescent City in November and, if the stars are in alignment, we can combine it with the crabbing trip."

This was good news. It meant Meg and I could spend some time together before she had to go.

"Bottom line," I summed up, "there's likely more than meets the eye. If there's a loss in the near future, it will all fall on Farmstead, and I'm looking at an underwriter III who may wind up with a target on her back."

I waited for her response but she seemed focused on the chips. "So, knowing that, do you think you might change your mind on taking the promotion?" I prompted.

"No. Big time no." she said. "Working with Clearheart on the policy doesn't exactly put me inside their operation, but it gives me a good place to watch them from. And I'll bet that all of those chains of shell companies, including Clearheart's, will lead back to the same source. I'm not saying it's Black Belt, but that's where I'd put my money."

"My God, you're sexy when you're determined."

"How about at other times?" she asked, scooping more guacamole.

"Those too." I said.

Chapter 31

Our case volume was starting to drop noticeably with the new geographic limits in place and I had begun to seriously inquire about openings at other firms. Beginning in October, things had started to really slow down for me, as my next hearings and depos were set after the holidays in the new year. I had also been able to settle a number of cases, which gave me some breathing room. We had had some heavy rain and it was far colder than usual.

But, true to my prediction, the case Mark had hit me with was a real monster. It turned out that the piece of equipment in question had been built about fifteen years ago by the guy who then owned the repair shop. It was known as a bankout wagon. Most of them were used during the rice harvest to shuttle back and forth between the combine harvester in the field and the trailers that were pulled to the rice dryers by the over-the-road big-rig tractors. It had an old Chrysler V-8 engine and enormous tires, which allowed it to navigate in the thick mud of the rice fields. Rice came out of the combine through a chute into the V-shaped bed of the wagon. Then, once the wagon got out to the road trailers, it would discharge the rice using a horizontal auger at the bottom of the bed.

In this case, the owner of the farm where the accident occurred was using the bankout wagon to harvest wheat rather than rice, but the principle was the same. The plaintiff had gotten a load of grain from the combine, then parked next to the trailer where it was to go. However, shortly after he started up the auger to make the transfer, grain stopped coming out the chute even though the bed was still pretty much full. This was a fairly common occurrence, known as "bridging," usually caused by the grain being damp. The regular practice was to use a pole or shovel to break the bridge and knock the grain down into the bottom of the bed where the auger could move it. For unknown reasons, the plaintiff decided he would walk out on top of the grain and stomp it down into the auger. For equally unknown reasons, he didn't turn off the auger before he did this. As I already knew, the grain bridge caved in and his leg was caught in the auger, damaging it so badly that it had to be amputated at the hip.

The issue in the case was one of product liability—basically, whether there were adequate warnings and adequate guards, given the function of the wagon and the state of the art at the time it was manufactured. But my guys hadn't manufactured the damn thing. The guy who had was one of the defendants in the lawsuit, but he had moved to Mexico after he sold the business and could not be served. So, the issue of whether we were stuck even though we didn't build it turned on a bunch of factual questions having to do with the details of the sale agreement and whether my guys promoted their connection with the old business. I had a sinking sensation that we wouldn't be able to skate on this ground when I saw the pictures taken by the adjuster who had done the initial investigation, which included a shot of the front of the building and a big sign reading, "Haysville Machine Works—Home of the Jenk's Bankout Wagon." They were touting the connection, and trading off of it—a factor which went a long way to defeating that defense.

The other issue—whether there were defenses under Arizona law which we could use in California—seemed more promising. I quickly found that Arizona did not allow product liability cases where the product was more than seven years old. California had a similar law regarding a cut-off on defective construction cases, but had nothing like that on product liability cases such as this one. So, the question was whether the Arizona law was procedural (governing how cases moved through the courts) or substantive (affecting rights and remedies). In the first case, we would be out of luck; in the second, we might defense the claim.

I was pondering all these variables, and looking out at the rain, when Rosa walked into my office.

"Hey, how's it going?" she asked.

"Okay," I responded, welcoming the chance to close my file. "Did you get a chance to look at my response on that writ in the Bellmont case?"

Rosa, being our deep source of wisdom on civil procedure and appellate law, was always willing to double-check any pleadings that we were filing. I had recently won a motion for summary judgment, and the writ was the attempt by the plaintiff's attorney to reverse the judge's ruling.

"Sure did. I know the track records of all the panels, and this got assigned to the one that's probably most sympathetic to your arguments. And your arguments are good ones, no matter which panel got it. Besides which, your guy would still be just a bit player even if he didn't have an out, and the big bad guy with the deep pockets is still in the case regardless, so you've got something of a sympathy factor going for you—not that it's supposed to be part of the analysis, but it doesn't hurt."

"I'm glad you liked it. Hopefully we'll get one of those cute postcards." When the Court of Appeals turns down a writ, it often does so without writing an opinion, and the postcard was how one learned of the decision.

"Yeah, it's a pretty efficient system," Rosa replied, "But I always worry about them getting lost in the mail. Thankfully, with the new on-line access tools, it's unlikely that something like that would slip through the cracks.

"Anyhow, that wasn't my main reason for coming to see you. I'm in a huge jam, and you're the only one with nothing on calendar this Friday. I've got a settlement conference in Modesto and a key medical witness deposition that got changed at the last minute. The case with the doctor is a big case and is almost certainly going to trial next month, and I'm hoping—pleeeeze—that you can handle the Modesto case for me." She clasped her hands together with a mock pleading look.

"I don't see why not," I said. "What sort of case is it, and do you want to try it or settle it?"

"It's just a run-of-the-mill auto case. In the abstract, I wouldn't mind trying it, because it's disputed liability, and I think it would wind up with fault split about 50/50. The problem is, if my case with the doctor's depo goes, I'll wind up trying the Modesto case back-to-back with it, and I really don't like the idea of two trials in a row."

"I know," I replied. "I'm always pretty wound up after a trial, and the one time I did what you're looking at, I couldn't sleep for at least a week once the second case was finished. So that's as good a reason to settle a case as any other in my book. Who's got it in claims?"

"It's Flora Hernandez. She's one of the new hires. Have you worked with her?"

"I've just met her; haven't had a case yet."

"Anyway, it probably doesn't matter. Alice Starr, the manager of our satellite office in Modesto, will cover it on the claims side. Do you know her?" I had talked with Alice many times on the phone and had met her several times at company functions, but I had never worked on a case with her.

"I do, and that will be fine," I said. "At least this way only one of us has to put in the drive-time. Sounds like neither of us will know much about the case, but I'm sure we can manage.

"So, how are you doing otherwise?" I asked. "We haven't really had a chance to talk about all the changes they're hitting us with."

"Wow," Rosa said. "Every week it's something new, and it seems that the strategy for dealing with any problem is to slap another layer of management on top of things. The latest, and this really fries me, has to do with that program we're supposed to use to figure settlement value. Have you used it very much?"

"Actually, not yet. I hear it's spitting out case values that are way too low."

"That's for sure," she said. "And, get this—there's a drop-down menu to use when you have a loss of earning capacity claim. You may not have seen this if you hadn't been looking there, but besides the usual parameters you would use to calculate the amount, you have to enter gender and ethnicity. So, I set up a test case with a white woman and a Latina woman, with everything else the same, and the valuation of the white woman's claim came back 200K more than the Latina's. So, what? I have to decide which ethnicity each claimant belongs to? Or do I have to ask them that in discovery? And am I supposed to perpetuate this racist crap in my settlements? You know how I hate the 'speaking as a Latina' business, but, speaking as a Latina, this really makes me furious."

"Wow. That is upsetting," I said. "And off-hand, I can't see anything we could do to work around it."

"Well, I suppose the good news is that I don't have any loss of earning capacity cases on my plate right now, so I can sort of ignore it, but if I get one with this kind of disparity, I'm likely to make a stink about it."

"You've got my support if you do. And don't worry about Friday. I'll find a way to make your case go away."

Chapter 32

That was easy to say, and true enough when I said it, but nature always bats last, as the saying goes. Tuesday's rain and south winds had turned into Wednesday's dry north winds as high pressure built in behind the low which had brought the rain. But Thursday was calm and cold, and Friday promised the same, which meant that I would probably be making the trip in a tule fog.

Tule fogs are named after the tule reeds which cover most of the shoreline of the Delta, where the San Joaquin River from the south joins with the Sacramento River from the north, ultimately flowing into San Francisco Bay and out through the Golden Gate. I'm no expert in fresh water botany, but identifying a tule is easy—if it's growing on the side of a body of fresh water and it's not a cattail, it's a tule. Anyway, the Delta is a perfect environment for tules—and for tule fogs.

I set my clock for an early wake-up Friday morning and could see as soon as I looked out my bedroom window that I was wise to have done so. The streetlight on the next block over was barely visible, and wisps of thicker fog moved across it, almost completely blocking

219

it out. I hurried through my shower, and got in the car just as the sky was starting to lighten.

Driving in a tule fog is no fun at all. It's thick, but inconsistent, so your visibility changes from second to second. I try to keep my speed down, but there are always idiots who will crawl right up your tailpipe if you do that. Chain-reaction pile-ups on the freeway are common, often involving 50 to 70 cars (and, ultimately, 100 to 140 attorneys). There's a debate as to which color car is safest in a tule fog. Personally, I think it's whatever color car you leave in the garage, but in my case, I had gone with a dark blue when I picked out my company ride. I left the radio and my cellphone off, wanting to keep distractions to a minimum.

My route to Modesto was to take Interstate 5 south to Stockton, then cut east over to southbound US-99. I-5 has the advantage of a fairly recent highway design, with generally broad shoulders and a wide median strip if you have to bail out. US-99 is older, and while stretches of it have been updated, it still has parts which are narrow, with tight on- and off-ramps.

The fog stayed pretty much the same the whole way down. It took me about thirty minutes longer than usual to get there, and I was pretty wasted when I arrived, but the extra time I had allotted gave me a chance to sit down with some coffee before going over to the courthouse.

I recognized Alice when I walked into the courtroom to which our case was assigned. When I had met her at company events, she had impressed me as one of the best-dressed of all the Farmsteaders. Today was no exception. I don't know very much about women's suits, but her royal blue ensemble looked expensive. She completed the outfit with knee-high suede boots.

"Good morning, Alice," I said as I sat down next to her. "You're making the rest of us here look pretty shabby."

"Thanks, Jake. Since this case is assigned to Judge Monroe, I had to look nice. He and I dated in high school, so this is old home week for me." She leaned over and lowered her voice. "He likes boots," she said.

"Wow—I didn't know we had a secret weapon today."

"Well, it's not likely he'll acknowledge the connection, but who knows, it could help."

"So, how are things going in your little slice of heaven?" I asked. The courtroom was filling up but we were still waiting for the judge.

"Not so good," she said. "We just got the word that they're closing all the field offices and laying almost everyone off, including me. Evidently, they figure they can handle the sorts of claims we take care of through a call center somewhere, and do it faster, better, and cheaper. Cheaper, I can see, at least in the short-term, but faster and better? No way. And my people—where are they going to find jobs? We were one of the biggest claims offices in town."

"How about your situation—are they offering any kind of compensation?"

"Very little. I offered to take a position in Sacramento, even if it meant a cut in pay, but no dice. I'm too old and too old-time Farmstead for the new gang to want to do anything for. So maybe I'll scratch something out doing consulting, or just hang it up."

"What would you do with your newfound spare time?"

"Well, I think you met my husband, Lew, at that Christmas party two years ago. He has a hobby, which is threatening to turn into a business, of restoring antique horse carriages. You'd be surprised how complicated those things are even with a hay-burning engine. And the hardware is mostly one-off stuff, which means we have to do a fair amount of blacksmithing. It's usually small fittings, so I don't need a lot of strength, but I've gotten pretty good at running a forge. It lets me work off some of my mad, too."

Just then the clerk came out and called our case into the judge's chambers. We chatted with the judge and outlined our respective positions. He didn't mention his connection with Alice, but he did take a long look at the outfit. When we were finished, he sent Alice and me back to the courtroom while he talked with the plaintiff's attorney.

"I forgot to ask—what authority did you get from claims?" I asked.

"Flora gave me 15K. I don't think it's enough, and I told her so, but she got pissy and told me that was it. I know Rosa wants this case to go away, so let's see what I can do."

A short time later, the judge sent to the plaintiff's lawyer out to get us, and we left him in the courtroom. Judge Monroe was brusque, evidently sensing a quick settlement might be in the cards. "Plaintiff's at 30K. I know he'll take 25K if you offer it. I think that's a reasonable figure. What can you do for me?"

I started to temporize by way of working up to the 15K we had to work with, when Alice cut in ahead of me. "If you can get the plaintiff to do it at 25, we'll pay that," she said.

"Consider it done," said the judge. "Just give me a minute with his counsel."

We went back to the courtroom, and I quizzed Alice. "I thought you only had 15K from Flora. Did I hear wrong?"

"You heard right, but 25 is within my authority as office manager, and I'm sick of all the BS games that they're putting us through. I'll just tell them I was the adjuster on the spot—after all, what are they going to do, lay me off? Screw them."

I was a little taken aback by this—you don't usually see this sort of attitude—but I agreed with what Alice had said. "If anyone asks, I'll back your play," I said.

"Oh, don't worry, Jake. They can't hurt me any worse than they already have. Anyway, I'd bet you that Flora had 25 in authority herself, and just wanted to look like a hero by making us sweat blood to do it at 15."

Once plaintiff's counsel came back into the courtroom and the judge took the bench and put the settlement on the record, Alice and I took our leave.

I shook her hand goodbye, knowing it would probably be the only time we would work together. "It was nice seeing you. If the Modesto office is going to do a farewell party, let me know. Some of us from legal might come down for the event."

"That would be nice. Hope the fog lets up before you get home."

When I got outside the courthouse, visibility was still poor. The freeway was as obscured as it had been going down, and there was more traffic than before. However, as I got to Ripon, a town about ten miles north of Modesto, some stray spots of blue began to appear above me. In a short while, I broke through one last dense wall of fog and into sunlight. At least it was sunlight on my windshield. My car, and every other car and truck on the road, was travelling through a fog bank that ended three feet off the ground. I couldn't see the tires of the cars passing me in the fast lane, but I could see their windows just fine. It was quite a sight, but dangerous as hell. I couldn't see the roadway or the lane markings, as the reflection of the sun off the top of the fog kicked up too much glare. Since I didn't have anything else on my calendar that day, I elected to get off the road and wait for the fog to either dissipate altogether or thicken up again. After about thirty minutes, it elected to do the former, and the rest of my ride was routine.

Chapter 33

The date for Don's crabbing trip had been set, and I was able to schedule my motion for summary judgment in the Eureka court to be heard on the day before. I also put in a vacation request for the following week, thinking Meg and I could spend some time together. She had been in Eureka for two weeks working on a couple of jobs, including Clearheart, and spending time with her family.

The drive from Redding to Eureka was more scenic than usual. A storm had come through the night before, and although it was still cloudy, I could occasionally see the snow-covered Trinity Alps to the north. Fortunately, the snow had not gotten down to the level of the passes on Route 299, and I made reasonable time.

The motion for summary judgment was set for hearing at nine o'clock. I got there at eight, as that's when the day's calendars were posted and I would be able to see which judge had been assigned to hear it. Well, as I said, my odds of getting one of the more favorable judges were good, but they obviously were not good enough, as I had drawn the joker in the pack. Oral argument on the motion went well, and the judge took it

under submission instead of ruling on the spot, meaning
I would get a soft, written "no" at the worst, but I didn't
have much hope. I got breakfast at an omelet place about
half a mile north of the courtroom, then went back to the
hotel and worked on cases.

I picked Meg up at her parents' house around five
p.m. She was just pulling in as I arrived, driving her
father's VW. I hadn't heard much about her meetings
with Clearheart and looked forward to the details. We
went to dinner at a pizza place a few blocks from the
hotel.

"Eureka does nothing for your tan," I said as we got
in the car and I put on my seatbelt. "And what's with the
bug? Isn't your car running?"

"As far as my tan goes, it's been clouds and rain the
whole time I've been here. The snow level was down
to about 2000 feet. You probably saw the snow on the
mountains. But it should be clear tomorrow. And my dad
asked me to drive the bug, since he's too busy to take it
out and exercise it."

"How's your family?"

"All well," she replied. "Ike's wife is pregnant again,
and Ike is walking on air. That man loves kids more than
most guys, that's for sure. But if this pregnancy works
out, he's going to see the doctor and get snipped."

"Well, I wish them good luck. So, what about you?
Did you sign Clearheart?"

"The short answer is yes."

"And the long answer?"

"Still yes. They took me to all of their operation
sites—the yards, the mill, the warehouse. Just like with

the hotel I felt like everything was staged and that I wasn't able to see the whole picture. But I can tell you a few things.

"One is that those yards out in the woods, where they consolidate the timber before trucking it to the mill, are just about empty. All that's on the deck at the mill is small stuff—nothing more than fifty years old at best—and a lot of it's pretty ugly, meaning they won't get much out of milling it. The warehouse next to the dock in Samoa is huge, and it was filled to the rafters with finished lumber and raw logs. There wasn't any sign of big stuff, but there's no telling what might be buried at the bottom of the piles. Anyway, they gave me the number for the value of what they have stored there, and it's not to their benefit if they low-ball it, since they won't get full value if there's a loss and they're underinsured."

"So, what you're telling me is that nothing looked suspicious unless you've got a suspicious mind."

"Just that. I mean, when I hit them with the quote, they seemed moderately pleased, and accepted it without trying to negotiate. So, what does that say? Did I go too low? We have a matrix to generate quotes, but in a risk as big as this one we work more with guidelines than hard and fast rules. Anyway, home office seemed eager to get the business, and I got a bunch of 'attagirls' in my email, so I'll leave it at that for now."

"What's Farmstead's own risk on this? Are we laying most of this off with reinsurance?" Reinsurance is the way that insurance companies spread the risk on large policies.

"Well, we can't automatically get reinsurance under our regular agreements—the risk is too big and too unique to do that. It's Jill's job as VP of underwriting to get that."

"So, until she's done that, Farmstead's on the hook for the policy limits with no help from our friends?"

"Well, now that you put it that way, yeah. But the paperwork's effective Monday, and I'm sure we'll have something in place soon. That's not my problem, but I see where you're going with this. If there was a huge loss at Clearheart before we got the reinsurance in place, we'd be on the hook for every dime of the claim. I don't know if I can monitor that from my end, but I'll see what my password will let me see."

We finished the pizza and started to go. "By the way," Meg said, "I don't think I told you, but since we're going out on sports licenses, we can't use *School's Out*. Dad made arrangements to go on a party boat that belongs to one his friends. Same marina; different dock. We each need to bring $5 and a copy of our sports license. I'll text you the location details."

I made it to the hotel and turned in fairly early, since time and tide don't wait. The next morning, I met up on the dock with Meg, Don, and Ike before there was any light in the sky. Don was talking with a heavy-set fellow with an extravagant beard when we arrived. "Hey, Jake, this is Cap'n Jack, as he's known around these parts. Jack, you remember Meg, I'm sure, and this is Meg's friend Jake from Sacramento."

"Nice to meet you," Jack said as he shook my hand. "Hi, Meg," he continued. "It's been a few years."

"So, to what do we owe the honor of going out on your boat?" I asked Jack.

"Well, I've known Don for ages. When he was shopping for the boat that ultimately became *School's Out*, he went out with me on my beauty a couple of times. If you look, you'll see it's from the same yard as *School's Out*, and it has the same hull design and engine. Since then, we've swapped back and forth whenever one of us needs a deckhand, so taking you out is no big deal, especially as the group I was supposed to take out today cancelled so late that I got to keep their deposit. So basically, this trip's paid for. I still need your five bucks and a copy of your license to make it all legal, and we're limited to ten crabs apiece under the sport regulations, but we'll make sure they're all jumbos."

Once we were well on our way, Don got us organized while Jack drove. "Jake, since you're new at this, I'm going to have Ike help me with the pots," he said. "No offense, but it's like doing ballet with eighty-pound barbells in your hand. Jack drives, and you and Meg can load bait jars and chase down any runners that don't make it into the box."

It's really unfair to describe what we were doing as sport fishing, since we were using commercial gear. "Sport," in my book, means the fish has something like a fighting chance. The crabs had none whatsoever.

We arrived at the first buoy, and Jack throttled way back. Ike leaned out with a pole and hooked the rope, pulling it up and looping it around the pulley of the hydraulic winch. The rope became increasingly perpendicular as we moved over the pot, and then it emerged. Don manipulated the controls, moving the pot inboard and setting it down on the deck. He popped the lid open, and there were about a dozen crabs scuttling around. Ike started picking through them, throwing most of them back into the water without any ceremony.

"We can only take males," Don said, "and they have to be a certain size. Since we're limited to ten apiece, Ike's picking out jumbos, so we may be at this for awhile. He'll leave the smaller legal ones in the pots, so Jack can pick them up next time he comes through."

Meg and I had been loading the bait jars with what turned out to be squid in a fairly advanced state of decomposition, but I guessed smellier was better when it came to attracting the crabs. Once the females and undersized males were overboard and the keepers were in the box, we clipped the new bait jars in. Don raised up the pot, set it down in the water, and pulled the loop off the pulley. As he did, Ike picked up the buoy attached to the next pot.

"It's more of an art than a science when it comes to spacing the pots so you're always doing something, but it looks like Jack called it right on this set," Don said.

We continued down the line of pots, taking the best two or three crabs from each, until we got to about the eighth one. This time, once the rope got perpendicular, the winch started pulling the boat into the water instead of pulling the pot up to the boat.

"Damn. Stuck pot," groused Don. "Sometimes they get filled up with sand, and you have to play with them. Looks like the weather will hold, so we've got some time to see if we can get it loose. Mostly we use the IBF method on this problem—ignorance and brute force."

Don called out directions to Jack while he manipulated the winch. Having the boat stuck to the pot emphasized the effect of the swell, and that, combined with Jack's maneuvers and the smell of the bait pots, made me wonder if I was going to make a sacrifice to Neptune. Fortunately, I had taken some Dramamine before we set off, so I didn't lose points in Don's eyes. Eventually, the pot came free, and we continued on down the line.

After another nine or ten pots, Ike called out, "By my count, we're at the limit."

"Let's quit while we're ahead, then," Jack replied.

Jack continued to drive while Ike and Don picked through the mass of crabs in the box. "Looks like we may be short one, but they're all jumbos, so it's no big deal," Don said. We got back to the wharf about forty-five minutes later, unloaded the box, and cleaned up the boat.

In the course of this, I found myself carrying the crab box with Ike. Meg was over by the truck and out of earshot, so I asked Ike how things were at the mill. "Still going like mad. It's funny. They're still running two shifts, and none of us know any of the guys working swing. They're nice enough to say hi to, but they don't want to talk with us. The mill has always had trouble hiring for swing until now, since the shift differential sucks. This time, they staffed it in a heartbeat. We're just running small stuff—what the loggers call 'pecker poles'—but sometimes when we come in on the day shift, the gear is obviously set up for much bigger logs. And there's no sign of what they've milled the night before when we get there. It's really got us scratching our heads."

By this time, we were up to where the trucks were parked. Don said, "I'll take these beauties home in the truck and we'll have some tonight. Ike's going to take some to my sister up in Grants Pass." He turned to Ike. "I'll pack them in ice with a lot of wet seaweed, and they'll be fine for the day. Just don't let them get loose," he smiled. "No telling what sort of trouble they might cause in the car."

Meg added, "Before 9/11, I used to bring them back alive to Sacramento on the plane. They didn't faze the security guys one bit back then, but I'd be afraid to try that now."

Chapter 34

After a fantastic crab dinner at her parents' place, Meg stayed with me at the hotel. We slept in the next morning and had a late breakfast at a diner near the harbor. The smell of coffee and maple syrup permeated the room. The place was full and several people sat by the door waiting for a table.

"I had a thought last night that might give us another way to prove this was arson," Meg said out of the blue.

"I assume you're talking about the inn?" I said, knowing exactly what she meant.

She nodded. The waitress had just brought our food—pancakes for Meg and an omelet for me. I found the ketchup, which poured more freely than I expected.

"What's your idea?" I asked. I scraped some of the ketchup off the omelet and took a bite. "I don't suppose talking about Buzzard's drug preferences would persuade anyone," I added. "Obviously, the easiest way would have been for Farmstead to pay for a full-on fire investigation."

"Yeah, right," she said. "But, like I said, no one—not Clearheart, not the authorities, not Farmstead—was interested. It was wham, bam, pay the claim."

Meg had doused the pancakes in syrup, which formed a smooth, shiny pool on her plate. "So, I wonder what's in a handmade varnish," she asked. "And why it burned so hot."

We stopped talking while the waitress refilled our coffee cups.

"Do you think it matters?" I asked. "Would it help us figure out what happened if we knew more about the varnish or the nature of the fire?"

"It could," she said.

"I doubt it," I replied. "I've never been involved in a fire investigation. I know they can often pinpoint where a fire started and what caused it, but if it's too hot there's just nothing there. From what the fire and police reports said, that seemed to be the case."

Meg took a sip of her coffee. "One thing I've been thinking about is all the antique wood molding," she said. "I bet that woodwork was pretty valuable."

"I would think so. If they were the original moldings from the hotel, they were beautifully crafted, old-growth redwood. That would be worth something."

"I wonder." Meg gazed absently around the room. "I wonder. . . you know, when I went up there for the inspection, the moldings were being refinished. They had been taken off the walls and were lying on the floor." She looked at me and wrapped her hands around the coffee cup as if she were trying to stay warm. "If I were going to burn down my hotel, I would take out anything of value. Wouldn't you?"

"Do you think they moved the moldings before the fire?"

She raised her eyebrows. "Could be. I think that might be a way to show that it was arson. Why would someone move the woodwork unless they planned to burn down the hotel?"

"Circumstantial evidence at best," I said, but Meg didn't seem to hear me.

"Where would you go to sell old redwood moldings? Ebay?" She thought a minute. "No, too risky to do it online."

Meg had her phone out and began typing into a search engine.

"I remember a place my mom told me about." She swiped her phone a few times. "Yeah, here it is." She passed her phone to me. The website read: "School of Traditional Arts and Millworks."

"They have a program with the schools that some of my mom's students were involved with."

I read a little more from her phone. "It's not too far from here," she said. "Curious? I am. Maybe we could learn something about antique redwood products. And the website shows they're open today even though it's a Sunday."

I shrugged. "Sure," I said. "It looks interesting. Let's do it."

The group waiting for tables had grown and we attracted their interest as Meg put on her jacket and I reached for my wallet. We made our way to the cashier and stepped out into the grey morning. The wind was picking up and fog covered the bay. Meg checked her phone again for the address. I turned on the heater and we drove a few blocks to the school.

The website had described it as a working mill shop that used modern as well as antique woodworking tools. Like many attractions, the mill combined a number of enterprises in an effort to make ends meet. They had a working job shop crafting custom woodwork for restorations, a demonstration mill and museum with antique equipment, a school program for hands-on learning, a low-power radio station, and a gift shop with wood toys, pottery, doll houses, and other gift items.

We walked into the museum and could hear the sound of shop running equipment in the back. A bell on the door signaled our arrival and a small woman of indeterminate age and a head full of grey-blond dreadlocks came out of the shop rubbing her hands with a shop towel. She wore overalls and a Giants baseball hat.

"Morning," she said. "Welcome. My name's Galadriel. The museum is $10 each."

That seemed pretty steep to me but Meg pulled out a twenty and filled out her name and address in a register.

"Thanks," she said as she rang up the sale on an old-fashioned cash register. "Need a receipt?"

Meg shook her head.

"Anything in particular you folks are interested in?"

"Just looking," Meg said, her eyes moving over the objects filling the walls. "We're interested in custom woodwork and redwood restoration, that sort of thing."

The woman seemed to brighten slightly. "Well, you've come to the right place. We do it all."

"Are you the owner?" Meg asked.

"One of them," she said, "for better or worse."

"Looks like you do a lot of custom work," Meg continued.

"We do. We do a lot of the traditional arts, a lot of things that might be forgotten otherwise. The custom jobs keep us in business. We work on historical buildings, old Victorians, and so on."

"I used to live in San Francisco," I said. "I saw a lot of beautiful custom renovations. I bet it's hard to find craftspeople like you." I looked through the door to the shop. "Do you work much with redwood?"

"Yeah," she said, nodding. "It's in demand—it's beautiful and it lasts. Of course, the redwood you get these days is not like the old-growth. I always tell people to repair their old redwood products if they can rather than replace them—it's just not the same wood it used to be."

"Is there much old-growth redwood around?" I asked.

"That depends what you mean. Almost all the old-growth trees have been logged. What's left is protected. But sometimes an old-growth tree falls on the highway or something like that, and if I'm lucky I can get a hold of the wood for special projects."

Meg was wandering through the room looking at the old milling equipment. She turned her attention back to the shop owner. "What about recycling?" Meg asked. "Is there a market for old redwood when buildings are torn down?"

"Could be," she said. "It depends on the quality."

"That was such a tragedy at the Eel River Inn," I said. "I stayed there years ago and I remember the beautiful wood moldings. It's so sad that all that work was lost in the fire."

"Such a tragedy," Galadriel said. "We were helping with the restoration—I handmade the varnishes myself." She paused for a minute and looked at the log Meg had signed. I thought we might be keeping her from her job. She turned to Meg. "Are you related to Judy Vann?" she asked.

Meg turned and looked at her with surprise. "Yes. How did you know? She's my mom."

"We have a continuation high school program here, and I've worked with your mother on it some. You look a lot like her. And Vann's not a very common name. I just put two and two together," Galadriel responded.

"Guess I can't get away with much around here," Meg replied with a smile. "Hi, I'm Meg and this is Jake." She shook Galadriel's hand. "Did you grow up around here?"

"A hometown girl, bred and buttered," Galadriel replied. "I've spent most of my life within twenty miles of here."

"It's great you were able to start a business," Meg said.

"Now that we're done with introductions," Galadriel replied, "let me show you the shop." She waved us into the back. We walked around the counter and through the doorway into a large room. There were piles of wood and a fine dust filled the air. Three young men were working on small jobs using the milling equipment and wearing respirators.

"Some of our students," she said. One of the young men stopped the drill and looked up at us. Galadriel gestured toward him. "That's Tom. He was working on the Eel River Inn project with me before the fire." Tom removed his respirator and raised his hand slightly to acknowledge the attention. "Tom was also fascinated with that woodwork at the hotel. He did some really beautiful drawings of it. Tom," she called, motioning to the young man to come over.

Tom got up slowly and walked toward us.

"Tom, this is Mrs. Vann's daughter Meg and her friend. . ." she paused.

"Jake," I said.

She smiled and continued. "We were just talking about the fire down in New Aberdeen and the beautiful moldings. Do you have your drawings with you?"

Tom's dark hair fell onto his face. He wore his brown baseball hat backwards. He shook his head.

"If anything like that woodwork in the hotel ever comes on the market, I'd be very interested," I said to Galadriel. "I have a friend who does restoration and I know he would pay top dollar."

"I'll keep you in mind," she said.

"Nice to meet you, Tom," I said. "Good luck with your class. It looks like you're doing a lot of interesting things here." Tom looked at us again and reluctantly shook hands with me.

"Well, that's the shop," Galadriel said, leading us back toward the entrance. "Feel free to walk around and poke your head in to anyplace that looks interesting. We have a gift shop, and if you find something you like, just bring it up to the front and I'll take care of you."

239

We wandered around the grounds, which contained a number of structures in what could best be described as arrested decay, then found our way into the gift shop, which was filled with amateurish work priced very cheaply.

As we turned to leave, we were startled to see Tom standing in the doorway. "I'm sorry, I'm not good at dealing with people I don't know. But I know your mother, and she's one of the kindest people in the world, so I guess I can tell you this." He was looking at Meg and avoided eye contact with me.

"Anyway, you're not the first people to ask about the molding since the fire," he said. Galadriel doesn't know anything more than what's been in the news, but I've heard rumors that not everything that supposedly got burned up there actually did. I don't know if this is about the molding, the kitchen stuff, or what, but there's something funny about that whole deal. Things got moved out before the fire. You're the first people I've told."

"How do you know?" asked Meg.

He shrugged. "Anyway, I'm on break and I've got to go." Tom turned and walked toward the shop without looking back.

"Well, there's something to think about," Meg said as we made our way to the car.

"Yeah," I responded. "I wonder who else might be asking about the fire."

"And I wonder what he meant when he said not everything was burned," she said. She started the car and navigated onto the road from the gravel lot.

"Well, it would hardly be the first time that someone claimed to lose more than they did in a fire," I said. "They already bought insurance on the completed value, so this would be double-dipping in a big way. As we know, some people see a loss as a free ticket."

Chapter 35

I had hoped to meet up with Drew in Eureka. His schedule was packed, so I jumped at the chance to get together with him when he had a free morning. We met at a small coffee shop on the north end of town. Meg said she would try to join us when she finished doing some things for her mom.

Drew was looking fit and healthy and handled my inquiries good naturedly as we ordered and sat at a small table in the corner. "Classes are fine," he said. "The sharks, not so much." he frowned. "More than half of what I'm catching these days are ones we've already tagged. It's not a big deal, as the transmitters don't last that long, and I just put a new one on, but I don't think we're building the data set very quickly."

"That's too bad."

"We have gotten some interesting information on the ones that have gone offshore, but it's kind of early days as far as that part of the project is concerned."

I heard my name being called by the barista. Drew picked up the coffees, along with a croissant. He took a long drink from his latte. "So, how are things with you?"

I grimaced. "Work sucks. The new boss gives empty suits a bad name. They're trying to turn the company on a dime and head off in a new corporate direction, and they respond to any inertia with hissy fits. And on top of it, I'm not likely to get any more Eureka cases. To tell you the truth, I'm looking for a new job."

"Wow, that all bites. I know you love it up here. In fact, your enthusiasm for this place helped me decide on Humboldt State."

"That's interesting. I don't think you ever mentioned that before." I watched Drew take a large bite out of the croissant.

"Anything else new?" I asked. "How are things with the double-wide? Has it sunk into the marsh yet?"

"It keeps trying, but it's light enough that it will probably float if it does. But, it's cheap and I actually have plenty of space, since my roomies are gone a lot."

"Are they Humboldt State students?"

"Well, they will be once spring semester starts. Summer and fall, they work as trimmers out in the backcountry."

"Trimmers?" I asked. "Do you mean for the marijuana? Do you know something about the marijuana grown up here?"

Drew snorted and began choking on the coffee he'd been drinking. "I have heard a few things about it," he said, wiping his mouth and smiling.

"About the farms? Tell me about the trimmers," I said, also trying to remain serious.

"Seriously," he said, "with a law degree you should be able to get a better job than that."

243

I laughed. "It's not for me, though any job sounds better than mine at the moment. I'm just curious."

"Well, the trimmers harvest and trim the marijuana buds so that there aren't any excess leaves to dilute the potency." Drew reached over to the counter and took a couple of extra napkins. "My roomies are busy in the summer and fall, and they earn good money because they've been doing it for a while and the farmers know them."

"When do they go to school?"

"During the winter and spring, they put in time at Humboldt. It's slow, but neither of them has anything much in the way of student loans, so it works out."

"What do you think will happen when recreational marijuana becomes legal?"

"From what I hear, I think prices will go way down. We get a lot of people coming through from other parts of the country—heck, from other parts of the world — looking for work out there. We even have a name for them—'trimmigrants.' There'll be a lot of disappointed people when that happens, and no one's especially happy thinking about what kinds of stress that's going to put on social services. Maybe someone will write *The Buds of Wrath*."

We talked about school, Elwood, and a number of other things until Drew had to leave. He didn't mention his mother and I didn't ask.

"Listen, before you go…" I said, as he got up. "Could you do me a favor? Could you ask your roommates if they ever came across a guy working on one of those grows named Frank Lyman, also known as Buzzard?"

"Isn't he the junkie who burned himself up along with the Eel River Inn? "

"He is," I said. "They probably heard about it."

What's your interest in that?" Drew asked.

"My old boss is working with homeless people in Sacramento now, and it's something I'm following up on for him." I felt bad about lying to Drew, but I wanted to keep Meg and my suspicions off his radar.

"Sure. Want me to call if there's anything?"

"Sure, or send an email to my home account."

Meg arrived just as we got up to leave and I introduced her to Drew. I wondered if they would find it awkward to meet each other but they didn't seem to. It turned out that Drew's advisor had helped Don with a summer science camp for high school seniors that Don organized. Drew sounded interested in possibly working in the program and gave Meg his contact information.

"We'll have to get you out on the crab boat one of these days," said Meg.

Drew smiled warmly. "I would love it, though if I'm out on the water much more, I may start growing gills." Meg laughed.

"Sorry I have to run off," said Drew. He shook Meg's hand and gave me a hug. "Good luck with your case."

"Thanks. Luck is always welcome," I said.

He smiled as he put on his jacket and waved goodbye.

XOXOX

Meg had arranged for lunch with Nancy Davis—a friend of an old friend of hers. Nancy was an activist in the environmental movement in Humboldt County and had agreed to meet with us at a Mexican restaurant off the central square in Arcata. We left one car at the coffee shop and drove to lunch.

Nancy turned out to be an energetic woman with short, prematurely grey hair. Meg and Nancy spent the first ten minutes catching up on news of their mutual friend, Mimi, and then we got down to my business.

"So, Mimi says that you have some questions about Clearheart Lumber, or as we around here call them, 'Clearcut.' I have to say that you're not alone in that. They've been acting weird for awhile."

"I hear that they're running their mill like there's no tomorrow," I added.

"That's actually an accurate way to describe it—no tomorrow. Clearheart has just about the only large, privately owned redwood properties left in this county. As you know, Meg, if you treat it right and don't overlog it, redwood will give you a steady stream of production year after year. But you have to be willing to wait, because it takes about a hundred years for a new tree to grow into something substantial."

Meg nodded.

"For the first few years it was here," Nancy continued, "Clearheart was doing just that. We'd see their trucks on the highway, loaded with decent size logs—nothing huge; nothing tiny. We'd also see their finished lumber heading south to market.

"Now, they're tarping all their loads—both the raw logs and what's coming out of the mill, so we can't tell what they've been cutting. Some of my colleagues have tried to get onto their land to see what's going on, but their security has turned tough and nasty. We tried to run a drone over one of their secondary yards, where the logs accumulate before they go to the mill, and those so-and-sos blasted its electronics with a drone killer. Those drone killer things are pricey, so you wouldn't have one just lying around unless you've got something to hide. You already know how hard they're working the mill. And they're sending all their lumber out by ship instead of trucking. They own the dock and that huge warehouse out on the Samoa spit, so they can keep people away while they're loading the ship."

"I've got some questions," said Meg. "First, do you have any idea why this change? Is what they're doing legal? Are folks up here doing anything about it?"

"As to why the change, no one has any idea," said Nancy. "Clearheart's owned by what looks like a shell company. We've got some pretty bright folks helping us, and they've been able to find the shell that owns the shell, but as far as who's ultimately at the top of the chain, we have no idea. We've confronted the local management, but they just blow smoke about improving yield through new techniques.

"Now, whether it's legal, I'm sure they're pulling more out of the forest than allowed by their THP—timber harvesting plan. We haven't been able to get any action out of the California Department of Forestry. Also, their property butts up to a Bureau of Land Management site which has some nice old-growth redwood on it and we have information that they are harvesting old growth illegally. But the feds seem to have even less interest in getting sideways with Clearheart than the state does. Even so, the worst that would happen would be a fine—

this is wrong and wrong-headed, but it's not criminal as in you're going to go to jail behind it.

"We've been trying to mobilize around this, but it's tough. Like you, Meg, I'm too young to have participated in Redwood Summer, but there's nothing like the enthusiasm for direct action that there was back then. We got about twenty-five people outside the warehouse and dock in Samoa for a protest two weeks ago, and it looked like we were going to get some reasonably good media coverage, but halfway through—well, you know what I mean if I mention antifa—the folks who show up at demonstrations wearing all black and with masks over their faces?"

We both nodded.

"Anyway, we seem to have a local version of antifa. We are not sure if they are homegrown or a franchise, but no one looked familiar to us. They turned up and tried to hijack the demo, calling on people to rush the gate and take the action onto Clearheart's property. It didn't work, but it sure took the air out of things, since it put us in the position of protecting Clearheart in order to keep the rally peaceful. Anyway, we're planning a larger rally soon with folks from all over. Hopefully, we can keep it peaceful, but I'm not sure. For one thing, Clearheart's ginning up local support using the old Redwood Summer playbook and trying to make it a fight between loggers' and millworkers' families on the one hand and the so-called 'tree-huggers' on the other."

"Speaking of Redwood Summer, I've seen some yellow ribbons on a few fences." Meg said. "It seems like an indicator that tensions are getting worse."

"It is," said Nancy.

"Yellow ribbons? What's that about?" I asked.

Nancy was finishing up her burrito and motioned to Meg to respond. "The yellow ribbons mean 'support our loggers,'" Meg said. "Which really means 'support the megabusinesses that control the mills.' They were all over the place during Redwood Summer."

"Hmm," I said. "It sounds like you have your work cut out for you," I continued, looking at Nancy. "I know Meg and I are with you on this, and I'll send a contribution to help financially."

"Really, that's not necessary," Nancy said, "but certainly welcomed. I appreciate the lunch." She began gathering her things, preparing to leave.

"Let us know if you hear anything else," Meg said.

"Sure. And we should try to get together with Mimi sometime."

"Would love to," said Meg. "Thank you so much for keeping us in the loop."

Chapter 36

O ur plan was to relax for a couple more days in Eureka
 before driving home to Sacramento. Meg suggested
that we do a little exploring. "Ever been to Petrolia? It's
near the coast south of here. You'll like the drive. It's
especially fun in the bug."

We headed south on 101 and, shortly after leaving
the outskirts of Eureka, took a long concrete arch bridge
over the Eel River. "This is Ferndale coming up—it's
sort of famous around here for its Victorian architecture."
I could see what Meg meant, as there were a number
of well-kept and brightly painted homes and businesses
clustered around the center of the town. With a few
early Christmas decorations up, the town looked totally
charming. Eureka might have looked this way if so much
of the downtown hadn't been transformed into utilitarian
concrete block buildings back in the 1940s and 1950s.

"This is lovely," I said as we passed a row of
refurbished homes. "And it looks like lots of those
yellow ribbons down here."

"I know," Meg replied. "I hoped the tensions and the
ribbons would go away if I stopped thinking about it."

She smiled at me. "I guess wishful thinking is never a good strategy.

"With almost everyone up here living paycheck to paycheck, and the mills paying the closest you can get to decent money, it's no wonder people have trouble looking down the road at what will happen when there are no more trees," Meg said. "Take Ike's job at Clearcut—I mean Clearheart. That mill is designed for redwood only, and there's no old growth and precious little second growth outside of state and national parkland. Right now, they're scraping the bottom of the barrel, and it baffles me why they've sped up the pace."

Meg turned onto a side road to show me more of the town. "It'll take at least a hundred years for the redwood on private land to grow back to harvestable size," she continued. "And I don't see Clearheart keeping people on the payroll with no logs. I guess they might convert to handling other types of trees, but my bet is that they'll just sell the equipment to an operation in some country where there aren't as many restrictions and leave town for good."

"Unfortunately, I don't see Ike moving to Siberia or Brazil along with his lasers," I said.

This discussion had taken us through Ferndale, and the road began to climb out of the Eel River valley on a series of switchbacks. Meg was obviously enjoying putting the VW through its paces. "When my dad was figuring out how to set up the bug, this was his test track, so it's also where I learned to drive twisty roads." We topped the hill and were presented with a marvelous view of a long beach to the southwest. Further south, mountains came down to the water, ending in steep cliffs.

"This is the north end of the Lost Coast. Those cliffs run almost the whole way down to Fort Bragg. When the state brought the engineers who built Highway 1 along the coast south of Big Sur up here with thoughts of doing something similar, they took one look at the terrain and said 'No, thank you.' I've never hiked the Lost Coast, but I'd sure like to do it someday."

The road dropped down until it was parallel to the beach. We pulled over and parked at a turnout where we could see for miles in either direction. There was only one other parked car, and it was about a mile south of us. Meg gestured at it and snorted, "Hmph, this beach is getting too crowded." The sand was dark yellow and coarse and not easy to walk on, but we made it up the shore for about a mile before turning back. "I'd like to stay and watch the sun set from the beach, but the road from Petrolia back to 101 is pretty windy and I'd rather do it in daylight. It's actually kept up better than the part we've already done, since logging trucks use it."

"Whatever works best," I replied. "I'm enjoying the ride and the scenery, and I don't mean just the beach and the mountains." My comment got me the elbow in the ribs it probably deserved, and we headed off.

The road turned inland, and we shortly arrived in Petrolia, which was the very definition of a wide spot in the road. A firehouse, a grange hall and a combo bar/grocery/deli pretty much covered the amenities. We stopped at the grocery and picked up a couple of sodas.

"Petrolia is pretty much the ass end of nowhere for Humboldt County, which is saying a lot considering

Humboldt County is so rural to begin with," Meg observed. "It's really isolated geographically."

"I can see that," I said. I looked at the mountains we had just come over and the ones I could see along the coast. "Looks like there's no cell phone coverage here," I said, glancing at my phone.

"Most of the people have satellite phones," Meg said. "Though rumor has it that there's some cell phone coverage at the top of the hill by the cemetery we passed."

I laughed. "Gives 'can you hear me now?' new meaning."

"As you might guess from its name," Meg said, "the town's claim to fame is that it was the site of the first producing oil well in California. I bet there's still oil down there, or maybe offshore, but I just don't see how it would be possible to get it out of the ground without trashing the environment."

We took a short detour, following the Mattole River to the ocean, to see the trailhead of the twenty-five-mile Lost Coast trail. The beach was cold and windy and the few hardy campers in the small campground were either in their tents or RV's, or further down the beach. Driftwood had been washed up by the waves and several rough sculptures and driftwood shelters dotted the sand. Next to the Bureau of Land Management information board at the trailhead was a yellow, diamond-shaped traffic sign saying only "DANGER." In addition to the ubiquitous shotgun holes in the sign, someone had written with marker in a flowery script: "Good Luck."

"Brrr," I said, putting my arm around Meg's shoulder as we got back to the car after a short walk. We then headed east, crossing the Mattole River several times. It looked like good steelhead water, and Meg said she had heard that there were decent runs at times, although she didn't know anyone who had ever fished it. I made a mental note to come back here some time with my gear and, hopefully, someone with local knowledge.

We passed a general store/post office with a sign saying "Welcome to Honeydew," and then crossed the Mattole one more time on a one-lane steel bridge with a wood plank roadway. We left the river and the road began to climb.

As she downshifted into third, Meg looked up in her rearview mirror with a puzzled frown. "There's a log truck behind us with a driver who must be late for a date. I think I saw him by the store when we left Petrolia. Now he's coming up fast, and I haven't been dawdling myself. Trouble with this road is there's really no good place to pull over until we get to the top of the pass. Here he comes. You should be able to see him."

I turned around and saw the truck. I noticed a large yellow ribbon on its radiator and one on its radio antenna. It was empty, and the pull trailer had been hoisted up onto the bed. I couldn't see a name on the door or a license plate. It gained noticeably on us in the short time I had it in view. "You're right about the hot date," I observed.

"There's a straight piece just ahead where I can slow down and he can get past me if there's no one coming downhill." We came around a curve, and Meg dropped the bug into second and moved as far to the right as she could, rolling down her window and gesturing for the truck to pass us. Although there was nothing in the oncoming lane, the truck pulled to the right and came straight for us. Just feet from us, it jammed on its airbrakes and blew its horn, slowing to our speed and then inching forward as if it wanted to give us a shove.

"That sonofabitch is out to get us!" Meg exclaimed.

"No shit" was my subtle rejoinder.

"Well, I'm not gonna stand for this. Bug, do your stuff."

I had thought Meg had been doing a thorough job of exercising the VW on the stretch before Petrolia, but she seriously topped her earlier performance. The bug couldn't accelerate faster than the empty truck on the straight sections of the road, but it could out-corner it in spades, and there were more corners than straights. Still, the truck got within inches of our bumper several times, and at one particularly hairy point, began to pull up beside us as if to force us off the road.

"I don't think this asshole is actually trying to kill us, because I can't outrun him and I'm sure he knows it. If he wanted to nail us, he could have had us for breakfast before this got serious. But I don't trust him to keep playing safe. I'm going to try something just on the other side of the pass, but if it doesn't work or he catches on, there may be some serious trouble. Makes me wish I'd brought my gun with me on this trip, but it probably isn't a good idea to carry heat on company business. Gives the wrong impression if you know what I mean. Anyway, here's the pass. Hang on and pray if you want."

We flew through a small clearing with dirt roads branching off to either side and running along the ridgeline. We immediately dropped into a different ecozone, with dark firs densely lining the road and limiting our vision. "It's just up ahead," Meg said. She double clutched and downshifted, turning the wheel and putting the VW into a skid with the passenger side leading. She then gunned the engine, breaking out of the skid as a side road appeared in front of us. Somehow, the bug regained traction, and we shot off the pavement and up the dirt road. It curved after about fifty yards. Meg stopped and turned off the ignition as soon as we were out of sight of the road. We heard the logging truck pass the side road and continue on past us until its sound faded away.

"There's a bunch of these little roads left over from the logging on this side of the hill," Meg said as she tried to catch her breath. "But this one is special, because it hooks up with the ridge road. If asshole comes back, he can follow us, but if we go south on the ridge, he'll never know which way we went at the four-way. Still, if I have to do that, I'll probably get daddy's beauty scratched, and we can't have that. Anyway, give him ten minutes and we'll see what gives."

We got out of the car and listened. I couldn't hear anything but the pinging of the bug's engine as it cooled down. I tried to put my arms around Meg, but she shook me off. Eventually, she took a deep sigh and sat rather abruptly on the forest floor. "Well, I think that's that. Now hold me while I cry. I had no idea if I could pull off that stunt."

I held her for a long time while she relaxed, millimeter by millimeter. When she appeared to have regained her composure, I asked, "What do you suppose that was all about?"

"Well, I don't think it was an old boyfriend. There are some who might pull a stunt like this, but none of them live in the county anymore. No, this is what happens when you start putting your nose into places you're not wanted and asking questions no one wants to know the answers to. One thing is for sure. The VW is too obvious. Everyone knows who it belongs to. Next time I come up here, it will be in a nice anonymous rental. But I better make sure I pay for the collision damage waiver just in case. Tell you what, would you mind driving back to town?"

I drove the car back to Meg's parents' house and Don, Meg, and I checked for damage. Nothing seemed amiss except for our nerves. I held Meg tightly for several minutes while we both regained our composure and then we went inside for a cup of tea with Don and Judy before going back to the hotel.

"I'm done here," Meg said later that night as we sat in a local Italian restaurant. She had hardly touched the pasta dish she had ordered and at first, I thought she was talking about her dinner. "Whatever is going on here is not worth our getting killed," she said. "Let's go back to Sacramento tomorrow and forget about Buzzard and the fire and all the rest of it."

I sighed. "You may be right," I said. "Honestly, I would be happy never to hear of Clearheart again, either up here or in Sacramento."

Chapter 37

B ack at work the next week, things seemed tediously
normal. I spent the first couple of days doing what
I call (but only to myself) feeding the animals at the
zoo. By that, I mean I sent in a big-time stream of status
reports and discovery updates on my cases. I wanted to
get my billables up and to drop off Mark's radar.

On Wednesday, I had to be in Placerville the first
thing in the morning for a motion to confirm a settlement
in a case involving a minor. These are routinely handled
by the plaintiff's attorney, but both the facts and the law
in this case were complex, and the firm on the other
side had a bad habit of sending attorneys who weren't
familiar with the file for hearings of this sort.

Placerville is in the Sierra foothills and was a hub
of mining operations during the rush that followed the
discovery of gold down the road in Coloma in 1848. It
is only about forty-five minutes from my house, but I
gave it more than an hour because parking around the
courthouse is tight. The courthouse itself is a Victorian-
era relic, one of many dotting the foothill and valley
counties. While the architecture is nice, all of those older

courthouses have one thing in common—the acoustics are terrible. I guess that one attribute lawyers needed a hundred years ago was a booming voice.

As I approached the courtroom door, it swung open violently and a young fellow in a business suit tore past me, taking the stairs down to the front door four at a time. I went inside, and noticed Mike James, a local lawyer I knew pretty well, looking at the door with a bemused smile on his face. "What was that all about?" I asked as I sat next to him.

"Oh, the usual. A lawyer from San Francisco assumed that Placerville must be the county seat of Placer County instead of El Dorado County. Now even if he drives like a madman, he'll be forty-five minutes late to court over in Auburn."

This confusion about county seats has tripped up many an out-of-town lawyer who isn't paying attention. It's not the only such courthouse oddity, as Yuba City is not the county seat of Yuba County (that would be Marysville, while Yuba City is the seat of Sutter County). Unlike Placerville, the right Yuba courthouse is only ten minutes from the wrong courthouse, so the mistake can often be corrected without much trouble. And then there are the misplaced mountains, where Mt. Lassen isn't in Lassen County (it's in Shasta County) and Mt. Shasta isn't in Shasta County (it's in Siskiyou County).

While I mused over these geographical peculiarities, the court calendar worked its way down to my case. The young plaintiff was there with her mother, along with a lawyer I didn't know who, as I expected, had not been briefed by his boss. Most judges take their role in these minor's compromise cases seriously, and today's judge was no exception. We weren't paying a ton of money to settle the claim since our exposure was pretty thin, so it was a good thing I was there to explain the warts on the case. In any event, the compromise was approved and I headed back to work.

That afternoon, Meg and I both got texts from Nancy Davis up in Arcata, asking us to call her. Meg's new position was keeping her busy so we decided that I would return the call once I was away from the office.

"Hi," she said, "I know I said I would let you know if anything new came up with Clearheart. Well, we have a contact in the Harbormaster's office who let us in on something. Clearheart has a freighter coming in tomorrow to pick up a load headed to Asia. Nothing new about that. What's interesting is that it's a much larger ship than usual—in fact, it's big enough that they had to time it so it would have an unusually high tide when it sails. Also, it's going to be at the Clearheart dock two days longer than usual."

"What do you think all that means?" I asked.

"It makes us think that Clearheart's going to be moving all that big stuff they've been cutting in one shipment."

"Hmm. What's the timeline like?"

"The high tide they need comes in early Monday morning, so we're calling a big demo at the warehouse for Sunday."

"Thanks, Nancy," I replied. I don't know if I can make it up there, but Meg and I will talk about it. I'll text you if we decide to come."

Actually, I had decided that I wanted to go before I had even put the phone down, but I wasn't sure what Meg might think of this. For me, I was now certain that something was going on that involved Clearheart and Farmstead and that if it was allowed to run its course, Meg would somehow be left holding the bag.

She came over later that evening, as we had already planned, and we discussed it. "I don't know if going up there is a good idea," she said. "For one thing, whatever Clearheart's logged is now lumber. Protesting isn't going to put the trees back in the ground. Everyone up there knows that this mini-boom at Clearheart can't last."

"Well, what if there's some kind of replay of the hotel fire? Isn't that going to fall into your lap as the underwriting lead?"

"Hmm, I could certainly see being the fall gal at Farmstead if something happened, but it would take a small nuke to wipe out that warehouse unless someone gave a fire a lot of help. Even if the locals put the blame on someone the way they did on Buzzard, there would have to be an investigation by some state or federal agency that would uncover anything suspicious."

"Well, I think you might be putting too much faith in what a government agency will do when there's an easy solution to a messy problem. It makes more sense to me to stop something from happening in the first place than hoping that someone hasn't completely covered their tracks after the fact."

I put my arm around her shoulder. "And anyway," I said. "If I can do anything to keep you from being hurt, I'm going to do it."

"Aw, you're too sweet," she said, holding me a little closer. "If you want to go, then go, but I'm going to sit this one out."

Be careful what you volunteer for. I was disappointed, but not completely surprised. Since the brush with the logging truck, the whole thing now seemed to be more my quest than hers.

Chapter 38

G iven the short timeline, I booked a flight to Eureka the following Saturday and called Drew to see if he could pick me up. I explained why I was coming back so soon. I told him the whole tale, and apologized for keeping him out of the loop until now.

"No worries about that," he responded to my mea culpa. "You know I was never a fan of conspiracy theories. It sounds like you and Meg have done some solid work on this."

"Thanks," I said. "I may need your help."

After hanging up with Drew, I went by Charlene's office. She had been out of the office most of the week, so I was glad to see her at her desk. I knocked on the doorframe. She looked up and waved me in. I shut the door, sat across from her, and brought her up to date on what I knew.

"Whatever is happening up there," I said, "it sounds like it's coming to a head."

Charlene leaned back in her chair and looked out the window as she thought. "So, the insurance policy Meg wrote for Clearheart is in effect?" she asked.

I nodded.

"And is there any reinsurance set up or would a loss be totally covered by Farmstead?"

"I don't know," I said. "I don't know if it's been set up yet. Let's hope nothing catastrophic happens."

Charlene nodded thoughtfully and tapped her pen on the side of her face. "I don't think you should go up there," she said. "It could be dangerous."

I laughed. "Oh, don't worry. You know me, I'm not the heroic type. I'm just going to look into things from a distance. Besides, I'm in too deep to quit now."

She continued to look concerned, but I assured her I would stay out of harm's way.

)(()()(

My flight left Sacramento midday on Saturday. The planes into Eureka are small, noisy and bumpy, and the airport was chancy when the weather was bad. Fortunately, the weather was clear and my flight was on time, which was a blessing. The airport in McKinleyville was originally built as an Army Air Corps training base during World War II. Rumor has it that the site was picked because it had some of the worst weather in the lower 48, and the pilots needed to learn how to handle it before being shipped up to fight the Japanese in the Aleutian Islands off Alaska. Even with today's instruments, there are still plenty of times that flights get cancelled or diverted due to fog or low clouds.

Drew was waiting for me with a fist bump and a quick hug when I arrived. I climbed into his truck and we headed south.

It was clear that he had been thinking about the problem. "It seems to me that what you need is some hard evidence that Clearheart is moving out prime stuff," he said. "Then if there's some kind of disaster at the warehouse and they claim it was lost, you've got proof that they're double-dipping."

"Yeah, but how are we going to do that? We can't get a search warrant."

"Well, I won't say there aren't people who know the harbor better than me, but all that shark hunting has to count for something. Clearheart's dock is private, but the harbor's not. If we go out tonight or tomorrow night, maybe we can get close enough in my boat to see what's going on."

"Have you been out at night before?"

"Not a lot, but enough to find my way. Besides, I've seen what it looks like when they're loading a ship. They work around the clock, and the whole area's lit up like Times Square. I'd have to be pretty stupid not to find them."

"So, what are we going to be doing if they spot us?"

"Who cares? Remember, public waters. We have just as much right to be there as they do as long as we don't go on the ship or the dock. If it comes to that, I'll take the shark gear along with us. Those babies don't usually feed at night, but we need to do some sampling just to be thorough."

"Well, I'm game if you are. Let's go tonight. What time should we leave?"

"Tide's right for the sharks from about one a.m. on. Let's get dinner and go to the movies and then hit the boatyard around midnight."

The temperature had dropped into the low 50s. We stopped at Drew's house in Arcata to change into warmer clothes and pick up the shark gear. Drew then took me to a Thai restaurant in Eureka that was one of his favorite spots and ordered what he thought were the best dishes.

He talked about his classes as we waited for the food. "I like Meg," he said. "It was nice to meet her."

"I'm glad you like her. I do, too."

"I don't know if you remember, but she mentioned a summer program her father runs with my biology professor. I looked into it and I think I'll apply to teach with them this summer. In fact, I called Don and spoke with him about it."

"That's wonderful. I think you'll like Don a lot. He has the patience of a saint."

Drew laughed. "Well, I don't know any saints, but I think the patience of someone who is both a fisherman and a high school teacher is probably greater."

"For sure," I said with a smile.

Drew told me more about the summer program and then our order arrived. It smelled delicious and I realized that I hadn't eaten since the morning.

"How's your mom?" I asked, spooning rice and eggplant onto my plate.

Drew shrugged. "Fine, I guess. I haven't talked to her for a while. Winter break will be here soon and I'm sure she'll want me to come down for Christmas."

"I'm sure she'd like that," I said. "Come visit me if you have time."

"I will," Drew said as he pushed the rest of the food onto his plate. He gave me some news about Beth's family—his cousin Ben was getting married and Beth's mom was in hospice care.

"I am so sorry," I said. I knew Drew was close to his grandma and I was sad to hear she was dying. She had always been very kind to me.

After dinner, we sat through some *Fast and Furious* nonsense with a handful of other people in an old movie theater in Eureka, leaving the theater around eleven-thirty.

Traffic was light as we headed toward the boatyard. We pulled in and hitched up the trailer.

"Let's not use the regular launch where anyone can see us," Drew said. "I know a better place. More private."

The better place involved taking the bridge to Samoa, then turning south along the narrow spit separating the harbor from the ocean. As we went down the road, we passed Clearheart's dock, off to our left. As Drew had mentioned, it was brightly lit. We could see the tops of the cranes mounted on the ship, but the warehouse blocked any view of what they were moving. There were a dozen or so trucks in a dirt lot near the road.

A few miles further down the spit, Drew turned down what looked like a driveway with a gate partially blocking the road. Signs on the gate showed it was a county park and that it was closed. Drew ignored the signs and drove around the gate in the left-hand lane.

"That gate is more of an advisory than anything else," he commented. "I've never heard of anyone getting into trouble for launching after hours. I think it's just a way for the county to limit their liability if someone does. Anyway, I've got an ID from the school I can leave on the dash which makes us look legit if someone does check."

Drew had brought a couple of camouflaged, non-reflective life vests, and gave me one. We got the boat launched without any trouble and headed north toward the Clearheart dock.

"I'll leave the navigating up to you," I said, "though I am starting to get a feel for the bay. The Coast Guard Station and harbor entrance are behind us, just a little further down the spit. Is that right?"

"Yeah," Drew said. "And this channel branches into two up ahead. I think Don probably moors his boat somewhere along the channel which goes off to the right."

"Glad you know what you're doing," I said. "Let's stay as quiet and out of sight as possible. Even though, as you say, it's public waters, let's try to avoid being seen."

Drew kept the engine throttled back, and we moved slowly and quietly against the outgoing tide. The air was cool. There was no wind. The moon had set and it was clear enough to see the stars. As my eyes adjusted to the darkness, I could see the shore but I wasn't able to recognize many landmarks. However, Drew seemed confident so I relaxed and enjoyed the ride.

I found the North Star and then turned toward Drew. "I remember looking at the stars together on camping trips. Do you remember any of the constellations?"

I could see his outline and heard the water gently lapping against the sides of the boat. "Hmm," he said. "I remember the hunter, Orion, and the Big Dipper. And I can usually point out Venus in the early evening."

"Well, that's something," I said. "How about Cassiopeia, the ragged W"?

"Yeah, maybe. We read about the ancient Polynesians in one of my classes," Drew added. "It's amazing how they were able to read the stars, the waves, and the birds to find their way across the Pacific."

"You've made a good start yourself in Humboldt Bay." I enjoyed putting my trust in this young man who had grown up to be an able navigator of the water and, I hoped, of life.

It didn't take much navigation to spot the dock and we were getting closer. We went up the middle of the channel until the ship was about a quarter of a mile away, off to our left. I pulled out a pair of binoculars Drew had brought along, and tried to focus them on the activity. No luck.

"Damn, it looks like they've not only lit up the dock and the ship, they've got really bright lights shining out into the harbor as well. I can't see anything but glare through these binoculars."

"Well, let's see if we can do anything about it." Drew continued north until we were about half a mile beyond the dock. "This is where it gets tricky, particularly with the tide going out," he said. "That dock is about as far in as the dredged channel goes, so where we are now is just mudflats with a natural channel down the middle. Luckily, the big lows are in the afternoon at this time of year. If I'm not in the channel, we'll know in about two minutes."

Drew made a wide 180-degree turn and pointed the boat straight toward the stern of the ship. It seemed that he had found the channel, since we didn't ground. I still couldn't see anything happening on board due to the dazzle from the lights, but I could see an area close to the stern that wasn't lit as brightly. I pointed it out to Drew.

Drew cut the engine. "Let's keep the motor off," he said. "We'll drift a little and the tide will take us closer to the ship. Since there's no wind, we should be okay." It was too bright to see anything and the sound of the machinery drowned out any other noise. Nevertheless, we kept our voices low.

We sat watching the ship and the activity onshore for about five minutes when we heard a warning over a PA system: "This is a private dock. Sheer off!" The voice was loud and coming from the ship.

Drew looked over at me. "Looks like our presence has been noted," he said. "What do you think we should do?"

"Nothing," I said. We continued to drift slightly toward the ship. We were still fifty yards away when we heard the warning again.

"UNIDENTIFIED VESSEL. SHEER OFF. THIS IS A PRIVATE DOCK."

"Start the motor," I said. "We're not seeing much from this side. Let's pass the ship and then come in from the south.

Drew restarted the engine and moved past the ship, getting closer as we did. We were now south of them and moving closer to the dock.

A searchlight lit up our boat, and the loud-hailer again blared: "UNIDENTIFIED VESSEL. SHEER OFF. THIS IS A PRIVATE DOCK."

"These are public waters," I shouted, though I doubted anyone could hear me. "We have a legal right to be here!"

The glare in our eyes and all around us made it impossible to see anything beyond our small boat. I heard a shot go off from the direction of the ship which splashed within ten feet of us.

The loud-hailer again: "UNIDENTIFIED VESSEL, THE NEXT ONE IS FOR REAL. SHEER OFF OR BE SHOT." Drew kept the boat steady. Again, there was a shot. This one whanged off the top of the outboard.

Then everything started happening at once. Almost simultaneously with the last shot from the ship, I heard another shot, this one from behind me. The searchlight turned yellow and then died. I turned and saw *School's Out* heading toward us from the south at the fast jog that passed for its version of full speed. Meg was up on the bow with the 30-06, working the bolt to put another round in the chamber. I could hear her yelling, "Pick on someone your own size, asshole!"

The next shots from the ship seemed to be aimed at *School's Out* rather than the skiff, but it didn't sound like they hit anything. Don's boat turned between the skiff and the ship, blocking any more fire aimed at me. However, in doing so, we caught the full force of the wake right against the side of the boat, and we turned turtle. As I fell in the water, something smacked me on the head. I grabbed the keel of the skiff, which was floating nicely, and called out to Drew. "I'm fine," he shouted. "Just hang on. This boat's got plenty of flotation. It can't sink."

I looked up to see what had happened to *School's Out*. It was still between us and the ship. There were a couple more shots from it, and one more from Meg, when another searchlight lit up, this one also from the south, and another loud-hailer declared, "ALL VESSELS CEASE FIRE AND DROP YOUR WEAPONS. THIS IS THE FBI."

By this time, the second boat, which was moving quite fast, was passing the skiff and *School's Out* with not much room to spare. I could see it was the big cutter the Coast Guard used for offshore patrols, and it was swarming with people armed with rifles and automatic weapons. It continued on toward the ship, and its wake knocked me off the skiff. The last thing I thought I saw as it went by was Charlene on the deck in a jacket with "FBI" stenciled on it. After that, things got very fuzzy.

Chapter 39

When I opened my eyes, I wasn't sure where I was. I was lying by myself in a double bed. I could see that someone had been sleeping next to me and I hoped it was Meg. The pillow beside me was balled up and the covers were tossed aside. Obviously, whoever had been there had gotten up. The room was dark, though I could see sunlight around the edge of the window shade. It must be morning.

I could hear voices speaking outside the room. I recognized Meg's voice. As I looked around the room, I realized that I was in her room in her parents' house. Above the desk was a picture of Meg, probably taken when she was in high school, smiling broadly and holding a large salmon. The desk was piled with papers. A bureau and mirror lined the wall next to the door. I could make out some kind of award ribbon hanging on the mirror.

I surveyed my situation carefully. My head ached. I reached up and felt a knot on the back of my head. Otherwise, I felt all right. Nothing a couple of Advils couldn't fix. I had been sleeping in boxer shorts that seemed too tight. I looked down and noticed that they weren't mine. I didn't see my clothes anywhere. The bed was comfortable and warm. I rolled on my side, looking toward the shaded window, and started to drift back to sleep.

I remembered being on the boat last night—shots being fired and hearing Meg's voice. Everything after that was foggy. Drew was there, too. Suddenly, I sat up. Where was Drew? What had happened?

Just then the door opened slightly, letting more light fall across the wall.

"You awake?" It was Meg.

"Yes. What's going on? Where's Drew?"

"Drew's fine. Don't worry. We'll go see him later." She closed the door behind her. She walked to the window and opened the shade. The sun was high and light filled the room.

"It must be late," I said

Meg sat down on the bed next to me. She looked at me with concern. "How do you feel?" she asked.

I sighed. "I've felt better, but seeing you helps. Do your parents know I'm in your bed?"

She laughed. "Yeah. I had to keep waking you to make sure you didn't have a concussion."

She lay down next to me and pulled the blanket up to keep us warm. I could hear Don talking to someone in the other room. I was falling asleep again.

After what seemed like a few minutes, Meg rolled over and sat up next to me. "What do you remember?" she asked.

I thought for a minute. "I remember being out in the bay with Drew watching the ship at the Clearheart dock.

I remember someone firing at us and then seeing your dad's boat racing toward us from the other direction. I remember the skiff capsizing. After that it gets vague."

Meg rubbed her hand along my arm. "You hit your head," she said. "The Coast Guard guys looked at it and figured you were okay. You were conscious, but I guess a little disoriented."

"Coast Guard?" I vaguely remembered being examined and having the flashlight in my eyes. "Oh my God," I said. "Coast Guard? I think you need to start at the beginning."

Meg got off the bed and tossed me some sweatpants and a t-shirt. "Ike's clothes seem to fit you well enough," she said. "Before I hit you with the rest of the story, you need to get up and get some breakfast."

"Are these Ike's boxers?" I asked. Meg nodded. "Who would guess that Ike would have smiley faces on his underwear." I continued, looking down at the brightly colored boxers.

Meg shrugged. "Your clothes were soaked. They're in the dryer, so you can change back soon."

I went to the bathroom and threw some water on my face. It was not a pretty picture. My hair was full of cowlicks and I tried to mat them down with a little water. "Oh, God. I need a vacation," I thought.

When I walked out of the room and into the kitchen, I could smell coffee and bacon. Suddenly, I was famished. Meg's parents began fussing over me, and I was happy to sit like a lump and be waited on. They let me eat several forkfuls of eggs and bacon before speaking.

"Well, I have to say, *School's Out* has seen a lot of action in the bay, but nothing like last night," Don said. "You're lucky Meg figured out what you two were up to."

Meg and I looked at each other. "How did you know?" I asked her.

"I don't know you as well as I want to, but I do know that once you've decided to do something, you're not going to stop. I was sitting in Sacramento, worried and afraid that whatever you did might be dangerous, so I took the late flight up. When I got in to the terminal and turned my phone back on, there was a text from Drew about your plan. I made him promise awhile back that if he couldn't keep you out of trouble, he should at least let me know what flavor the trouble was going to come in."

"So, who picked me up in the water?"

"The Coast Guard had a couple of their surf rescue boats following the cutter, and they fished you and Drew out, got the skiff righted, and hauled you two and it to their base by the harbor mouth. That's where we met up. Drew and I explained what your part in all this was, and it doesn't look like there's going to be trouble for any of us, but they don't want you leaving town without making a statement.

"Well, we may not be in trouble with the feds, but I'm sure Humboldt State can't be too happy to have their skiff mixed up in all this."

Meg nodded in agreement.

"So, what was a boatload of Coasties and Feebees doing in the middle of Humboldt Bay in the middle of the night? And one thing's surreal—I thought I saw Charlene on the cutter. Or is that just the concussion talking?" As I was asking this, I heard a car door slam outside, and before anyone could answer, Charlene came into view through the breakfast room window.

"What the hell?" was all I could say.

Chapter 40

It turned out Charlene had been hired by the FBI months earlier. Black Belt had been on the FBI's radar for years, and when it acquired Farmstead, one of the agents in the local office remembered the connection from her application. So, for her first assignment, the FBI had her stay at Farmstead and learn what she could about Black Belt. The giant private equity fund was under investigation for fraud and tax evasion.

Charlene stayed for a cup of coffee. Then Meg drove me back to the Eureka Inn and Charlene followed in her car. They waited in the café next door while I took a shower and changed into my own clothes. I felt much better when I joined them a half an hour later.

"Black Belt controlled Farmstead and, through another corporation, they also secretly owned Clearheart and several other companies as well," Charlene explained. "They planned to bankrupt Farmstead through a monster claim by Clearheart. Then they would move the money from Clearheart to other companies that are registered offshore."

"How were they going to make that happen?" I asked.

"It was pretty simple," Charlene continued. "These were not the smartest guys in the room. All it would take would be a fire which burned up all the inventory Clearheart's been stockpiling. Clearheart has been harvesting every redwood tree it could find, both legally and illegally. That ship was filled with the nicest redwood logs and milled lumber you'd ever want to see—all of it headed to countries where's there's a lot of demand and very few questions. All that was left in the warehouse was trash, but very burnable trash."

"Yeah, but how does the fire start?"

"Oh, you'll love this," Charlene continued. "You know the demonstration that was supposed to happen today? They had some goons set to get tricked out as protesters who were going to bust down the gates and lead the others into the warehouse, at which point one of the workers there would 'accidentally' start the fire while responding to the chaos. If some of the protesters got caught in the fire, that would just be too bad. And the ship was going to sail this morning instead of tomorrow, so it would be away from the dock and in international waters before this all came down."

"But I don't see how all this connects, and who all was in on it, anyway?" I asked.

"It's a shell game," Charlene said. "Black Belt funnels money from Farmstead to Clearheart through this claim, which is probably big enough to bankrupt Farmstead. They lose their stake in Farmstead, but the cost of that is nothing compared to the amount of the claim. Clearheart sends the money it gets on the claim through the shell companies to Black Belt, sells off what it can, and then closes down. And the redwood buyers, instead of paying Clearheart for the lumber, pay a different shell corporation in the Bahamas.

"As far as who was in on it, it looks like at the Farmstead end of things it included Abercrombie, Jill Dodge, and Ann Baxter, but we're still looking into whether there's anyone else involved there. There are warrants out on them, and I don't know if they're in custody yet, but several of the folks we picked up when we raided the dock know pieces of the puzzle and are falling all over themselves singing."

"So, Clearheart gets paid twice," I said, "Once by Farmstead and once by folks buying the lumber."

"Yeah," Charlene said. "As usual, it's all about the money. And guess what. Way down in the hold, we found molding which looks like it came from the Eel River Inn. Not a lot of it, so I bet most of it has already been sold, but enough to connect someone there with the hotel fire and Buzzard's death on top of the fraud."

"Were you able to show that Buzzard was murdered?" I asked.

Charlene nodded. "We've had agents on the ground here working on the case for a while. The forensics can prove he was murdered."

We sat silently for a minute and Meg shook her head. "Poor guy," she said. "Just a pawn in this money grab."

"But what about all the other madness at work?" I asked. "Was that somehow connected?"

"Not directly," said Charlene. "The whole idea was to gut Farmstead and force it into bankruptcy, and the shift to commercial was a way to make writing the Clearheart policy look unremarkable. I think Abercrombie thought that stirring up dust would make it less likely that anyone would have enough time or energy to start asking questions, so there may have been some method to the madness, but I think a lot of the craziness was just what happens when you put folks in positions they don't really care about."

"Wow." I looked at Meg, who already knew what Charlene was telling me. Meg took my hand under the table and gave it a squeeze.

"I told you it was dangerous," Charlene scolded me. "You could have been killed."

"I didn't expect an armed response," I said.

"There was a lot on the line for Black Belt," Charlene continued. "The deckhands were told that you and Drew were ecoterrorists trying to blow up the ship."

I took a deep breath and sat back in my chair. "Thank you both for fishing me out of the bay," I said.

When we had finished our coffees, Charlene said goodbye and Meg and I headed over to Drew's house. As Meg drove across the bay, I looked in the direction of the Clearheart pier, but we were too far away to make out the details.

Drew's truck and the skiff were parked next to his mobile home and we pulled in next to them. I walked slowly around the boat and could see that there was a lot of damage. I thought I could make out a dent in the shape of my head.

"Ugh," I said, rubbing the bump on my head.

Drew heard us and came down the stairs. I gave him a hug which was a little longer than usual.

"I am so sorry that I put you in danger," I said. "If anything had happened to you. . ."

Drew put his hand up to stop me. "I'm fine," he said. "I had fun. You're the one who took the beating." He looked at the back of my head and frowned. "Ouch," he said.

"And the boat," I said. "Have you talked with the school?"

Drew nodded. "Actually, my boss, the faculty person responsible for the gear, is a good friend of some of the people who organized the protest. He told me that as long as everything's fixed or replaced, there'll be no problem."

"That's a relief," I said. "We can work out the details. Just let me know how much it costs and if there is anything else I can do."

We talked for a while longer, standing outside, until Drew said he had to go.

"And don't worry," he said as he walked back into his house, "I won't tell mom."

I laughed. "Well, I guess I hadn't thought about that but, now that you mention it, thank you."

The sun was getting higher in the sky and the air was warming. Meg and I got back into the car and she pulled onto the road.

"Are you ready to go home?" she asked.

"I am. I miss Elwood." I paused for a moment. "I don't know what to expect at Farmstead."

Neither of us said anything for several minutes.

"Do all your relationships start off this dramatically?" I asked.

282

Meg turned and gave me a Mona Lisa smile. "The gun battle was new," she said.

She turned the car onto the bridge and we headed inland.

Authors' Acknowledgements

It has been our good fortune over the years to be able to spend time in Humboldt County with Pam Sowerwine and her late husband, John, at their home in Arcata and, later, in McKinleyville. Their generous hospitality gave us a chance to experience and explore California's North Coast and many scenes in this book are based on memories of those visits. John was a commercial fisherman out of Trinidad Harbor and all of the fishing trips described in the book (including shark tagging) are based on trips we took with John. We also thank Pam for being our first reader.

Many thanks to all our early readers for their insights and for sharing their skills and knowledge: Mark Blackman, Detta Penna, Kathy Lee, Judith McKibben, Kary Shender, Marge Matoba, Donna Davis, and Nancy Mandelberg.

We also thank Detta Penna for allowing us to include Peter Penna as a character in the book. Unlike the fictional character, Peter was not a lawyer. He was a talented musician, a natural entertainer, and another friend who was gone too soon.

The scene on the road from Petrolia was inspired by a portion of Judi Bari's book, *Timber Wars* (Common Courage Press, 1994).

Jeff March and Marti Childs at EditPros LLC in Davis, California, have been invaluable in their help with all aspects of self-publishing. We thank them for their patience and professionalism.

About the Authors

Susan and Randy Padgett have shared a love of mysteries and the attractions of California for over forty years. Susan is a retired legal secretary/paralegal/ university staffer. Randy is a retired attorney. He is a California native who grew up in a family where long road trips were a common way to spend a holiday. The authors live in Davis, California, and can be reached at randyandsusanpadgett@gmail.com.